ROBIN SCHADEL

Carmilla's Ghost

Cursing Raven Books

First published by Cursing Raven Books 2021

First edition

ISBN: 978-1-63752-080-2

This book was professionally typeset on Reedsy.
Find out more at reedsy.com

I would like to dedicate this book to my fur babies:
To Zuzu, who inspired Sandy Paws
To Bit Bit, who provided snuggles while I wrote
To Salem Binx, who provided entertainment and love
To Legsie, who will always be the Dudeliest Dude of all the Dudely Dudes
And to Bailey, who is a perpetual good boy.

1

Chapter 1

"Do you need some help, Miss Hain?" The sales associate, Ashlyn Starsinger, asked as I growled to myself while browsing the dress racks at A Needle in Time Clothiers. Ashlyn was a petite woman in her mid-twenties with ghost white skin, light blonde hair she kept in a neat bun while at work, big sapphire eyes that would have blended seamlessly in whatever Destiny's anime obsession of the month happened to be, and a nearly imperceptible limp in her right leg from a soccer injury that didn't heal properly.

I shrugged and replied, "I don't know, Ashlyn. I need something that works for an elegant dinner in an Austrian castle, looks good on me now, and will be fucking amazing when I drop my ten birthday pounds over the next few days. Anything like that in stock?"

She traced her index finger along the black satin-trimmed lapel of the gray blazer of her skirt suit, and her eyes scanned the fluorescent lights of the ceiling absentmindedly in thought, causing her to wince in pain before saying, "I know we have a decent selection right now in your aesthetic. The retro look is making a comeback thanks to a handful of fashion and lifestyle YouTubers. And you've got an impressive figure, Miss Hain. But I'll be honest, we don't get a lot of requests here for something appropriate for an Austrian castle. Why do you need… oh!" Her jaw dropped before curling into a smile as she continued, "Are you and Carmilla back together again?"

I rolled my eyes and snorted. "No," I said, "It's not going to happen. I just accepted an invitation to spend Christmas with her this year. Why does everyone think we're getting back together?"

Ashlyn chuckled and answered, "Well, aside from the betting pool… What? You didn't know we had a pool here in the Heights on when y'all would get back together?" Her eyes and smile softened, and she added, "Look, Miss Hain, you've done so much for so many families here, brought us safety, given us a chance at happiness. We want that for you too, and you were at your happiest when you two were together. That's all. And it's all in good fun."

The fucking truth was that Ashlyn was right. My mother was right on my birthday. Destiny has been right countless times. Of all the women I've dated, Carmilla made me the happiest. The fact that five fucking years after I broke it off, the slightest touch of her hand still took my breath away. Butterflies danced in my stomach whenever she said my full name in her noble Austrian accent. And when, in broad daylight, knowing she could burn to ash or be killed by overzealous agents, she confidently strode into a Duilearga stronghold to ensure my safety after that fight with that demon Zozo on Old Tom's Hill in Bannagh, it took all my composure not to squeal like a giddy schoolgirl whose crush acknowledged her existence for the first time. She's smart. She's confident. She's charming. She's

2

a more amazing watercolorist than she gives herself credit for being. It's just that—well, it's not that she's a vampire *per se* that was the problem. I had no problem with her being what some would call a supernatural creature or undead, but it wasn't easy waking up to a corpse at my side. Her pale, naked body was beautiful, but it was also cold, stiff, and lifeless.

I sighed wistfully. Then, shaking my head and sighing, I refocused my gaze on Ashlyn and asked, "Anyway, how's your brother James doing?"

She laughed and smiled. "See that," she asked, pointing a finger at me. "That is an example of the happiness you've brought us that we want to see returned to you. But he's doing well, starting Butcher's Bend Community College in the fall. We've had no more trouble with the Inola boys since, well, you know," she pointed to her eyes and added, "or from the S-T's."

"Old hatreds die hard sometimes," I mused. The Starsingers were what the Cherokee called "moon-eyed people." They were a race of short, pale, blue-eyed, nocturnal people who lived here over a millennium ago. And they lost a war to the Cherokee before even Leif Erikson sailed west and were driven from their subterranean homes. The Starsingers came back a few generations ago, and, though they still had trouble seeing in daylight, they've adapted to the schedule of the modern world. The Inola boys saw the crescent moon glowing in James' eyes and started trouble. That drew the attention of the S-T's, the Stith Thompsons, or the U.S.' branch of the Veil Watchers, a government sanctioned, independent organization who preserves the secret that we share a world with creatures from lore and legend, and they often do so through a body count. Over the years, I've developed a reputation for helping those who run afoul of the Watchers with a minimal body count. My last case had a larger count than I would have liked.

"Yeah," Ashlyn mused before perking up and rushing to a dress at the far end of the rack. She returned with the dress and asked, "How do you feel about orange?"

I shrugged and said, "I usually use it as an accent color when I'm wearing blue. Can't say I've ever thought of it as a primary color."

"I think you should," she said with a smirk as she produced this orange velvet wiggle dress with a v-shaped portrait neckline and gently flowing ruffled cowl. "And," she said, "there's enough built-in support around the waist that you wouldn't even have to worry about those five pounds." With a wink, she added, "And Carmilla will be begging for permission to enter."

I rolled my eyes and chuckled. This was why I preferred to shop in the Veiled Heights district of Butcher's Bend. Since most of what our government classified as "NHMs" or "Non-Human Mythics" who had integrated legally and secretly into Butcher's Bend society lived in this district, I never had to fear a misspoken word when talking about my life. Normal humans who lived in blissful ignorance of this truth of the world sometimes wandered into the Heights, but they rarely stayed long, claiming that they just felt uneasy and jumpy while in the area. It was like that realization at Pride of being with your true family. You might not always like each other. You might not always get along. But you can be yourself without fear. It was empowering and humbling.

I took the dress from her and said, "I'll give it a try."

I stepped into the fitting room and removed the black pencil skirt and burgundy fitted cardigan with gold polka dots I was wearing. I stared at my reflection in the mirrors and pursed my lips. I haven't been skinny since I was ten, but I have kept in decent shape. And the vintage-inspired black lace lingerie I routinely wore helped camouflage small imperfections. I liked my curves, and Carmilla loved them. My nose was still too wide, and I started to wonder if I should lighten my deep brown hair to better coordinate with this dress. I wiggled into that orange dress and did a few spins and twists in the mirror.

I called out, "Ashlyn, you didn't say this dress would push up the girls this much."

"Vampire-slaying cleavage is a free bonus when you buy the dress," came her reply.

I changed back and carefully folded the dress over my arm. As I returned to the shop floor, a beaming Ashlyn greeted me, "And we have the perfect lingerie and shoes to pair with this dress, should you be interested."

"Lingerie is my weakness, so let's go all out," I said before finishing my shopping here before meeting Destiny for lunch.

Decembers in Butcher's Bend, South Carolina, were cool and clear. The fallen leaves provided a vibrant blanket for the dying grass. The local coffee shops and bakeries all stocked homemade hot cider along with their assortments of seasonal pastries and cookies. Homes and businesses sported festive decorations, and even the city decorated the streetlights and trees with simple but elegant white lights. The Blue Ridge Mountains to our west sported snowy caps, which always made me hopeful for an early snowfall.

Nestled in the Conroy and Wollensky Shopping Center just south of Veiled Heights, Hassel & Beck's Baked Potato Cottage was one of our favorite places for a lighter but satisfying lunch, and I needed to drop a few pounds quickly. Like a good strip mall, the Cottage's exterior was boring and unassuming, but after stepping through the glass door, Mackenzie Davenport-Hassel and Charlene Beck transported customers to a country cottage in southern France with its golden oak flooring, tables, and shelving; chairs covered in white and green checkered upholstery; and white linen tablecloths with a subtle, golden fleur-de-lis embroidery. Destiny arrived before I did, and I walked in on her raiding a nearby gym in *Pokemon Go*. When she succeeded, we hugged, and then followed the hostess to our table.

As our server, a middle-aged man with used-car-salesman slicked black hair, brought our chardonnay, bread, and herb butter, Destiny brushed a chin-length blonde ringlet behind her right ear, smiled, and asked, "So, Sam, all set for your big romantic Christmas vacation?"

I furrowed my brow and narrowed my eyes at my best friend and assistant before responding, "It's not a romantic vacation, Des. I'm just spending time with a friend… who happens to be my ex-girlfriend."

Destiny pursed her lips and rolled her eyes. She sighed and said, "She's the ex you haven't gotten over - even after you broke up with her. And you made a promise to an Old World vampire, and that…"

"Is an oath sworn to be kept," I interrupted her. "Yeah, I know. It's one step below a blood oath, and they hold those oaths as sacred. But no, I haven't finished shopping. I've got no idea what to get 'Milla for Christmas. I mean, she's nearly three hundred, runs a successful investment company, produces amazing watercolor paintings, is the matriarch of a major vampire clan, and…"

"Just happens to be the one woman who causes the heart of the great private investigator Samantha B. Hain to flutter like a crushing schoolgirl," Destiny finished.

"Yeah, that too," I said into my wineglass. Yes, I was still in love with Countess Carmilla Karnstein five years after I ended our relationship. I sipped the fruity wine and added, "And I leave in four days."

"Well," Destiny said as she spread the herb butter on her bread, "what have you gotten her before?"

I sighed as I thought back to those few months when we were together. Shaking my head, I said, "A scarf; a Book of the Month Club subscription, which she continued at her own expense after the year; and a locket with miniature portraits of both of us. I mean, it's not easy to buy for someone who rarely eats human food unless its highly seasoned, can buy anything she wants, and has lived for three hundred years. I'm stumped."

Destiny tilted her head and nodded. Her blue eyes stared into her wineglass as she drummed her right index finger against the back of her spoon. She smiled, highlighting her perfectly German features, and said, "I don't know what to get her, but I don't think the what of it really matters to her as much as the fact that you're the one giving it to her. And let's face it, you spending time at her castle, which is something you never did when the two of you dated, is something she's wanted for a long time. We could hit The Luv Shack after lunch so you could buy some of that lingerie that has a bow to wrap around your boobs."

Her smirk told me that she noticed my blushing. Destiny has been my best friend for years, and she was the first to see through my attempts to date after ending things with Carmilla. Even if we weren't friends, the daughter of Werther Grimm, head of the German branch of the Veil Watchers, was both smart and perceptive enough to see through my bullshit. I tugged at my cardigan's neck, suddenly feeling the air grow warm, and my right foot tapped like I was a bored teenager in church. I took several deep breaths to focus, closing my eyes to avoid her triumphant smile. And as I ran my fingers through my hair, I said, "I can't think about that, Des. I need to focus. And we're just friends now. We're good friends. We work as friends. Maybe she's allergic to cats. So, friends it is."

Destiny's laughter drew the attention of the room. She apologized and took a large gulp of her wine before saying, "Really? Allergic to cats? That's your excuse?" She sighed. "My family has collected lore on Non-Human Mythical Beings for centuries, Sam, and you may want to ask whether she can turn into a wolf or a cat. Anyway, I know it's cliché to say that it's not the gift; it's the thought, but in this case, I think the fact that you are spending time with her in her home is the gift she wants. So, just get her something special and heartfelt, and you'll be fine. Want me to watch Sandy Paws?"

But I didn't want things to be fine. I wanted them to be amazing. I wanted Carmilla, but as adamant as I've been on keeping our relationship platonic, I couldn't just come out and say that. Fuck! I sighed and said, "I'd thought about boarding her for the two weeks I'm gone so she's be around more cats and people. I mean, thanks to both my fee for helping the Vernal Prince's banshee friend and then Lady O'Cuinn's generosity, we've had a nice surplus that put us back in the black for the first time in two years. Plus, it's a holiday, and I didn't want you to feel obligated to giving up your holiday to cat sit."

Destiny shook her head gently. "Oh, Sam," she said, "I appreciate it, but I'm not going anywhere. I can't. I've joined the Junior League's Inclusive Holiday Choir, and we have our retirement home tour as well as a few other performances scattered about the season. So, I don't mind watching Sandy. Just pick me up an ornament at a *Christkindlmarkt.*"

I nodded and smiled. I turned my attention to our server who brought our potatoes, thanking him, before responding to Destiny, "Well, I do appreciate it, and I'm sad that I'll miss your performances. But at least I know Sandy will be in good hands. And I expect updates on how it goes when Jeremy's parents come for a visit."

"Yeah, well, at least you don't have to meet Carmilla's parents," she replied.

I chuckled and replied, "No, but there is that entire clan of vampiric offspring, relatives, courtiers, and allies. Some of whom I've met, and some I'm sure I'll meet in the future."

* * *

For over fourteen centuries, the gray and black stone walls of Castle Karnstein have stood proudly amidst the Alps in the Austrian state of Tyrol. It has weathered countless storms and assaults from without and within and remained strong but not unwounded. As a waning crescent moon shone amidst a vibrant starry sky, Countess Carmilla Karnstein sat in a leather-upholstered mahogany chair behind the green and gray marble-topped mahogany desk in her office. She held a cell phone in her left hand, and the manicured fingers of her right hand drummed upon the marble. A crimson flame tinted her eyes, narrowed in annoyance to match her scowl as she listened to Franz Gruber, Chief Manager of the Supernatural Investments Division for her investment company, K-B Investments, drone about exceeding the quarterly goals and about setting more ambitious goals for the next quarter.

As her desk tapping grew more frantic, an older man with a white tonsure and thick mustache who was wearing a navy suit with polished burgundy shoes entered her office carrying a silver tray atop which sat a crystal glass, a carafe of wine, and a note. He placed the tray on her desk, poured her a glass of wine, and stepped back, standing in the doorway. As she sipped the wine, her shoulders sank into the chair's leather padding and her head fell back with a smile. She looked at the note, which simply read, *Gräfin Karnstein, I believe that you would prefer to spend your evening planning for your upcoming visitor?*

She smirked toward her servant and nodded. Then, in a firm tone, she said, "Franz, these plans are good, but I have other matters to attend this night. Perhaps you could send the report to me by post or by email? Thank you." She then ended the call.

With a sigh of relief, she looked her servant in the eyes and smiled, saying, "Thank you, Martin. You are ever a blessing."

He bowed his head and replied, "Thank you, my Countess. I have served your family faithfully since your grandfather was the same age as you were when you entered immortality. And it has been both a pleasure and an adventure watching you mature into a capable and confident matriarch of the Karnstein-Bertholt Clan."

Carmilla smiled and then sighed as her eyes turned to the framed photograph of Sam and herself that she kept on her desk. With a wistful tone, she said, "And I need everything to be perfect. I know she won't change her mind, but I still want it to be a perfect visit."

Martin nodded, collected the tray and wine bottle, and said, "We will do our best, Countess. Now, the thralls have returned with three choices for the tree to be placed in your drawing room. Do you wish to select the tree, or shall I?"

"I will choose and decorate this tree," she said, rising from her seat. She paused mid-rise as panic washed over her face. She added, "Do you think I should? Should I wait for her to arrive so that we could decorate it together? Will she think me a terrible hostess for choosing incorrectly? Martin, what do I do?"

He chuckled and shook his head. "I think that the choice is yours," he said. "I personally think that either would be lovely, but you may wish to not appear overly eager to rekindle what you both once enjoyed."

Carmilla nodded, "I understand. I will choose and decorate the tree. Take the bottle to my drawing room and then instruct the thralls to decorate the Great Hall, the courtyard, and the gardens per our usual manner."

"Yes, Countess," he said with a bow.

As Martin turned to leave, Carmilla called out, "And then double the locks on the dungeon's door, but make sure that she's comfortable first. I want no trouble from her during these weeks."

Martin turned and nodded, saying, "If I may be so bold, Countess, perhaps now is the time to forgive and find freedom." He then exited her office.

Carmilla sipped her wine slowly. Her mind traveled both to her past and to her future. A single bloody tear fell from her right eye. She wiped it away with the backs of her index and middle fingers, shook her head, and exited her office, whispering, "If only it were that easy, Martin."

Rich mahogany walls decorated with gold-tasseled medieval tapestries, a few of Carmilla's own watercolor landscapes, and bookcases filled with leather-bound volumes framed the Countess' drawing room. A burgundy velvet sofa and two crushed burgundy velvet armchairs sat atop a gold-trimmed burgundy rug so that all seated could feel the warmth of the stone hearth. An old phonograph with updated technology played *"Stille Nacht"* from Carmilla's Spotify account. Carmilla, in her burgundy dressing gown, decorated the mantle above the hearth with a miniature Alpine winter village. She sipped the rich purple Sanguinovese wine Martin brought her as she arranged and rearranged every miniature building, person, animal, or streetlight to display the perfect image in her head. She had already decorated the fifteen-foot tall Austrian pine with white candles, dainty glass snowflakes, and a single pickle. Carmilla then packed up her easel, canvas, and watercolors and moved them into a chest against the wall.

After she finished decorating her drawing room, Carmilla walked through the drafty and damp stone corridors, stopping at the guest chamber near hers where Sam would sleep. Inside, she removed the blue comforter with a subtle pattern of golden heraldic eagles from the wooden chest at the bed's foot and placed it lovingly atop the blanket of the queen-sized, four-poster oak bed. She glanced at the two-centuries-old mirror beside the wardrobe that reflected only the image of her wine glass floating beside a standing dressing gown. She frowned and mentally noted to have a servant clean the smudges on the mirror's right side. She decided the nightstand needed a vase with violets and Christmas roses and an Advent wreath.

Carmilla stood in the door frame, gazed upon the room with downcast eyes, and whispered, "I pray this room pleases you,

Samantha; although, I wish you would join me in mine."

"You continue to place yourself at the edge of happiness only to torture yourself through denial, 'Millie," a woman's voice rasped from behind her.

As a hand rested on her left shoulder, Carmilla slouched and sighed, saying, "I know what I desire, Lisa, and I know what I deserve."

"Almost two centuries have passed, dear sister," the spirit said. "None alive have personal memory of those events as time flows like water beneath a bridge."

Carmilla clenched her fists, snapping the wine glass' stem, causing the glass to shatter on the floor. Her face contorted as she buried it in her right shoulder, bloody tears falling from her eyes. She shook her head and replied, "You're wrong, Lisa. You're wrong." And with that, Carmilla spun around and walked through the empty hallway, the bedroom door open behind her.

Exiting the main keep of Castle Karnstein, Carmilla entered the rear courtyard where the castle's gardens stood. Her eyes glowed as she stepped into the snowy night air. A gentle snowfall descended from the cloudy sky. The snow-draped holly bushes that both framed the gardens and formed the hedge maze presented their crimson berries. Per her instructions, the servants had placed white candles in the wrought iron candlesticks that rose from the soil at regular intervals throughout the gardens. Though leafless now, the stately branches of the ancient oak trees that stood in the garden's four corners hold the ropes from which hang white pillar candles. Though only a few of the violets and Christmas rose bushes bloom, Carmilla smiles as she walked the labyrinthine path toward the fountain at the garden's center.

The winter night's air warmed her, and Carmilla mused over that fact as she listened to the water spraying from the chest of a dragon, thrown to its back by the assault of the badger actively clawing it, that in life, the winter night's cold terrified her. She sat on the fountain's edge, as the moon's waning form caused the fountain whose central statue, a badger attacking a dragon, the symbol of House Karnstein, to cast its long shadow over Carmilla as she wiped the bloody tears and ruined mascara from her perpetually young face. With a heavy sigh, she turned her attention toward the stone door in the garden wall to her left, a wall that stood against Stubai Alps. The Karnstein-Bertholt mausoleum lay beyond that door, and Carmilla heard the voices of the dead cut through the gurgling of the water. The voices of those who taught her, those disappointed in her life choices, and those offended by her ascendance to clan matriarch reverberated through her mind, drowning out her own as they screamed, "Failure! Traitor! Unworthy!"

The voices aligned, reminding her of one specific night. She gnashed her teeth and growled. Trembling with sorrow and rage, Carmilla wailed into the night. Wolves howled in response, and a cloud of bats screeched as they circled overhead. Her wailing became dolorous weeping. Bloody tears plummeted from her eyes as she cried through the night, passing out as the sun crept over the mountains.

The next sunset, Carmilla awoke to find herself tucked beneath the burgundy comforter in her mahogany canopy bed. Her coughs rasped from her throat, and she smacked her lips and grimaced at her dry mouth. Her head throbbed as her veins pulsed, begging to be filled. Groans and whimpers slouched from her lips. She fell into her plush down pillows and turned her head toward her nightstand where a silver tray presented her with a filled blood bag, a bottle of wine, a crystal glass, and a note. She grabbed the blood bag and pierced it with her fangs, gulping its contents with animalistic ferocity. Her muscles relaxed as she drained the bag. She sighed with relief and read the note.

Gräfin Karnstein, at the last hours of night, I heard your sorrow from my chambers, rushed to the garden, and carried you to the safety of your room. There, I cleaned you and dressed you for bed. I have taken the liberty of placing sustenance, physical and emotional, by your side so that when you awaken, you will be able to mitigate the suffering of your sorrow-induced hunger. Please take care of yourself, as you have a Clan Council Meeting at 7 o'clock. And I know you wish to continue preparations for your special guest's arrival. If I am not present at the time of your waking, I am in Karnsburg purchasing food and bourbon for Miss Hain.–Martin.

* * *

The Butcher's Bend Holiday Makers' Village occurred every year on the second weekend of December. Dubbed "The Farmers' Market of Independent Craftspeople," the tents, stalls, and wheeled kitchens filled into the H.D. Magus Memorial Park with handmade crafts ranging from homemade quilts to blown and etched glass to wooden toys and furniture to blacksmith creations to art of all varieties. Mobile kitchens sold seasoned popcorn, seasonal cookies and pastries, smoked meats, jams and preserves, and street food snacks from hot dogs to Frito pie to cheeseburgers to soup-filled bread bowls. Cinnamon, coriander, and clove perfumed the cool winter air, electrified by holiday excitement, conversation, and alcohol.

The three of them moved through the crowd, handmade ceramic mugs filled with mulled wine in hand as they talked, laughed, and shopped. Sam Hain's blue pencil skirt peaked beneath her blue and gold hounds tooth trench, and her brown riding boots hid most of her stockings. Destiny Grimm's covered most of her blonde curls in a gray cat-eared beanie that coordinated with her tacky holiday sweater that had several images of young anime girls fainting and shouting with a single line of text announcing that "Senpai" had noticed them. On Sam's right, walked a woman whose rich umber skin possessed bronze undertones and whose springy coils danced lightly over the top of her purple and black paisley scarf. Laura Kelsington, though heavier than Sam but almost as tall, wore a flowing, open-front, purple cardigan over a black turtleneck and dark wash jeans.

"So, Sam," Laura began, "aren't you glad I dragged you here?"

"I am," Sam replied before sarcastically adding, "Who knew that having a friend on the Metro Art Council would lead to being invited to artistic events."

"Yeah, but this is a great place to finish Christmas shopping," Destiny added.

"Finishing shopping would be a good idea," Sam mumbled into her mug.

Laura took another sip of wine and asked, "Who's left on your list?"

"No one here," Sam said. "I've got yours, Des', Kina's, Angie's, Jim's, Devin's, Liz's, and of course a new bed and fancy treats for Sandy."

"So, it's just a gift for Carmilla then," Laura said. "What do you buy the woman who has everything?"

"Except for the woman she really wants," Destiny added,

causing all, even Sam, to laugh.

Laura smirked and quipped, "I'm sure someone here has a box large enough to fit Sam in. Although, it might be a bit cold being shipped naked to Germany."

As Destiny giggled, Sam shot both of her friends an incredulous look, clutching the pearls around her neck that she was not wearing. She said, "If you're going to ship me like freight, you could at least let me wear my new lingerie and a trench coat."

After a series of squeals and laughs, Destiny stopped abruptly and held her arm out to stop Sam, saying, "Wait. What new lingerie?"

Sam rolled her eyes and said, "I bought it with my new dress and shoes at A Needle in Time, Des. I told you about it at lunch that day."

"You said you bought new underwear," Destiny said. Her voice trailed as she sipped her wine, and then her eyes shot closed. She stomped once and added, "And I know you don't wear any normal underwear, so yeah, I should've realized it was lacy and fancy."

"And," Laura added, "at least we didn't offer to tattoo 'Bite Here' on your inner thighs."

Laura and Destiny laughed. When Sam blushed, they laughed harder. Sam downed the rest of her mulled wine and, while running her index finger along her collarbone, mumbled, "It's not like she needs help knowing where I like that."

They continued eating, drinking, and shopping for several hours. Sam purchased Carmilla's gift from a man who burns custom images into wood using modified Tesla coils. Destiny added to her collection of glass animal Christmas ornaments by purchasing a pair of silvery white and gold swans, a brown tinted beagle, and shimmering silver and blue swordfish. She also purchased three bags of cotton candy in blue raspberry and pink lemonade. Laura purchased a set of three Afrofuturistic holiday village buildings and four dozen cookies to give as gifts for her colleagues.

After leaving the Holiday Makers' Village, Sam returned to her small apartment on the second floor of the Palmetto and Pine Apartments. The small complex was gated in name only, as the entrance gate, flanked by two palmetto trees, remained open because of a faulty mechanism that the management company had yet to replace. Sam drove through the uneven, pothole-laden parking lot with its faded yellow lines and broken speed bumps until she reached a space in front of her door. She unloaded her car and brought her purchases into her apartment. As she unlocked the door, her calico cat Sandy Paws, wearing a green collar with a bell, leapt from her place on the windowsill and paced in front of the door, meowing plaintively as Sam entered.

"I'm sorry, Sandy," she said, setting her packages and purse on the perpetually cluttered dining table that often doubled as her desk when she needed a more professional setting working from home than her bed. As she knelt to pet her cat, who was darting around her legs and mewing for attention as she added, "It took a little longer to get all my shopping done for the holidays. Come on, let's go snuggle a bit before I check the mail and fix us supper."

As they walked toward the old sofa, decorated with scratch trails, Sam noticed that Sandy's water dish was nearly empty. Taking a slight detour, she refilled the ceramic bowl with Sandy's name on it in the kitchen sink. Sandy paused to lap some fresh, cool water before joining Sam on the sofa, shedding all over Sam's clothes while rubbing her head against Sam's face.

"Oh, I'm going to miss you too, baby," Sam cooed as she stroked Sandy's back while the cat purred happily. "But don't worry, Auntie Des will come and keep you company, and I'm sure she'll call me so I can talk to you at least twice a week. I know, don't meow at me like that. If it were anyone but 'Milla, I wouldn't be doing this. You know that."

After an hour of snuggling and conversing, Sandy jumped from Sam's lap and walked to her litter box. Sam took this as an opportunity to walk downstairs to the complex's mail room. She unlocked her rusted gray mailbox. She jerked the box's door, and it slowly creaked open. Sam frowned, as Our Neighbor and Occupant had more mail than she did. And then she saw the only piece of mail addressed to her. This burgundy envelope felt like it contained a letter, but as Sam ran her fingers over it, there was something more solid and firm than paper. When she saw the letter's postmark was from Austria, she inhaled sharply as her body tensed. Her cheeks flushed, and she beamed. She threw the junk mail in the mailroom's garbage can before power walking back to her apartment.

As soon as she closed the door, she opened the envelope and found a letter, folded in the Regency style and sealed with burgundy wax bearing the coat of arms of the Karnstein family. Sam sniffed the golden parchment and smelled Carmilla's custom Otto of Roses and violet perfume. She rolled her eyes at her own behavior before popping the wax seal and unfolding the letter containing Carmilla's measured and elegant calligraphic hand.

My dearest friend, Samantha,

19

As I pen this letter, ten days remain before I am given the honor, privilege, and pleasure of spending the Christmas season with you in my castle. I hope that this letter finds you well, and I hope that you receive this letter before you depart. Though I may use the cellular phone to speak to you, I have spent the entirety of my life and much of my immortality communicating through handwritten letters. And when communicating in a language that is not my native German, I feel more confident when I write. Therefore, I pray that you indulge me, my dearest friend, in what may be a longer letter than you are accustomed to receiving.

Although I am certain that you have observed the forecast in Innsbruck, the nearest large city to my castle, the small town of Karnsburg that rests at the foot of the path that leads up the mountains to my home is closer, but I do not know how much information you may find upon it. That said, you must know that our winters are cold and dry. The snows have begun to fall, providing a lovely blanket on the bushes in my gardens and the roofs of our buildings. The nights can be below freezing, and my castle is often said to be drafty and cold, and, given the altitude of my home, our nights are often colder than those in the cities.

However, your room is not without warmth, and I hope that it is to your liking. I have placed my finest and warmest blankets in the trunk at the foot of your bed, and I have instructed my servants to keep the hearth in your room burning with pine and scented sachets for your physical and emotional pleasure. You will also find an Advent wreath on the nightstand and an ample wardrobe for your clothing.

Sam's heart skipped and quickened as she read these words. A smile crept across her face and she bounced at the ankles. She bit her lower lip as she continued reading.

In addition to your Advent wreath, you will find that I have decorated my home for the season. The white candles are traditional, and although you will find electricity and modern plumbing in my castle, I still continue the tradition of decorating with candles instead of electric Christmas string lights. You are familiar with the Christmas tree, yes? The main tree has been placed in my study, and while my servants decorated most of the castle, I decorated the tree in the traditional style as my family has done for centuries. I had thought about waiting for you to arrive to see if you would join me in decorating the tree, but my nature evoked a great fear that, were my decorating unfinished, you would be unhappy with me. Therefore, my home is fully decorated for the holiday and for your arrival.

I hope that you will want for nothing during your stay. Any food or drink you desire will be yours for the asking. If your room is not to your liking, I will change anything about the room you do not like. Though I do not live in a luxury resort hotel, you will find many diversions through which to seek entertainment. Martin, or another servant, can easily drive you to Karnsburg should you wish to spend the daylight hours in town. Should you have need of anything, please inform me so that I may ensure it is provided to you.

While there is much rejoicing in your coming, and I long to see you, there is an unfortunate circumstance that must delay our reunion. On the evening of your arrival, I have a meeting with the Directorial Board of my investment firm. As a result of that, I will be unable to greet you when you descend from the airplane onto Austrian soil. This overlap of scheduling is unfortunate, and I am unable to reschedule this meeting. My trusted estate steward Martin will be waiting with a car to drive you to my home. I will, however, be waiting in the forward courtyard to greet you upon your arrival. Should fortune smile upon us and circumstances change in *our favor, I regret that I will likely be unable to inform you of the change in a timely manner. Regardless, I am overjoyed that you accepted my offer, and I count the days until your arrival as if it were my own Advent calendar.*

Yours eternally,

Countess Carmilla Karnstein of House Karnstein-Bertholt

Her heart sank momentarily upon learning that Carmilla would not greet her at the airport. When she finished the letter, she involuntarily pressed it against her chest and slid down to her floor. Sandy walked over and licked her hands and the parchment on which Carmilla wrote her letter. The rough cat tongue brought Sam back to her immediate reality. She sighed, smiled, and pet Sandy, saying, "I've got thirty-six hours until I leave, Sandy. I guess I need to get packing."

2

Chapter 2

When the Chief Purser directed, I returned my seat to its upright position and looked out my window to see the lights from the city of Innsbruck poking through the dark night. I rolled my shoulders as needle pricks of pain shot through my stiff muscles. I had hoped to get some sleep on the eighteen-hour trip, but even in the first-class cabin with its generous leg room, a double bourbon on the rocks, a perfectly seared filet, and warm chocolate chip cookies, my in-flight insomnia reigned. Maybe I should've taken Destiny's advice and listened to that podcast, *All Work No Play* or whatever it was called, she mentioned. When our red-suited attendant came to ask for our final requests, I asked him for three bags of honey-roasted peanuts. He tilted his head in surprise, commented on how Americans always asked for these, and then handed me my prize.

The inside of Innsbruck's airport looked like a generic shopping mall with its white walls and giant windows showing what the various shops had for sale. They decorated for the holiday season with wreaths, candles, holly, and even a large bronze statue of Krampus chasing children. Through the massive windows, I could make out the shadow of the Alps, and I had a twinge of sadness at not being able to see them as soon as I stepped off the plane. But that would put Carmilla in danger, and that would have made me more nervous right now. Both for her safety and for my own feelings. I stopped at the Testa Rossa for an overpriced cappuccino before heading to the baggage claim area.

As I saw the baggage conveyors, I chuckled, remembering how mad my mom and my asshole father were when I treated one of the ones at JFK like a merry-go-round. I was five-years-old, and it was my first flight. I saw what looked like a fun thing to ride on, and I crawled between a pair of large suitcases. The area behind the rubber curtain was boring, but the workers waved back as I rode along my way. Both my parents yelled at me, and my asshole father threatened to spank me if I didn't provide a good explanation for my "irresponsible behavior." I chuckled as I remembered how Mom's anger turned on him when I told him it looked like one of those faerie caves he described in the stories he told me that he explored while growing up in Ireland.

A man's voice shocked me from my memory when I heard him call out, "*Fraulein* Hain!"

I looked in the voice's direction and saw this older man with a silvery gray monk's haircut, what a linguistics professor of mine once called a "reverse beanie." He wore a navy frock coat with matching trousers, a burgundy vest with gold buttons, a white tuxedo shirt, a burgundy ascot, and white gloves. I walked over to him and the luggage carrier beside him and asked, "So, I suppose you're Martin?"

He bowed and said, "Yes, Miss Hain. Countess Karnstein

24

regrets greatly that she is unable to greet you upon your arrival, as that was her plan when she purchased your ticket. Unfortunately, she has a meeting that she could not reschedule; however, her business should conclude by the time we arrive at the castle."

Sipping my cappuccino, I nodded and asked, "How far is the castle from here?"

"About three hours, Miss," he said. As I looked at the clock on my phone, he added, "I know that you will be dining late, and so I have a light meal waiting for you in the car."

"Alright," I said with a smile. "I guess let's just get my suitcases and head into the mountains."

Martin nodded and requested that I simply point to my suitcases, both of which had a royal blue and orange checkerboard pattern. He placed them, and my burgundy carry-on the luggage carrier and led me to Carmilla's black G12, the car she picked me up in after the events in Bannagh. As he opened my door, I texted Destiny to let her know I had arrived. I stepped inside and saw that the light meal he provided me happened to be a charcuterie board of local sausages, cheeses, pretzels, pickles, and a small bottle of Booker's bourbon in a wooden serving tray garnished with a single violet.

As we drove off, Martin informed me that we had a two-hour drive to the village of Karnsburg, and from there we had another hour into the mountains. The castle was not far from the village, but the mountain road demanded careful travel in the winter. I sipped the bourbon as my phone vibrated. Destiny sent me a video of Sandy playing with a catnip mouse. Before I could respond, she added a single, pointed question, "What are you wearing under your trench?"

I rolled my eyes and shook my head. With a chuckle, I

responded, "Burgundy turtleneck, white jeans, brown riding boots."

Destiny then texted, "Oh, the jeans that make your butt look good? Have fun!"

I rolled my eyes at the winking emoji that followed, but Destiny had a point. I chose these jeans—my only pair of jeans—because of how they make my ass look. Jeans and riding boots also made traveling easier than a swing dress and stilettos did. I finished the light meal as we reached the halfway point between Innsbruck and Karnsburg. Downing the last swig of bourbon, I asked, "Hey, Martin. Since you mentioned a meal later, will I be dining alone?"

I winced at how my voice halted and lilted like an awkward baby lesbian's. If Martin even smiled, I couldn't detect it through the rear-view mirror. His voice acquired a strange but comforting timbre as he answered, "No, Miss Hain. Countess Karnstein will join you for evening meals in the family dining hall. If that is acceptable?"

"Of course it is, I," I blurted out with a blush before forcing a cough, straightening my posture, and correcting, "It is her home, after all, so she may do as she likes. Given that she invited me, I had hoped she would grace me with her presence when both our schedules aligned."

I blushed again, running my fingers through my hair and silently cursing my sudden lack of a poker face. I buried my face in my chest, scrolling idly through my Twitter feed, as Martin chuckled and said, "As you wish, Miss Hain."

About an hour-and-a-half later, we turned south at Karnsburg and headed up a gently sloping mountain road. The road kept straight enough with only a few gentle curves as I peered into the unlit darkness. When I lamented not being able to see even a fraction of the landscape, Martin informed me that though the Karnstein-Bertholt family offered to pay for upkeep, the resultant electrical cost to establish and maintain the lighting on the road made it undesirable. He mused that with the upswing in solar and wind power in Germany and Austria, perhaps the issue would soon be revisited. I nodded and then said, "Yeah, I guess also that the only people driving it at night would be 'Milla or another vampire in the family, right?"

"Not all who serve the Countess are vampires, Miss Hain," he said.

"Sorry," I said. "I just assumed the human servants would be asleep at night, so the ones with night vision would be on the road."

He nodded and said, "Mostly correct, Miss Hain. Those who provide security work in shifts, as I'm sure you understand."

"How long have you served, Martin, if you don't mind me asking," I asked.

He chuckled and replied, "I have served the Karnstein family since the Countess' grandfather was the Karnstein-Bertholt patriarch."

I thought for a moment and then asked, "So then, you knew 'Milla when she was…"

"Since she was both your age and mortal," he interjected. "I have had the privilege of serving her and the pleasure of watching her as she matured into the strong, confident, and independent matriarch of our clan. Speaking of the Countess, there she is."

I saw the dash illuminate as Martin's phone played that generic ringtone most Boomers use. Without perceptible movement to switch to a hands-free mode, he said, "Yes,

Countess?"

I forced an unaffected composure as I saw his brown eyes smile at me through the rear-view mirror when I heard her voice, "Martin, what is your location?"

He chuckled and said, "My Countess, we are approximately twenty minutes from the castle gate. Shall I increase our speed?"

"No. No, no, no. No. Your rate of travel is fine," I've never heard Carmilla sound so flustered over the telephone. Or in person, for that matter. But she continued, "I still have preparations to make for Samantha's arrival."

My body tensed with a blushing smile because I know she purposefully emphasized every linguistic nuance as she pronounced my name. Martin nodded and said, "Of course, Countess."

I didn't have the most robust German vocabulary for describing things not related to food, travel, shopping, and work, but I swear I heard Martin mumble advice to not step into a hole in the courtyard. I wanted to ask, but I thought it better to remain silent.

We soon reached the gray stone walls and wide portcullis that formed the gates of Castle Karnstein. As we approached, I could see some flickering lights on the higher floors of the keep and throughout the courtyard. When I asked, Martin assured me that there was solar-powered electricity in the castle and that the flickering lights were the white candles used to decorate the keep and courtyards in the traditional style. We waited for the iron gate to rise so that we could pass into the snow-blanketed courtyard where statues held white pillar candles to illuminate paths around the leafless Austrian oaks. As we approached the main keep, Carmilla stood before its door with a three-pronged candelabra in her left hand. Her pale skin seemed more flushed and lifelike than I remember seeing it—even after a feeding. I inhaled sharply as Martin brought the car to a stop before the stairs that ascended to the keep's entrance.

* * *

Carmilla tensed, drawing a deep breath into her lungs as Martin emerged from the G12. Sam placed the violet in her hair, just behind her left ear. Carmilla exhaled and composed herself as he opened the rear passenger door and stood at attention. Sam sat inside for a moment before realizing that she had not yet exited the car. As her mahogany brown riding boots set foot on the stone path leading to the stairs, a southwestern wind offered her nose the violet and rose scent of Carmilla's perfume in the hazy darkness of the cold, winter night. They beamed and locked eyes. Though wearing only a knee-length burgundy pencil dress with black satin tuxedo stripes on the skirt, Carmilla instinctively reached to hike up her skirt as she descended the stairs.

They hugged, and as they embraced, each woman's muscles relaxed in a way neither had in years. When Carmilla opened her eyes, she saw Martin nodding with a smile before he drove the car to the garage. Each stepped back and, with hands still touching the other's shoulders, smiled. Carmilla broke the silence by saying, "Welcome to my home and my family's home, Samantha. It brings me great pleasure to have you here at this time."

"I couldn't refuse, 'Milla," Sam said, her right foot bouncing. "I'm still trying to remember why I never accepted this offer when we were dating, but here we are."

Sam shivered as a north wind blew through her. Seemingly unphased by the cold, Carmilla chuckled and said, "Let us get you inside so you can warm by my fire. It has been so long since I have felt the cold that I forgot how it can effect mortals."

"And I forgot that the cold doesn't hit you the same way," Sam said. "I wouldn't turn down a glass of wine or cider, but I would like to come and walk through the courtyard at night to really see all the decorations."

"Well then," Carmilla said, "it is settled. After you unpack, we will dine, and then I shall give you the tour of my home unless you are weary from your travels."

Sam yawned as they began ascending the stairs. "Sorry," she said, "I'm a bit tired, but that's just from the flight from JFK. I got a decent nap during my layover. Plus, I'm not working, so I think I'll try to keep a schedule similar to my friend and hostess."

Carmilla escorted Sam through her castle, stopping first at the room prepared for Sam. The room smelled of orange, cinnamon, coriander, and clove. As Sam opened the wardrobe, she saw that Martin had taken the liberty of unpacking for her, hanging her clothing, and storing her other items in the appropriate shelves or in the attached bathroom. Sam's jaw plummeted toward the floor as she saw the massive claw-foot gray marble bathtub with gold fixtures.

Sam asked, "And all of his is heated and lit by solar power?"

Carmilla nodded, beaming with pride. "Aside from the hearths that burn wood, yes," she answered, "We are completely powered by solar energy for heating, cooling, refrigeration, illumination, and communication. And that reminds me, you will find the password for the wireless internet in the drawer of the nightstand. We also compost and recycle eighty-seven percent of our waste. A vampire is an efficient hunter, and, while many clans disagree, the Karnstein-Bertholt clan will be efficient citizens acting in the world around us. What benefits the whole ecosystem benefits us."

Sam squinted at Carmilla, mockingly searching her expressionless face, before saying, "You know, that makes sense. I know a lot of hunters don't want the ecosystem fucked over, because it hurts their fun. I'm surprised more vampires aren't as up on this as you are. That makes me even prouder to know you, 'Milla."

The vampire's smile broadened. She nodded once and said, "That pleases me. Come. There is more of my castle to show you before we dine."

Carmilla, candelabra in hand, guided Sam through the drafty, otherwise darkened halls of her castle's highest floor. She explained that mortal guests never came here unless they knew what she was and were escorted by either herself or Martin. She confined business and pleasure with other mortals to the ground floor and to her office on the second floor. They first stopped at Carmilla's bedroom, where Sam remained mostly silent, as voicing her thoughts on Carmilla's four-poster bed would have broken her illusion of platonic affection. They reached Carmilla's drawing room, a lavishly appointed room where Carmilla herself decorated the fifteen-foot tall pine tree with small white taper candles, class snowflakes, and a Christmas pickle, which elicited a giggle from Sam. The Countess then opened the French doors that connected the drawing room to the library with its leather and velvet furniture and floor-to-ceiling mahogany shelves filled with leather volumes whose musk perfumed the chamber. Sam's

31

jaw dropped at the sight, and she let out a soft moan as she smelled the old book leather.

Carmilla continued showing Sam her home as they descended from floor to floor. While in her office, she said, "This was once a war room where my father, at the request of an old friend, helped equip and train a black band of peasants. The rebellion failed, and the Karnstein-Bertholt clan had to find a way to appease two princes displeased with our actions."

"I'm sorry that I don't know that much about local history," Sam said, "but do you mean princes in Germany and Austria?"

Carmilla shook her head. "No," she said, "the mortal prince and..." Her face contorted into a disgusted scowl as she spat, "Tepes."

Sam blinked and bit her lip. She exhaled, nodded, and said, "I've gathered from your reactions to even adaptations of Stoker's work that you don't like him."

Carmilla thought for a moment, softening her face before adding, "My issues with *him* are personal in nature. They are unpleasant memories, to say the least. Let us continue."

They descended to the ground floor, and Sam smelled meat being roasted with ginger and clove. Carmilla's pace slowed as they turned down one hallway that felt like it sloped down into the mountain. There were no electric lights along this hallway. Portraits of clan patriarchs, their wives, and other ranking members lined the walls. Sam noticed that Carmilla kept her head down, as if she wished to avoid their gaze. Sam placed her hand gently on Carmilla's back and offered a compassionate smile and nod. Carmilla inhaled sharply at her touch and bit her lip to stop herself from tearing up. She smiled at Sam. They continued down this hallway until it ended at an ancient iron-banded wooden door with three locks.

"Wow," Sam exclaimed. "This is like something out of an old vampire movie."

Carmilla forced a chuckle and replied, "Beyond this locked door is the staircase to the castle's old dungeon. It is no longer in use, but it does contain the Karnstein family shame and curse." She took a deep breath before adding, "I will tell you that story when I am ready to do so, my dearest friend, but for now, I ask that you do not attempt to try and enter the dungeon. The rest of my home and my servants are at your disposal. Should you wish to visit Karnsburg or Innsbruck during the day, Martin will drive you. Please, Sam, give me this one kindness."

"Of course, 'Milla," Sam replied, thinking, "I already know she's a vampire and a lesbian, so I don't know what this curse could be."

From there, they toured both snow-draped courtyards. Leafless oaks stood tall in the winter night, their branches cradling white pillar candles. The statues in the front courtyard, marble replicas of Athenian and Renaissance statuary, held candles in their hands. Carmilla explained how this area once held practice grounds for the knights and archers who swore fealty to her family, but as times changed, the family slowly redecorated the front courtyard. Sam found herself drawn to a statue of a triumphant Medusa standing beside the keep's wall, and Carmilla demonstrated how to run a hand along the right side of Medusa's waist and find the switch that opened a secret passage that led to her chamber.

With a wistful smile, she said, "As a young girl and before my turning, it was my habit to sneak away from my tutors and family in order to explore the life in the village below. At my turning at the age of twenty-one, Father sealed over

33

the passage. Upon my ascension to matriarch, I unsealed the passage. Those were happy memories."

Sam smiled and said, "And why the Medusa? She hasn't been an image of empowerment for that long."

Carmilla turned her gaze away from her guest and lowered her eyes, saying, "I too am a monster, and her victory over those who would destroy her gives me hope."

Sam grasped Carmilla's hand and gave it a gentle squeeze. "You're not a monster, 'Milla," she said lovingly, "you're a vampire. Aside from that and the fact that you're really old, you're no different from me. After some things I've done, I have my own claim to monstrosity. And you're still human, flawed like the rest of us."

Carmilla sniffed as she wiped her eyes. Sam noticed a red mark on Carmilla's otherwise flawless alabaster skin. The vampire forced a smile as she gazed into Sam's eyes and said, her voice trembling, "I pray I never lose your compassion."

They then walked through the keep toward the rear court-yard. As they passed the dining hall, Martin informed them that the evening meal would be ready in half an hour. Carmilla apologized for the lack of flowering plants, promising that the gardens were awash with color and fragrance in the spring and summer.

Sam brushed a strand of hair behind her right ear and said, "But they're beautiful. The snow blanketing them, the candles providing gentle light so I can still see the moon and stars, and a fucking hedge maze with a fountain at its center. 'Milla, I know this is your life, so it probably seems boring to you, but it's something I've always dreamed of having. I mean, I grew up well off, but nothing like this. I fell in love with Austen and the Brontes because I dreamed of owning a manor with

a garden that had a hedge maze I could run through. This…
this is beautiful."

Carmilla's honest smile returned, and she extended her arm,
saying, "As I have said, you have the freedom to wander my
home. If you desire to run through my gardens, you may do
so."

Sam's gaze turned toward the darkened Alps. She pointed
toward the stone door and asked, "What's in there? Secret
weapons manufacturing facility?"

Carmilla chuckled and shook her head, replying, "Nothing
so evil, I fear. Beyond that door lies the Karnstein-Bertholt
clan crypt. As you know from previous cases, vampires do
not turn into ash but instead return to the moment of death
that we avoided during our turning. The older generations are
embalmed therein, but the younger ones are cremated. Their
ashes in decorative urns line shelves carved into the mountain
itself. Perhaps one night I shall tell you stories of my noble
ancestors."

"I'd like that," Sam said with a smile. She sighed, watching
her breath drift away as a cloud of icy vapor before adding,
"My family's greatest claim to fame was my father, and we both
know how that turned out."

Sam felt a familiar squeeze on her hand as Carmilla said,
"Your family's greatest claim to fame has yet to have her story
concluded. Come, Martin should have our meal prepared."

The Karnstein-Bertholt dining hall was smaller than Sam
expected, but the varnished oak table had space for twenty
diners. Carmilla sat at the table's head, and Sam sat in the
seat to her right. Martin placed before each of them a golden-
rimmed porcelain plate full of sauerbraten topped with a red
onion and mushroom gravy, roasted potatoes and carrots, and

sauteed asparagus. He filled glasses with a dark crimson blood wine for each of them, provided Sam a glass of water, and set a sliced loaf of a crusty bread and a dish of herbed butter on the table. He then exited silently, leaving the two to dine by candlelight.

After several moments of idle conversation and dining, Sam asked, "This is a lovely setting, 'Milla, but do you always dine here? It seems like it would be lonely."

"I normally dine, such as I do, in my office while I work or in my drawing room," she replied. "I dine at this ancestral table of mine on special occasions."

Sam smiled and fidgeted with her hair. "I'm honored," she said, "but the thought of eating in your drawing room, especially while you paint, perhaps, has an intimate appeal. And as much as I enjoy wearing pretty clothes, I almost feel like I need formal attire for this room."

Carmilla laughed, bearing her fangs, as she sipped her wine. "At one point in time," she said, "that would have been expected of you. But I agree. A more informal setting would be nice, and it would be far less wasteful."

"Wasteful?" Sam asked, looking at the table. "Um, 'Milla, we've emptied a bottle of wine, and devoured a loaf of bread already. And if Martin brings a cake out, I can promise you that I'll eat at least half of it, so you don't feel it's wasted."

Carmilla shook her head as she sliced a small square from her sauerbraten and said, "It's not the food that is wasted. What we do not eat, the servants will eat. It's more the amount of spices and extra energy and time taken to prepare such feasts for vampires."

"Oh, that's right," Sam said as she used a slice of bread to sop up the gravy on her plate, "you can't digest food as well as

36

we can, but you can eat it. It's just more efficient to get your nutrients from blood."

Carmilla swallowed her bite and nodded, saying, "That is correct. Nor do we taste spice and seasoning in food as we once did, except in unusual circumstances, unless it is over-spiced for mortal palettes. I remember that table game you showed me—the *Masquerade* or something—and asked how close it was to the truth. I still remember that special ability that allowed vampires to eat food when all of us can do that. We simply must wait longer to process and digest than a mortal would. As a result, most of us eat only on special occasions when either we prepare our own food, or a specialist prepares it for us."

Sam tilted her head to the side and asked, "Do I want to know what those *exceptional circumstances* are?"

Carmilla dabbed the corners of her mouth with her burgundy cloth napkin before answering, "A fledgling, freshly turned, can taste food as they did in life. Also, when a vampire begins turning a mortal, and after the exchange of blood between them but before the mortal passes into immortality, the parent vampire may taste food through their progeny."

"That makes sense," Sam replied. She leaned forward as she sipped her wine and added, "I thought you were going to mention some kinky vampire sex ritual or blood sacrifice."

The Countess smirked and leaned forward. She rested her chin in her hand as she purred, "I've never participated in a kinky sex ritual, kinky sex, yes, but you are well aware of that, Samantha Blake." She winked, causing Sam to blush and fiddle with the collar of her sweater, before Carmilla continued, "And blood sacrifices are powerful but wasteful. A last resort, but nothing kinky."

They continued their conversation as Martin cleared the table and then brought a chocolate Yule log with marzipan leaves and mushroom-shaped cream puffs. Sam's eyes widened as she watched him cut level, inch-thick slices of that gorgeous ganache-covered, rolled chocolate cake with a Swiss meringue buttercream. He served them both and exited. Sam presented her fork as if it were a fencer's blade, looked Carmilla in the eyes, smirked, and said, "Challenge accepted."

* * *

After two hours of post-meal conversation, Sam's lengthy travels and the amount of food she ate overcame her desire to stay awake with Carmilla. She fought hard, yawning and nodding off randomly during conversation; she infrequently interjected the random thoughts that entered her mind. Carmilla smiled and laughed warmly as her friend lost her battle against sleep. In the end, sleep prevailed, and Carmilla guided Sam to the guest chamber and then bid her a good night. As Carmilla closed the door to the guest chamber, she heard Sam mumble something about seeing her in an hour into her pillow. Carmilla smiled and returned to her drawing room.

In her slumber, Sam's dream returned her to events occurring just over a month earlier. The moon had just started to wane, and it was the day before her birthday. She raced through the forest north of Bannagh toward Old Tom's Hill alone. She saw the lit torches and heard the chanting as both the Hermetic Order of the Astrum Argentum and the Order of the Dragon worked to summon the Sumerian entity Zozo.

As she surveyed the carnage at the hill's northern base, she recalled the stench of burning flesh as the thick clouds of smoke peeled away and formed a swirling boundary to a battlefield between herself and the goat-headed fiend. Her breaths came in short, quick bursts as Zozo bared his rotting, yellowed fangs through a terrifying grin. Lowering its four wings, the fiend stalked toward her. Sam's eyes shot wide. Her arm quaked as she aimed her Walther at her foe. She pulled the trigger. Click. Her heart sank as her eyes lowered to gaze upon the unloaded gun she held. She cursed.

Zozo backhanded Sam to the ground and dragged her to the center of the burned and broken bodies surrounding an altar by her hair. She screamed as his claws, covered in black fur, ripped at her hair, dragging her across thorns and broken bodies. Tears rained from her eyes, clenched shut to avoid seeing the bloodied, mangled bodies surrounding her. He kicked her in the stomach, and she folded, grunting in pain. Zozo grabbed one of the torch poles and jammed its butt into her throat. She sputtered blood. With a brittle and hollow laugh that reverberated through her mind, Sam watched as Zozo spun the torch and thrust the flame into her abdomen. Sam screamed through gritted teeth as the tears mixed with choking coughs from smoke. Zozo hurled the torch to the side and began pummeling Sam's body and face, his fists crushing her bones and his claws tearing into her flesh and muscle. Her eyes closed.

They opened. Sam found herself in the middle of a hedge maze. Through the fog that surrounded her, she saw the outline of the crescent moon as it waxed in the night sky. Wearing a flowing dressing gown of white lace and carrying a three-pronged golden candelabra, Sam called for Carmilla. Her heart pounded. Her breaths came in quick, short puffs. She received no reply to her calls. She raced along the grassy corridors, retracing her steps at dead ends, and peering as far as the fog allowed when she came to a crossroads. Her head darted frantically from side to side as she found neither Carmilla nor an exit.

And then Sam heard the distant but distinct sounds of a chamber ensemble playing Bach. She followed the sound, breathing a deep sigh of relief when she heard the murmur of conversation ahead. She knew Carmilla must have been hosting a garden party, but why she was not invited, she had no clue. Sam followed the sounds as the maze condensed into a single path, and then that path opened into a large garden where a dozen guests sat around wicker tables in in velvet cushioned wicker chairs as the chamber ensemble, all wearing black suits and emotionless white masks sat as the violinist and harpsichordist played Sonata in F Major. Hurt by believing she was excluded from this party, Sam steeled her visage, adjusted the dressing gown to be as modest as possible, and sauntered purposefully into the gathering.

The guests paid no attention to her as she walked amongst them. They continued drinking from crystal glasses and conversing with their table mates as if she were not present. Scanning the party scene, she saw servants in black domino masks providing refreshments while moving silently through the scene. She saw a table with one person who sat with their back to her. This person had long black hair and wore a burgundy dress. Believing this to be Carmilla, Sam sauntered toward her, taking a crystal glass of wine from one of the servants' trays as she walked.

Sitting in the chair opposite this woman, Sam saw that it was not Carmilla, but the woman's face, her beautiful, alabaster, proud face, had an aura like Carmilla's. They talked for what felt like hours. Sam saw the woman's mouth moving, but she heard no sound emerge. Sam responded to each silent utterance by providing deep personal information. They leaned toward each other and smiled as they talked. Sam twirled her hair around her finger as she spoke. Everything felt natural. When the woman licked her lips, Sam blushed. The woman crawled atop the table toward her, and the mask Sam believed to be the woman's beautiful face fell and shattered on the table. Sam screamed as the woman's serpentine face lunged forward on an elongated neck and sank its fangs into her neck.

Sam shot awake, finding herself in her bed in the guest chamber of Carmilla's castle. She wiped the cold sweat from her forehead before breathing deeply. The fire had begun to smolder, so, naked, she rose from the bed and threw another log into the hearth and watched as it caught fire. She donned her brown-belted blue bathrobe and walked back toward the bed. Picking up her cell phone, she frowned when she saw the hour. Sam switched on the flashlight and walked toward Carmilla's drawing room.

Carmilla, in her burgundy lace dressing gown, reclined on a chaise, reading a book and drinking blood wine. Sam breathed a sigh of relief when her hostess raised her eyes and asked, "It is an early hour, Sam. What troubles your sleep?"

Sam ran her fingers through her hair and asked, "What gave me away?"

Carmilla smiled and said, "Well, the sun is not up, and the clock says it is three in the morning. Aside from that, your hair is a mess and matted as if you had been sweating. And finally, you came to seek me. Combined, those observations suggest a troubled sleep." She then motioned to the chair nearest her

41

and said, "Sit, and we can converse until you feel calm enough to sleep again or until Martin prepares the morning coffee for you."

Sam smiled and curled up in the chair, leaning toward Carmilla who shifted position to mirror her friend. Carmilla listened attentively as Sam rambled the details of her dream as she could remember them. Her voice trembled as she sped through the fight with Zozo. The Countess poured Sam a glass of wine before refilling her own. After a few sips, Sam relaxed. Her vocal pace returned to normal, albeit tinged with confusion, as she recounted the events in the hedge maze and the garden party. When she finished recounting her dream, Sam downed her glass.

As she raised the empty glass and watched the firelight sparkle in its crystal, she gazed wistfully at Carmilla and said, "I remember when you finally convinced me to try blood wine. So much smoother than I thought, and not a hint of blood's iron taste."

Sipping her wine, Carmilla smiled and nodded. "I do as well," she said. "And inexperienced vintners produce swill by mixing blood with wine instead of fertilizing the soil with sanguimantic rituals to infuse the vivification powers inherent in blood into the grapes and, consequently, into the wine. And there is only one who has smoother blood wine."

"Nick Scratch," Sam said. "Yeah, after I said goodbye to my mom this year, he gave me a glass on the house. Can't say I'm not curious as to his angle there."

Carmilla shook her head and chuckled. She shrugged and said, "First of the Fallen, but still an angel when it suits him. You seem to be calming down, Sam."

Sam beamed and nodded, blushing slightly, before saying, "I

am, thank you, 'Milla. What were you reading?"

"A biography of Maximiliane Ackers," she said. "I remember discovering her work in the gloriously fun days of Weimar Berlin. The little Fuhrer and his twisted cultural morality police disapproved of her work and burned many copies, but I happened to have my own autographed first editions."

"Her books offend fascists," Sam said, nodding. "Perhaps I'll try to read them while I'm here—a powerful jaw, if you don't mind."

"Of course you may read my books. My home is yours," Carmilla replied. She then leaned forward, allowing her dressing gown to open, revealing her pert breasts, before she added, "You may enjoy all manner of pleasurable diversions you find here."

Fuck, I forgot how perfect those are, Sam thought as her breathing stopped momentarily. She swallowed hard and shook her head, shifting in her seat before replying, "You are persistent, 'Milla. If I thought it would work out, maybe."

Carmilla shrugged and winked. "I know you no longer desire a relationship, Samantha," she said. "However, perhaps a night here or there would be amenable. Besides that, you opened the door for me to walk through."

"I did," Sam said, shaking her head and chuckling. She raised her right eyebrow and added, "I don't think I've ever seen you yawn, 'Milla."

"I don't yawn often," she replied, "but a tedious meeting, this late hour, and a lot of wine still impacts me now as it did when I was a mortal. If you will excuse me, it is my turn to drift into sleep."

Sam nodded and snuffed the fire in the drawing room's hearth. Carmilla left the book on her oak side table. Sam rose

43

and shifted her robe, saying, "Well, you escorted me to my room, let me at least escort you to yours."

* * *

Paul Byron walked through the empty hallways of the Oberon Center at the corner of Willow and Yew. His thick fingers ran through his shaggy mop of strawberry blond hair, pushing back the hood of his oversized purple Hercules' Labors Gym and Crossfit Center hoodie. He was an average-looking man with hazel eyes, a bulbous nose, and a strong jaw with a cleft chin. He checked his phone conversation with his senior officer who gave him the address. His gaze shifted toward the ceiling as the fluorescent lights flickered. He grumbled as he read the signs on the various doors.

He turned toward the door marked Hain Private Investigations. The door was locked, and it appeared the light was off. He knocked three times on the glass. There was no response. It was then that he noticed the "Closed" sign hanging from the doorknob. He knocked again, and silence again responded. The same result occurred when he tried again. He cursed and turned to leave.

As he started walking, he paused and turned to his left. He tilted his head as he saw a door on the wall—a door he swore was not there when he approached Hain Private Investigations. The door had a frosted glass panel with the word "Enter" etched onto it in an elegant, calligraphic font. A pale blue light from beyond the door was visible through the frosted glass and around the door's edges. This seemed to be the only door on this floor with someone behind it. Byron shrugged, and thinking he had nothing to lose, he opened the door and entered.

Byron halted as he scanned the scene that greeted him. In the hallway, the only sound he heard were the echoes of his footsteps. Inside, he saw a lively bar with elegant tables and booths illuminated by candles set in bronze candelabra. A pack of werewolves sat in a corner booth, feasting and drinking. Byron thought he saw a handful of members of the Court of Earth and Winter, including satyrs, redcaps, and a dullahan taking the tables by the stage where a statuesque, caramel-skinned woman whose brown hair and horns curled elegantly sang "Stormy Weather" accompanied by an ensemble led by a man with reddish skin, slicked black hair, and a pointed goatee who played a French horn. From behind the bar, a tall, classically handsome man with slicked black hair, piercing green eyes, and three-day stubble called out in his aristocratic Londoner's voice, "Welcome to the Four Winds where all who enter are welcome to sit, drink, and share their stories. And the first one is always free."

The patrons shot Byron quick glances but paid him no mind as he walked to the bar. The bartender, in his white starched shirt and charcoal vest, leaned forward and said, "First time here? What would you like?"

Byron shrugged and scratched his head, and, in a marked Scouse dialect, he said, "A beer. I'm not picky."

The bartender smirked and nodded, responding, "Easy enough."

He turned and busied himself at the taps, pouring a rich, amber draught with a caramel head. He passed it across the bar with a smile and said, "Here you go, private stock."

"How much do I owe you," Byron asked.

"Didn't you hear me when you entered? The first one's free," the bartender said. "So, what brings you here?"

"I was trying to get some help for my fiancée," he said, looking toward the stage, "and I heard from somewhere that this Samantha Hain chick could help with her problem. Do you know where she is? She's not answering my calls or knocks."

"Samantha Hain, you say?" The bartender squinted as his eyes searched the man. Scratching his chin, he said, "Very few call her by that name. Ah! But where are my manners? I've not introduced myself, and this is my establishment. I am Nicholas Scratch, and you are?"

He held out his hand, and Byron shook it, saying, "Matthew Walpole. Say, you know that you share a name with the devil?"

Mister Scratch chuckled and said, "Well, we're both devilishly handsome, charming, and horny."

Byron chuckled and downed half his pint and said, "Damn, this is perfect. I'm going to need a second one. How much, by the way? I never pay more than five bucks for a beer."

Mister Scratch poured another drink and, with his back to Byron, said, "Money's not my desire, as I have plenty. If that's all you have, I suppose I can take it. If you're willing to put off payment, I suppose I could act like my namesake and take your soul. But my preference is a bit of barter—an exchange of information or services for a drink or information. The choice is yours."

As the singer began crooning "Trust in Me," Byron scratched his head and looked around. He realized he was underdressed for the establishment and began shifting from foot to foot. Byron looked down, unable to meet Mister Scratch's piercing gaze. He sighed and said, "Fucking strange but whatever old man. What info you want?"

Mister Scratch gazed lovingly at the singer. With a wistful

sigh, he said, "After all these years, my wife is still the most stunning creature ever created. And yes, I heard you, Matthew. And if you want another round, all I ask is that you tell me what your business with Miss Hain is. Is that fair?"

Byron shrugged and nodded. He downed the rest of his beer and pushed the pint glass toward Mister Scratch. As the bartender poured him a second round, Byron said, "My fiancée, June, and I were on a holiday road trip that started in Zurich and was supposed to end in Vienna. Well, we stopped in Telfs for that Krampus-loaf thing when we met this charming man who promised to show us the 'true nightlife' of the city. Well, I went to the loo for a crap, and when I got back, I saw him bite her on the neck. Now, I'm a real man, so I punched the wanker in his crooked face. Fucking coward ran. Now, June is all anemic and can't stand being in the sun. That's why I want this Samantha Hain."

"That's a terrible thing to happen on holiday," Mister Scratch said. "Would you happen to remember the assailant's name?"

Byron shook his head while drinking his second pint. "No," he said, "We'd had a lot to drink, you see, so I barely remember talking to anyone. What's it to you?"

Mister Scratch shrugged and winked. He poured himself a glass of red wine and said, "Nothing personal, but I can put you in touch with Miss Hain, so…"

Byron sighed. Shaking his head, he asked, "What info you want now?"

Mister Scratch shook his head, saying, "Oh no. Miss Hain will want to speak in person about the specifics of your issue, so that requires divulging her specific location at present. And that would require a favor."

Byron slammed the pint glass on the bar, cracking it. The

nearby conversations went silent as they turned toward the bar. He shouted, "Bullshit! I didn't come here to get mocked by some twit who fancies himself a devil-wannabe and asks for favors and personal information. I ought to fucking leave. What you say about that?"

The performance stopped. The crowd turned away as Mister Scratch's laughter bellowed through the bar. With a shrug, he extended his arms and said, "I fancy myself a great many things, Mister *Walpole*, but what I am is someone who has the information you need. Ask yourself what price is too high for your *fiancée's* health and safety. Oh yes, if you need Miss Hain's assistance, then your fiancée's medical malady is the least of your worries. If you desire not to hear my terms, you are free to walk through any of the four doors that exit my establishment. Of course, if you choose to walk that path, your fiancée will face a Grimm fate."

Byron tensed and bowed up against Mister Scratch, who stood motionless with a confident smile on his face. Byron clenched his fists. His heart thundered against his ribs. He snarled like a bull preparing to charge. Two burly men dressed in sleeveless vests made their presence felt, but Mister Scratch waved them aside. They retreated into the bar's shadows, their eyes glowing through the darkness.

The patrons busied themselves in their drinks as the silent standoff lasted for five minutes before Byron's shoulders slumped with a sigh, and he said, "Name your price."

With a practiced smugness, Mister Scratch sipped his wine and said, "I thought you'd see things my way. Oh, don't look like someone kicked a puppy. I'm evil, but I'm not cruel. What I ask of you is simple and will be easy once you are in Miss Hain's vicinity. By the first bell announcing Christmas Eve's midnight mass, I want you to deliver to me the black Madonna statue from St. Januarius' Cathedral in Karnsburg in the Tyrol state of Austria. Fail to do this, and I'll find another payment." He winked.

"Stealing from a church isn't the worst thing I've done, I guess," Byron said. "I suppose negotiating another price isn't possible?"

"I'm afraid not. My prices are firm but fair," Mister Scratch said.

Paul Byron sighed and nodded. "Yeah," he said, "I need to get in touch with her. I'll pay it."

They shook hands, and Mister Scratched handed him Sam Hain's business card with her email address. Byron left The Four Winds by the same door through which he entered. As the bar returned to its normal level of activity. As the performers shifted and played "Sympathy for the Devil," Nicholas Scratch smiled.

3

Chapter 3

I slept for most of the daylight hours after seeing Carmilla drift into her sleep of death as dawn approached. My feelings for her aside, she has remained one of my best and most trusted friends, so I wanted to spend as much of my vacation time here with her as possible, which I couldn't do if I kept to my normal hours. It's not like I haven't done this before on several cases for both human and folkloric clients, and at least this time, no one's life is in danger.

The next three of my inverted day and night cycles reminded me both why I fell in love with Carmilla and why I ended our relationship. From the drawing room where I read some of her gloriously leather-scented antique books, which she gained when they were new, I heard her remain calm on business calls when, even with my broken German, I could tell that other parties attempted to talk over her or to explain things to her that she already knew. The calm but firm tone with which she shut down any disrespect always impressed me. My response has always involved two middle fingers and included the phrase, "Fuck you, shit stain!" Both of us had confidence, but she had a far more even temper than I did.

And maybe it was that vampiric mind control shit, but our conversations have always been open, deep, and without reservation. Tonight, however, we did little talking after she convinced me to pose for a life-sized portrait. To her credit, she neither asked for me to wear only lingerie nor be naked. She asked me to dress as I would for an investigation, so I wore a white button-down blouse, a burgundy pencil skirt, black, back-seamed stockings held up by a garter belt, and black pumps. Then she sat me in one of her velvet-cushioned chairs with a glass of bourbon in one hand and a fountain pen, held like a cigarette, in the other. She denied me the bourbon until she finished the pencil sketch that she would then shade with various charcoals. For a cold winter's night in a drafty castle, I found myself afraid to sweat through my clothing.

I lingered for a while at Carmilla's door as we parted for the morning. Leaning against the cold stone of the castle's wall, I lingered for a while after she closed the door. Then I sighed. The dusky rose scent of her perfume lingered in the air. It sucked being so physically close to her, but knowing that I would likely freak out the moment her sleeping body went cold. I wouldn't scream—not again—but I would cry and curl into the fetal position. I gazed at the door and the darkness emerging from beneath it and sighed again. Candelabra in hand, I walked to my chamber, stripped, and curled into bed, holding a pillow tightly.

"Follow me," came a voice that pierced my dream.

I woke, covered in cold sweat, from a nightmare-plagued sleep. Groaning, I blinked and saw my door was open. I cursed and rolled over, pulling the blanket over my head. A freezing wind blew through the room and extinguished the hearth. I shivered. Then I felt someone shake my shoulder the way my mother would wake me for school in the morning. I swatted at the source of the touch with a hand, but I touched nothing.

"Follow me," the voice repeated with greater urgency.

I groaned again and rolled over. Without opening my eyes, I mumbled, "Ugh, 'Milla, we just went to sleep ten minutes ago. You should be in bed."

"Follow me," the voice ordered.

I rubbed my eyes and blinked to see Carmilla, in a white nightgown, standing in my doorway and calling out for me to follow her. She had a three-pronged candelabra with blue flames in her left hand, and she beckoned me with her right. She appeared hazy, like an out-of-focus image, so I blinked a few more times. Nothing changed. Confused and groggy, I stumbled to grab my phone and the bathrobe, so I didn't walk through a cold, drafty castle naked. I switched on the flashlight and stumbled through the door after her.

I followed her as she glided along the stone floor of the hallway. That's one vampire ability the movies always got right. And fuck, I'd be a liar if I said that wasn't cool or, in this case, hot. She was unusually silent. I asked her what was so important and where we were going, but she never answered. I followed because I trusted her and because I was curious. This was not normal for Carmilla and for our friendship, so I had to get to the bottom of this hall.

I followed her down the spiraling stairs all the way to the first floor. We passed the family dining hall and the great hall, which now stood empty. We followed the only corridor on this floor not illuminated by electric lights. As we reached the double-locked door that went to the dungeons, I watched as Carmilla floated through the door without causing so much as a lock or chain to rattle.

Stunned and confused, I stood in silence, my jaw open, until I heard Carmilla's voice from behind me say, "Samantha? Sam? What are you doing here?"

I spun around and saw Carmilla standing there in her burgundy dressing gown. My eyes shot wide. My jaw slammed against my chin. I spun back and forth, pointing alternately at her and at the door, and stammered, "But you—how did you—from my nightmare—and you glided through the—weren't wearing—white gown—how did you change clothes—what the fuck is happening?"

I dropped to my knees on the cold stone floor. Carmilla glided over, knelt, and wrapped her arm around me. Instinctively, my head flopped onto her shoulder. She held me, and for whatever reason, I cried. Smelling her natural spiced honey scent penetrating through her dusty rose perfume made me smile and sigh wistfully. I felt her hand stroke my back gently. She started to run her fingers through my hair and stopped. And I whimpered.

Apparently, Martin heard this and descended the stairs to investigate. He and Carmilla helped me to my feet. We ascended the stairs to the drawing room where they helped me to the chaise. Martin excused himself and returned carrying a bottle of blood wine, a full blood bag, and a bottle of bourbon. He again excused himself, and Carmilla sat next to me. She popped the blood bag as easily as I used to pop Capri Suns and drained the entire thing. She then poured herself a glass of wine and me a glass of bourbon.

I took a swig of the bourbon and slowly sighed. Still confused, I looked into her eyes and asked, "That wasn't you I saw walk through the locked door?"

She shook her head. "No," she said, "I cannot walk through solid forms. I am not even of a line that can transform into mist."

I tilted my head and asked, "Then what exactly did I just see?"

"I do not know why she would appear to you," Carmilla said, "but the spirit you saw was the ghost of my younger sister, Elisa."

"Your sister," I asked, sliding closer to Carmilla's chair. "I know you've mentioned her, but I thought you said she died as a mortal."

Carmilla nodded, her eyes closed as she sighed and said, "She died one year before it was tradition for us to be turned. She has remained here since that day. I am surprised, as much as you mean to me, that she was not more conversational. Perhaps it would have been less confusing for you if she were."

I sipped my bourbon and shook my head. Chuckling, I said, "You know, 'Milla, I've spoken with faeries, lycanthropes, fallen in love with a vampire, even made a deal with the devil. You'd think that a simple ghost wouldn't have caused me to react like that."

She smiled warmly. I bit my lip as my eyes focused on the movement of her lips. And then she said, "You have been under mental stress with everything that happened in Ireland. I knew I should have immediately traveled there when word reached us of the murders."

I smiled, blushing, as she finished and then said, "No, 'Milla, I mean, I would've loved to have you by my side - er, to have your help - but I wouldn't want you to put yourself in danger. I know you're strong, but there was something about what happened there that I still can't quite put my finger on. Something doesn't add up."

"You will find the answer," she said with a yawn. "However, I am afraid that I must retire for the morning. You are welcome to remain awake or to return to sleep. Regardless, I have already instructed Martin to check on you throughout the day."

I nodded and followed her to her bedroom. She turned and smiled, and I said, "Thanks, 'Milla. All of this means a lot. Thank you."

She bowed her head and replied, "It is I who should be giving you thanks, Sam. Well, good morning." And then she closed the door behind her.

I exhaled again. Running my fingers through my hair, I chuckled. Of course she lived in a haunted castle. And then I sighed, my mood darkening, as I realized that maybe being haunted by the ghost of someone you love wasn't the best thing. She told me that her sister passed on, but she never went into details about the death or about her sister's life. I didn't push for them, knowing how I hated when people asked about my mom's passing. I respected her privacy and figured that if she wanted me to know, she would have told me.

* * *

Church bells announced the witching hour to all who remained awake in Karnsburg. Stray scraps of paper, pine needles, and evergreen leaves danced in widening gyres along the paths of the icy winter winds. As the last bell tolled, the last light of the town's Christmas Market dimmed and went dark. Streetlights, the signs of the few still-open businesses, and house lights provided some illumination, but darkness covered the small town. All was still. All was quiet.

The loudest noise in Karnsburg pulsed from inside of *Klub Abweichend*, the larger of the town's two discotheques. Blue, purple, and green lights pulse in rhythm with the bass, illuminating the darkness around this converted guardhouse with the Athenian temple-style pediment supported by three Corinthian columns that kept the bouncers safe from rain and snow. Inside, the near-capacity crowd gyrated to the bass-heavy electronica provided by the dancing, pink-haired woman in the DJ booth. The blue, purple, and green light from the wall panels pulsed and reflected from the mirrored ceiling above the dance floor. Behind a clear glass bar, the bartenders served cocktails that glowed in fluorescent hues beneath the black lights that hung over the bar.

A young woman with a copper-highlighted, auburn side-swept pixie cut approached the bar and ordered her drink. Her bright clothing, though appropriate for a discotheque, would leave her cold as she left the club. She bobbed her head along with the music as the bartender, a thirty-something man with buzzed blond hair and grayish blue eyes, handed her a fuchsia concoction in a martini glass from which dry ice smoke bubbled over like fog rising from the sea. When the smoke dissipated, she sipped the cocktail and reveled in the bubbling, cold rush the dry ice imparted to a spiced apple martini. She looked back at the dance floor with a searching gaze. She checked her cell phone and saw its battery had died. Stomping the floor, she cursed under her breath and returned to her drink.

As she sipped, sweat beading on her forehead and her chest rising with her rapid breathing, a well-dressed man with blond curls that fell to the bottom of his shoulder blades approached and stood next to her. She glanced in his direction and found him attractive enough, if nondescript in any feature other than his hair. He smiled and winked before ordering a coffee-colored beer. He turned and surveyed the dance floor, drinking his beer in silence.

Without taking his eyes off the dance floor, he leaned toward her and said in a tipsy British accent, "Having a good night?"

She nodded, her drink in her mouth, and replied, "Yes."

He extended his right hand to her, saying, "I'm George Ruthwen."

"Sofia," she replied as she shook his leathery hand, rolling her eyes at the clichéd approach.

"I haven't seen you here before," he said, "but it's always crowded these days. Are you from here?"

She shook her head and said, "I'm here on holiday with a friend. Can't seem to find her."

"She's probably still here," George said as he downed half his beer before adding, "The bar is a good place to stay and wait. Easy to find you."

Sofia nodded and continued searching for her friend. She hated conversing with strangers in discotheques because the loud music made hearing challenging and because they always had an awkward hollowness to them. She pretended to send a text message on her cell phone as she neared the end of her drink.

"You seem worried," George noted. "Do you think your friend is in danger?"

"No," Sofia shook her head as she answered. "It's just not like her to not return my texts. We even text during classes."

"What do you study?" He asked.

"Engineering at TU in Berlin," she answered.

"Oh," he said, "I am an engineer. Been working on improving waste heat recovery through cascading Rankine cycles so that we can have cheaper and more sustainable eco-friendly power options."

Sofia's eyes lit up, and the two began talking about work and research. The bartender rolled his eyes and chuckled silently as they filled their conversation with technical jargon. He wagered that neither had many chances to talk about such things as openly and animatedly at a discotheque. It made him smile. Sofia gently squeezed his arm as they leaned toward each other. Neither focused any attention on the dance floor. After half an hour of animated, engaged conversation, George suggested they find a late-night snack, and so they left together.

George led her to a small restaurant that was little more than a glorified food cart in a shopping center near the discotheque that stayed open for police officers, first responders, and club goers. George claimed they sold the best vegan currywurst and spiced apple chips in Karnsburg. Though this town was far smaller than Berlin, Sofia enjoyed the snack. They continued talking, and George promised to walk Sofia back to her friend's house because he knew the town well and could easily find it when given an address.

They walked through the dark streets, and the flickering streetlights cast stop-motion shadows across their paths. As a gentle snow fell, he led her on a shortcut through a series of alleys that avoided municipal government buildings. As they moved beneath a heavy shadow, Sofia leaned against the wall, smiled at George, and licked her lips, parting them slightly as she gazed into his eyes. He met her gaze, and the left corner of his lips quivered as he stroked her cheek with the back of his right hand. Her breaths came faster as she leaned toward him. He raised an eyebrow. She nodded affirmatively, arching her back. He slid his right hand around her head and his left into his trench coat's pocket as he leaned.

Their lips met. The roughness of George's lips shocked Sofia momentarily, but her tongue danced around them and helped moisten them. She clutched his back and purred into his mouth. His right hand cupped the back of her neck and held her close. Hidden in his pocket, he slid something metallic onto his left hand. He pushed her against the wall, shocking her momentarily before slamming his open left hand into her neck. She cried in pain and surprise as she felt two sharp points puncture her skin. George held her in place with the weight of his body as he used his right hand to draw back a syringe-like apparatus that sucked the blood from her veins. She called for help once, but he thrust his lips onto hers in a deep, rough kiss that muffled her words. In vain, Sofia tried to push the larger and much stronger man off her.

After a few minutes, Sofia ceased her struggle. Her body fell limp against George's body. He removed the apparatus which resembled a set of brass knuckles with a pair of fangs attached to a syringe from her neck and then dropped it back into his pocket. He looked at her lifeless body beneath an awning that would keep it from being covered by snow. Kneeling, he folded her arms across her chest, closed her eyes with his thumb, and stood. He then made the sign of the cross and nodded.

"Nothing personal," he said, "I'm sure you're a good person, Sofia, and I hope you'll forgive me. But it's for the greater good of bringing light and truth into this dark, vile world." Stepping over her body, he then walked into the darkness of the night as the church bells tolled Lauds.

* * *

Sam awoke two hours before sunset the following night. Wearing a blue and orange striped cardigan over a white button-down blouse with a Peter Pan collar and pecan brown maxi skirt, she sprawled on the chaise in the drawing room, sipping a cup of black coffee and eating toast with apricot jam. The fire crackled in the hearth, and the scents of cinnamon, cardamom, and clove, emerging from two large pillar candles atop the mantle, perfumed the air. Martin walked in quietly and handed him the day's issue of *The Karnsburg Crier*.

Sam shrugged and said, "Well, I guess we can see how well that Duolingo app helped me over the past month."

He smiled and chuckled once, saying, "I know that the Countess does not have a television set, preferring her books and art to other such diversions; however, I thought perhaps you would desire for knowledge of current events while inside this house."

She smiled gently and asked, "She tends to live in the past, and not just the time when we were together, doesn't she?"

He nodded. "She has survived for nearly three centuries, and many regrets weigh upon her." He refilled my cup and added, "Perhaps you will have a positive influence upon her."

He excused himself to perform other duties, and Sam sat in silence. She stared into her coffee cup, wishing that, like tea, there were leaves she could pretend she knew how to read for divinatory purposes. Her own feelings toward Carmilla were complicated, and she suspected that Carmilla knew that. If Carmilla knew that, then Martin likely knew that as well. But she cared about Carmilla, and she wanted her to be happy. She always sensed a darkness hung over the vampire, but she let herself believe it was the pressure of being her clan's matriarch. Since encountering Elisa's ghost, Sam began contemplating other causes.

She opened *The Crier* and skimmed the headlines. The newspaper devoted only two pages to politics, which Sam found refreshing. Most of the twenty-page daily newspaper featured recipes, local events, editorials, and an advice column that covered etiquette, gift giving, apologizing, and even gardening. The police blotter caught her attention with a headline that she thought read, "Young Woman Found Drained of Blood by Neck. Police Seek Murderer."

At 0545 this morning, Ada Bauer discovered the body of one Sofia Pichler, 21, in an alley behind Bauer's Bake Box. Police arrived two hours later and found Pichler died from blood loss caused by two puncture wounds on her neck. Police have no leads at this time. Any with information are invited to call Polizeiinspektion Innsbruck.

Sam folded the paper and set it on the side table. She grabbed her coffee cup and slid her feet into her slippers. She sighed and looked down at the paper before picking up her cell phone to text Destiny, "Let your dad know I'm going to call him tomorrow. Maybe fish for information on open cases. Thanks!"

With her coffee cup in hand, she walked through the drafty castle halls to Carmilla's bed chamber. She held her breath as she walked. Her mind raced faster than her feet moved. Carmilla could have done that, but she did not leave the castle. She has not killed any mortal since she and Sam met. From the photograph, the girl appeared to be Carmilla's romantic type, which meant that she would consider feeding from her but not to the point of death. Carmilla had more restraint and control than most in these situations. She had too much to lose. She reached the wooden door and stopped. Sam inhaled deeply and bit her lip as her hand slid on the frigid iron handle.

Sam's phone vibrated as a British phone number called her. She cocked an eyebrow and answered, "Sam Hain, Private Investigator. What do you need?"

The accent was unfamiliar to her, but it was a British man who answered and said, "Miss Hain? Ah, good, this number was correct. So sorry, I'm Matthew Walpole, and I need your help."

"I'm on vacation," Sam said. "I can't promise that I have time to help. And I can't just get to England."

"No, no, no," he said, "I'm in Innsbruck right now. My fiancée, Mathilda, and I were in Karnsburg a few weeks ago. I think she was bitten by a vampire as she's anemic and claims the sun burns. I'm sorry to interrupt your holiday, but I don't know who else to ask, and my cousin, Mabd Donovan, said you helped her out of a fix, so…"

Sam recalled Mabd's situation after she ran afoul of the Duilearga and several other groups for posting a TikTok video of a banshee singing on the moors, and how no one but Sam proved capable of helping her. She inhaled deeply and said, "I've got plans for the night, but I can meet you tomorrow afternoon in Karnsburg to discuss the situation. But I can't promise anything."

"I'll take what I can get," he said and ended the call.

It worried her that Carmilla slept with her door unlocked, but it made tonight's investigation easier. She pushed the door open and stepped into Carmilla's bedroom. No windows opened to the outside. Her eyes widened as she saw the beautiful antique vanity, dresser, and wardrobe of mahogany with gold fittings that Carmilla had likely owned for centuries.

Sam smiled when she saw both Carmilla's watercolors and a photograph from their first date hanging on the walls. She inhaled sharply when she saw the ornate carvings on the four posts of Carmilla's mahogany bed.

"Fuck, that's sexy," she said as she ran her hand along the bedpost.

Sam crept toward the side of the bed, holding her breath as she moved through the cold room. Her fingertips brushed against the translucent burgundy silk canopy that pooled along the floor. When she reached the head of the bed, Sam tensed her muscles. She paused for a moment and closed her eyes as she pulled back the canopy to see Carmilla sprawled on her left side, naked, and surrounded by velvet pillows. Sam exhaled. Her shoulders relaxed. Carmilla was pale with angular features, signs that she had not recently fed. Sam hesitated but touched her icy, lifeless cheek.

Sam cried as memories flooded her mind. She recalled the first night she spent with Carmilla and her scream upon waking to find how cold and dead a sleeping vampire truly was. And yet she smiled because she knew Carmilla was both innocent and safe. Her phone vibrated in her hand, shocking her back into the present. Destiny replied that the Grimms were conducting investigations in Dresden, Munich, and Vienna and then asked why Sam wanted to know.

"Just a local news article about a college student who was killed," Sam texted. "Someone drained her of enough blood to kill her and dumped her in an alley."

"You think it's a vampire?" Destiny replied.

Sam frowned as her fingers sent the words, "Killed by two puncture wounds. I just want to be careful."

"Ok," Destiny responded. "I told dad you would call. I'll keep an ear out. Did you check your suitcase liner pocket?"

Sam rolled her eyes and chuckled. "Yes," she replied, "I found the dental dams. We don't need them."

"Just want you safe, since you don't have a gun," she said and punctuated her text with a winking face and one that laughed so hard it cried. Sam shook her head, laughing in response, and then sat on the floor by the door.

Sam scrolled through her social media and then read one of the tawdry, dollar romance novellas she downloaded through the Kindle app. Unknown to her, the sun set on the Austrian countryside as she finished the second, poorly written sex scene. Carmilla groaned from the bed, snapping Sam's attention back to the present. She heard Carmilla rolling around and yawning. Her mind flooded with memories of the Countess' naked form, her back arched, as she returned to life from her daily death.

"Martin," Carmilla called out with a slight pout, "is that you? Do I have a meeting tonight or can I take my time waking?"

Sam smiled, having never seen this cute side of Carmilla before. She stifled a giggle and said, "No, 'Milla, it's me. I was just checking up on you."

"Sam?" Carmilla frantically shot her head and chest through the canopy. Smirking, she purred, "My bed is far more comfortable than the floor."

"Not the way you were sprawled out on that bed," Sam countered.

Carmilla cocked an eyebrow and crawled forward. Sitting atop the chest at the foot of the bed, she then covered herself in mocking modesty as she said, "Samantha Blake Hain! We are not married, and yet, you snuck into my chamber and spied upon me as I slept. When did you become so forward?"

Sam stood and folded her arms across her chest. She walked forward and stood in front of Carmilla. Leaning forward, placing her face just a breath from the vampire's, Sam's breathing trembled. She bit her lip and then said, "What are you going to do? Spank me?"

Carmilla stood and, in an instant, moved behind Sam. Breathing on her neck, Carmilla chuckled as Sam trembled. The Countess purred, "Not until after we visit the *Christkindl-markt* tonight." She then blew Sam a kiss and glided to her wardrobe to find clothing.

* * *

The Karnsburg Christmas Market stood within and sprawled out from the town square at the center of Karnsburg like a village within a town. Two dozen stalls, shaped like tiny houses made of maple and mahogany and illuminated by strings of white lights, rested in little streets surrounding the massive, eighty-foot tall fir tree adorned with solar powered white candles and strings of light at the main village's center. Amidst the chatter and laughter of adults and children, the sounds of fryers bubbling, the smells of pretzels and pastries baking, and the siren song of a hand-carved, wooden carousel filled the winter night's air. Though the stalls had painted their roofs to be covered in snow, only the faintest hint of that decoration was visible beneath the blanketing of snow that had fallen that afternoon and continued to fall gently that evening.

Sam and Carmilla walked through the crowd, both enjoying a blend of calmness and anonymity. Though neither was a celebrity mobbed by fans, both knew the feeling of being watched while going about their daily routines. Beneath her white wool trench, Carmilla wore a black turtleneck, white trousers, and black riding boots. Sam wore a white lace collared black sweater with a white outline of the late Justice Ruth Bader Ginsburg that read, "Judging You;" a pair of dark wash, boot cut jeans; and a pair of gray snakeskin ankle boots with a chunky black heel.

They stopped at an L-shaped stall selling hot and cold mead and decorative but functional drinking horns. Carmilla purchased a cold black mead, because the black currants used to flavor the wine brought back Christmas memories with her family before the Countess was turned. Sam purchased a horn with her name painted on the side in golden letters filled with a smooth, hot acerglyn mead whose maple flavor reminded her of breakfast.

As they walked through the crowd, Sam giggled as the white clouds of her breath floated through the air. Carmilla kept her plastic mead cup close to her face to camouflage her lack of breathing. Sam's smile lowered as she saw Carmilla's skin had grown paler than when they left. Sam leaned in and whispered, "Do you need to feed?"

"You watched me eat before we left," Carmilla replied.

Sam nodded as they walked, musing, "It's just that you're growing pale. I guess I assumed your cheeks would get flushed in the cold like mine do."

Carmilla chuckled, shaking her head and running her fingers through her hair, as she said, "I used to be that way, but as the centuries have passed, I find myself feeling more comfortable in the cold. It stings me far less now than it did a century ago. I do not know what that means." She shrugged and then added, "or if it means anything."

"This is nice," Sam said, "and knowing Martin isn't waiting

in the car makes it easier to enjoy everything."

"He has been an invaluable servant and friend," Carmilla said, smiling wistfully. She glanced at Sam and then turned her head as their eyes met before saying, "But it is nice for it to be just the two of us."

"So, what's in that little forest," Sam asked, pointing toward a grove of fir trees with a few stalls illuminated by white candles. "It looks like fun."

"Oh," Carmilla said, tensing her muscles in excitement. "That's an area for adults. There are more sophisticated foods, higher quality wines, and softer lighting. Traditional crafters both sell and demonstrate their work. And there are diversions such as axe throwing, knife throwing, and a simple archery range."

Sam squeezed Carmilla's hand for a moment as she quickened her pace and said, "Let's go then."

As they walked through the wooden arch that read *Liebhaberhain* in golden letters, Carmilla silently whispered a hopeful prayer. The scents of the fir trees paired with the rich aromas of rose, cinnamon, clove, coriander, orange, and ginger to create an intoxicating miasma that flushed the skin and warmed the heart. Carmilla purchased two glasses of glühwein while Sam marveled at the intricately sculpted and painted marzipan treats for sale alongside chocolate-dipped strawberries and mirror-glazed sacher tortes. A chamber ensemble played soft, seasonal music from traditional medieval songs through contemporary carols.

They laughed and talked as they watched a master glassblower create intricate ornaments with pinpoint-sized snowflakes suspended inside a pale blue glass globe. They made their way to the archery range, which contained three targets affixed to hay bales set thirty yards from the firing line. After failing to even hit the bales after a dozen arrows, Sam handed the simple red bow to Carmilla and picked up her glass of wine. Carmilla smiled over her shoulder and winked before taking aim and hitting the target eight times, and of those eight hits, she hit the bullseye five times.

"I'll stick to the gun," Sam said as they continued exploring the grove, "but you're good. I didn't know you were an archer."

"Growing up as an heir to a noble house," Carmilla said, "I was expected to learn the bow. Lisa was far better than I am. But you are more skilled with the gun than I am, and the sound of it firing hurts my ears."

Sam rested her hand on Carmilla's lower back and asked, "Human or vampire trait?"

"The latter," the Countess said.

They walked side by side, occasionally touching the other as they enjoyed the Christmas market. As the bells tolled nine o'clock and the lights began to dim, Carmilla's phone rang. Upon seeing it was Martin, she answered, "Yes, Martin?"

"Forgive me, my Countess," he said, "I would not disturb your date—er, your evening out—were it not important. However, you have a visitor. Lord Volny has arrived from Budapest, and he expects to speak with you soon."

Carmilla's eyes narrowed, and her lips pursed. She said, "We will return within the hour."

Carmilla sped home so that they arrived in under an hour. Sam white-knuckled the car's armrest as the Countess refused to slow down as the mountain pass curved and snaked. As they pulled into the front courtyard, two men greeted them as they stepped from the car. Martin bowed to Carmilla, took the keys, and drove the car to the garage. The other man remained stone-faced and motionless. He stood tall and slender with salt and pepper hair, a stern face, and commanding gray eyes. The man tied his white, lace-trimmed ascot in an oversized bow and tucked it into his gray pinstripe waistcoat that matched his frock coat and trousers. He over-starched his collar so that it stood as stiff as he appeared.

Carmilla curtseyed and said, "Lord Prvan Volny, High Elder of the Volny-Novikov clan, I, Countess Carmilla Karnstein of the Karnstein-Bertholt clan, welcome you to my home. You may enter and leave freely. May your visit bring glory, honor, and happiness to both our clans."

He bowed in return and answered, "Greetings, Countess Carmilla Karnstein, Elder of House Karnstein-Bertholt." Disdain soaked his voice as he said her name and title. "I, Prvan Volny, Elder of the Volny-Novikov clan, accept your offer of hospitality, and I pray that glory, honor, and happiness shine on both our clans."

Carmilla smiled a practiced smile, gestured to Sam, and said, "And this is Samantha Hain."

Lord Volny flicked his right hand dismissively and said, "I care not to know the name of your midnight snack. We have pressing matters."

"Samantha is not a midnight snack, Prvan," Carmilla said, the smile and tone growing more forced as she continued, "I would be surprised to find you did not know that she is my friend and my former lover. And yes, I gather that we have pressing business. Let us see to it."

Lord Volny nodded and waited for Carmilla to enter the keep first. Sam noticed that the Countess's fists clenched as she stepped through the door. As she went to follow the two vampires, Lord Volny closed the door in her face, saying, "Wait here, human. It is not that cold outside."

"Fucking asshole!" Sam screamed to the door, kicking the snow as she spoke.

"He is," Martin said from behind her. She turned, and he continued, "Follow me, Miss Hain. There is another entrance that will allow you to reach the drawing room without disturbing their business."

He led Sam into the garage and through the passage that connected to the kitchen. As they walked, she said, "Martin, do you know what's going on? 'Milla scared me as she sped up the mountain road."

The old servant shook his head and answered, "A clan patriarch does not visit unannounced unless it is of great importance. He would tell me nothing of his intentions beyond that rooms were needed to be prepared for him and six of his men."

"Your eyes tell me you don't want him here," Sam said.

He nodded and opened the door to the kitchen for her, saying, "Your attention to detail speaks of the quality of your professional work, Miss Hain. And no, I would prefer him to leave; however, the Volny-Novikov clan is one of our oldest remaining allies. This is likely to be…"

"About that little blurb in the newspaper," Sam mused.

Martin stamped his right foot as he halted. His eyes searched her as he asked, "You do not suspect her, do you?"

Sam shook her head and replied, "No, I know she didn't. After I read the police blotter, I checked her room. She was asleep, pale, and gaunt, which we both know means that she had not fed since she went to sleep the night before. I know she's innocent, but I have this feeling that he thinks otherwise."

Martin nodded and said, "We shall see."

Martin emptied a bottle of one of Carmilla's favorite blood wines into a crystal carafe to aerate and then placed it and two crystal glasses on a silver tray. He escorted Sam to the drawing room and asked if she needed anything before excusing himself to see to Lord Volny's living quarters. Sam opened the doors to the library and busied herself reading a few small antique novels while she waited for Carmilla's meeting with this unpleasant vampire to end.

Three hours later, Carmilla stormed into the drawing room, muttering, "Insufferable, archaic fool. How any can think I would endanger all of our clan by acting like a fledgling after all these years."

Sam looked up from reading *Ella the Outcast*, one of the many penny dreadfulls Carmilla owned, to ask, "Meeting with Count Patriarchy go as swimmingly as I expected, 'Milla?"

Carmilla took a deep breath and closed the drawing room's door, locking it. Sam poured two glasses of the 1987 Sanguinovese Martin aerated and left in preparation for her arrival and handed her a glass. Carmilla slipped out of her boots and curled up inside the chair, leaning toward Sam. She drained the glass in one gulp and then said, "I'm sorry you saw that, Sam. I never wanted you to see such an ignoble outburst."

Sam sipped her own wine and walked to sit on the chair's armrest. She wrapped her arm around the Countess and said, "I've said this before, 'Milla; you may be a vampire, but you're still human. And I'm your friend, I'm here for you. What's up?"

Carmilla leaned into Sam's shoulder and inhaled her scent. She smiled. Sam refilled the empty glass. Carmilla looked up, a thin layer of blood covering her eyes as she said, "It appears that a young woman was murdered by having her blood drained.

71

Lord Volny wishes to ensure that I am not guilty of this action. As such, he and a handful of his operatives will remain in our home until the murderer is apprehended." She gulped a quarter of her glass' contents before continuing, "He says that I am free to go about my own home and country, but if I leave the castle grounds, I will be watched. As if I am a child or a fledgling again."

"I saw a headline about a murder," Sam said, "but I know you. You don't lose control. He'll see that it's not you soon enough, and he'll be gone. Then, it'll be just us… and Martin and the rest of your servants and thralls."

Carmilla smiled and said, "I hope you are correct, Samantha. I hope you are correct."

4

Chapter 4

Martin drove me into Karnsburg for the day. I told him I had some shopping to do, and I would text him when I needed to be picked up. We agreed to meet at a local coffee shop whose name roughly translates into *Bean There a Latte*. Besides meeting with this Matthew Walpole, I had shopping to do. I had such a good evening at the Christmas market with Carmilla that I forgot to pick up an ornament for Destiny. So, I had to accomplish those two things, and I wanted to pick up something for 'Milla to show support, given that I know she's upset about Lord Patriarchy creeping around her castle.

The Karnsburg Christmas market was still fun during the day, but it was nowhere near as pretty as it was last night. The lights, the candles, and the company really made it magical. On this cold but sunny day, I grabbed myself a pretzel, some knockwurst and chips, a marzipan mouse, and a cup of spiced cider. I then returned to that enchanting little grove and purchased Destiny a glass ball that contained glass snow falling over a chalet. While I thought about getting her some chocolate or marzipan too, I knew no Christmas sweets would last until I flew home. I rarely ate sweets, but that always changed when I was around Carmilla.

Using Google Maps, I found my way to a florist to get something for Carmilla. I knew flowers would be a cliché gift, but I honestly couldn't think of anything aside from a stupid card. I've never been a part of vampire aristocracy, but I've been around asshats like Lord Patriarchy. Since killing him would likely be politically dangerous for 'Milla, I settled on flowers. I purchased a nice, tasteful bouquet of violets surrounding a single pink rose. The florist kept asking if Carmilla and I were just friends in that knowing way, but one elderly customer crossed herself and looked away when I said the address. I hoped they could deliver the flowers before I returned and before 'Milla woke. I then walked into an alley and made a call.

"Hello," Werther Grimm's stern bass voice answered, "Samantha, how is Austria treating you?"

"I'm doing well, Mister Grimm," I said, "but depending on what Des told you, probably not as well as she would like."

He chuckled and said, "I take it that you and Countess Karnstein are not yet a couple again?"

I shook my head and replied, "No. We're great as friends. It's nice to have a friend like her. But…"

"You would like more than that," he interjected.

I blushed and twirled my hair as I blurted out, "Yeah, but that's not why I called you, Mister Grimm. I was just wondering if you could tell me about any investigations in Karnsburg?"

"It is a very good *friend*," he said with a laugh before continuing, "that is concerned for her *friend's* safety, yes? I will tell you this, Samantha. Our agent, whose name and

74

information I shall not disclose to you, is currently searching for the vampire. Our agent is watching Castle Karnstein, but no present evidence suggests that your *friend* is guilty. But stay safe and stay out of trouble."

"Funny you should mention that," I said as I paced in the alley. "You see, the fiancé of the first victim called my cell phone. I'm about to meet with him. I think he wants me to take the case, but with a murder attached to it, I'm pretty sure any vampire will face the stake."

"And you know better than to inhibit a police investigation of a crime," he said flatly.

"Of course," I said. "As I've done before, if I do take the case and uncover evidence that might mitigate punishment, I'll bring it forward. If the vampire is just an asshole killing for fun or sport, I'll step out of the way. I just want to protect 'Milla."

"Then be careful and be smart, Samantha," he said. "And come to Oktoberfest next year."

"I will, Mister Grimm. Goodbye," I said as I ended the call.

I still had over two hours before I needed to meet Mr. Walpole, so I made my way to Karnsburg's public library to do a little research on the situation. Like a small town's library back home, the town converted a traditional home into its library. I walked up the stairs onto the porch of a raised, stone-framed, half timber house. They kept the gaslight fixtures and left the windows open during the day for added natural light. The archival librarian, an absent-minded older man who wore an argyle sweater vest, directed me to the Municipal Archives in the basement, which had some records that went back to the seventeenth century.

I learned that the village I'm wandering around wasn't really that old, being rebuilt in 1872 after it was razed in 1827. After several village girls disappeared and were later found murdered, a young woman died after being visited in her bed by a spectral woman. Then a group of angry villagers grabbed their torches and pitchforks like extras in an old Universal monster film and started razing the town on their way to Castle Karnstein. This history claims they then dragged Carmilla through the streets to the town's church, a St. Januarius' Cathedral, where they bound her to the altar and drove a stake through her heart. Odd. We spent the evening together last night, so I think the mob grabbed the wrong person. Typical. The history records that as she died, lightning struck the town square, causing a madness to grip the mob who then looted and destroyed the church.

This historian then claimed that when the madness left the mob and they saw what they had done, they saw the body of the young girl on the altar, dead but not burned. Believing it to be a sign of her innocence, they spent fifty years living in tents and eating only nuts and nettles as penance for their actions. I rolled my eyes as I read the historian's extreme efforts to justify the murder and destruction caused by human stupidity. And when they finally started rebuilding the town, they recalled the folk knowledge that seeds scattered before a door protected against vampires because the vampires had a compulsion to count the seeds first. So, they scattered seeds inside and on top of all the bricks used in construction for protection.

I snapped a picture of that and sent it to Destiny with a text that said, "Think 'Milla will kill me if I drop seeds in front of her to watch her count them?"

A few minutes later, Des replied, "You know that's BS, right? When the lore got collected, that was one of the things changed so that people couldn't fully protect themselves from vampires and would thus need the Veil Watchers. It's as fictional as that whole bat thing, which Stoker invented. I'd suggest wearing a white dressing gown with nothing underneath and leaving your neck and thighs exposed instead as you lay on a stone bench in a garden as the light of the full moon illuminates your milky flesh."

She punctuated her text with a laughing emoji. I rolled my eyes and pursed my lips before typing, "My life isn't an erotic retelling of *Bram Stoker's Dracula*. Plus, we both know how much 'Milla hates anything remotely connected to Vlad the Impaler." And that image and the narrative it implied didn't help my wavering resolve to remain only friends. Then I sent another text, "Ready for tomorrow, love bird?"

Destiny responded with three faces laughing so hard they cried before she added, "Yeah, sure. I just found out that he's bringing his parents over to my place first for coffee. So, stress cleaning."

I smiled a bit at that and said, "Well, have fun, be yourself, and use protection–just not a gun!" I then added a winking face emoji and finished making notes for later study.

I thanked the librarian and then walked to *Bean There a Latte*, which also happened to be where I was to meet Matthew Walpole. The coffee shop was a small, cute little café with natural maple tables and chairs set in wrought iron scattered in a planned haphazardness around the counter and illuminated pastry case. A handful of people filled the shop with the chatter of conversation and the clacking of keyboards. I ordered my coffee and a slice of Black Forest cake and found myself a table in the corner. I texted Matthew to let him know where I was sitting. I decided that if Mister Walpole did not arrive before I finished my cake, I would let Martin know I was ready to head back to the castle.

Halfway through that rich, oversized slice of chocolate and cherry heaven, this large man in a gym hoodie so oversized I couldn't get a sense of his physique, the hair and eyes of a ginger version of Shaggy from *Scooby Doo*, and a face that looked generic and forgettable approached and sat in the chair opposite me. He had a strong, broad jaw that was as wide as his neck, and a cleft that was about a pinky nail's width left of center. Axe Body Spray would have been an improvement to his smell. In a Scouse accent, he said, "You Miss Samantha Hain?"

"I am," I replied. "You must be Mister Walpole?"

He nodded, "Matthew, yes. I thought you might not show, given your vacation. Thank you."

I shot him a sympathetic smile and said, "I'm not promising anything, but I will listen. How's your fiancée?"

"She's conscious," he nodded and said. "Weak but conscious."

"What hospital is she in," I asked. "I may call her later to see if she's up for a visit."

"No, no, no," he spat out. "It might be dangerous, depending on how far along her *condition* is. Besides, Vienna is a bit far."

"I could always call her," I offered. "While I do have some questions, I really just want to see how she's doing and, if I decide to help, to keep her updated."

"You don't got to worry about that," he sputtered. "I'll keep her up on things. You just do your thing here and leave her to rest."

That sounded like an odd response to me. Maybe it's just me, but if my fiancée were bitten by a vampire, I'd want the person who was going to help me have all the information available. Also, if she were to turn into a vampire, she would have already done so by now. Shrugging it off, I assumed she may have contracted porphyria or a temporary hemophilia from the bite. On a happier note, nothing he had previously told me suggested a bacterial illness brought on from a bad batch of synthoflavin. I chose not to push the issue at this time.

"I understand," I said, nodding. "Why don't you tell me what happened on that night?"

Matthew Walpole nodded. He looked around, leaned forward, and spoke in a low voice, "Like I told you, Mathilda and I, we, were on holiday heading from Zurich to Vienna to do all the Christmas stuff. We stopped in Karnsburg for the Krampus run nonsense and had a bit too much to drink at this club–don't remember the name–looked like a Greek temple or something—after the parade. We started chatting with this nice enough local bloke who promised he could show us the *real nightlife*. What a fucking wanker. Might have been a girl. Was pretty. Dykes can have long hair, I guess."

I glared and interjected, "Yes, we can."

"Anyway," he said. His dismissive hand wave earned a further glare, and he added, "I went to the loo for a good piss, and when I came back, this fuck hole had his lips on Mathilda's neck. I mean, as you can see, I'm a real man, so I hauled off and punched him in his crooked face. I was gonna curb stomp him like we do back home when some foppish dandy comes to the wrong side of town, but the coward fucking ran off. That's when I saw Tilly's neck had bloodstains on it. Docs say it's a special case of anemia, but I'm not so sure. And that's why I called you—to fix this."

I leaned back and sipped my coffee, taking this in. He didn't want me to talk to Mathilda, because he was afraid the visit would put her in danger, but he also didn't believe the doctors' diagnosis. I knew how I would usually handle this situation, but I doubted that he wanted my methodical, rational investigation. I set the ceramic mug on the table, leaned forward, and said, "I don't know what you think I do, Mister Walpole, but I'm not a monster hunter. There is a group of people who do that; I know some of them, and they told me they are already investigating."

"If you're not going to fucking kill the beast, what do you fucking do," he asked, pounding his enormous fist on the table, and drawing the disdainful side eyes of the other customers.

"What I can do," I said with a sigh, "is to protect you and Mathilda from those same hunters. I see you're a bit confused, so let me explain. These same hunters who will kill this creature if they can prove it exists and has done what you claim it has done, also ensure that no word of it reaches the public by killing the humans who recognized it. What I do is try to keep all parties involved alive."

"So, you're not going to kill the bloody thing? Fuck, waste of that airfare to the fucking States," he complained.

Sensing his frustration, even though he clearly gave no shits about mine, I changed tactics and said, "I will let the professionals handle whatever this person is. There are special courts. There will be a trial. And if he is found guilty, he will be executed within twenty-four hours of conviction. These hunters are the best there are. Don't worry about that. Worry about Mathilda's and your own safety. And that's what I offer."

We both reclined in our chairs. I sipped my coffee. He stroked his chin. He fidgeted with his phone as his left leg bounced like Destiny after her fourth Red Bull of the morning. And then with a sigh, he said, "They told me your fee was five thousand American, yes? That's a right pretty penny."

"It is," I nodded, "but I put myself in danger, so you don't have to be. I think it's worth that. Also, I only charge half up front to cover expenses. And normally, an international job would be seventy-five hundred, but since I'm already here, I'll charge my home-state fee. So, what did this guy look like? You haven't told me."

"He looked like what you'd expect here," Matthew Walpole said with a slight shrug. "Blond hair, long and curly; blue eyes; pale skin; almost fancy dress type clothes. Handsome enough, I guess, if you're into that."

I nodded. It almost seemed like he was describing Lestat de Lioncourt. We were in Austria, so there were quite a few people who matched that description. It seemed almost too generic a description, but it's not like I haven't seen vampires who looked like that. Put him in a curly blond wig and that description would have fit Lord Patriarchy a few centuries ago. I chuckled at that thought and then said, "Well, that gives me something to go on, so if you want my help, I'll need twenty-five hundred dollars, please."

He groaned and then handed me a crumpled envelope from his hoodie's pocket. I counted the money inside and thanked him. He rose and left, saying he would contact me if the situation changed. I nodded. After he departed, I texted Martin and waited for his arrival.

* * *

Paul Byron opened and powered on his silver laptop in his small hotel room at the western edge of Karnsburg. Even by British standards, this room was small, spartan and basic. He draped his gym hoodie over the edge of the twin bed. His ribbed white tank top revealed his muscular frame, and he ran his thick fingers through the mop of red hair on his head. His nose wrinkled in the stale air. He tensed himself as he saw notification of a requested video chat.

A middle-aged, dark-skinned man with thick, curly black hair, piercing brown eyes, and three-day stubble appeared. He wore a fitted gray blazer with a French-cuffed, white, button-down shirt and a red and black striped tie. A flag hung from the wall behind him with a black dragon, curved into the shape of a circle with its tail coiled around its neck and a red St. George cross on its back, emblazoned upon it. Byron greeted him by saying, "Greetings, Knight-Commander Paul Bertalan, Squire Paul Byron reporting as you requested, Sir."

Knight-Commander Bertalan nodded, and in his thick Hungarian accent said, "Then report, Squire. Time is of the essence as we seek to recover from the Order's failure in Ireland."

"Yes, Sir," Byron said, straightening his posture. He cleared his throat and continued, "I flew to Great Bend, South Carolina in the United States in order to meet with and contract the services of Miss Samantha Hain, daughter of our ally Arch Magus Donal Hain of the Hermetic Order of the Astrum Argentum. She was not there, but I entered this bar on the other side of the hall where the fucking strange bartender, a Nickie Scratch, offered to trade me her cell phone number in exchange for a stupid favor. From there, I…"

"You did what?" Bertalan screamed as his lips curled into a snarl. Byron's eyes widened as he saw his superior's hands tighten into fists. Bertalan continued, "Why did you not request intelligence when you could not find Miss Hain in the States? Do you know what you've done?"

Byron shrugged his shoulders and said, "I talked to some bloody wanker of a bartender who acted like he's the devil or something, making deals and calling himself evil."

Knight-Commander Bertalan massaged his temples with his right thumb and index finger and sighed. "You dolt," he said before returning his gaze toward the camera, "You walked into a strange bar and met a bartender named Nick Scratch. You made a deal with him. You made a deal with the actual devil, and now you owe him something. This endangers not only your mission here but also the resurrection of our great Voivode Vladislaus Dracula Tepes, who was betrayed to that Dutchman. Beyond that heinous blunder, how have you progressed?"

His reddened cheeks revealed his pride to be visibly wounded, Byron continued, "Yes, Sir. I have made contact with Miss Hain and engaged her services as directed. I don't know why I can't just kill her."

"We want her spirit broken," Bertalan said. "If we can accomplish that, she may join us in the Great Working. If that is not possible, we will probably have neutralized her threat. What is the status of the ground plan?"

Still stinging from the dressing down, Byron said, "I've followed your ancestor's path and chosen my first victim based upon the traitor's preferred type. I'll choose another tonight, and probably two more after that. Or should I do more?"

Knight-Commander Bertalan shook his head, saying, "No more than four. Perhaps stop at three. More than that may draw the Grimms to investigate the matter. That would give Miss Hain more allies in the area. We want her broken and alone so that she has no one to turn to but us or to death. So, continue with the mission as directed. We have agents moving into position to execute the traitor. The world will come into the light—even if we have to chain and drag it there for its own good. Over and out."

"Bloody fucking hell," Paul Byron closed his laptop, donned his hoodie, and exited his hotel room, slamming the door behind him.

The new St. Rita of Cascia Catholic Church sat on at the eastern edge of the town square where Karnsburg's Christmas market stood. Built on the ruins of the old St. Januarius' Cathedral, this late-nineteenth century cathedral's architect modeled the architecture on traditional Gothic cathedrals. Byron flipped the hood over his head and shoved his hands in the hoodie's pockets as he trudged through the gathered crowd. He ascended the stone stairs and opened the left of the two double doors. Ignoring the parishioners who lit candles, he examined every statue present, observing and touching them until one of the local priests walked to greet him.

"Most normally don't touch the statues, my son," he said.

Byron observed that he was a younger man with skin the color of milk chocolate and thick, black curls on his head. He smiled warmly and stood about as tall as Byron did, but he had a thinner frame. Byron backed away from a statue of St. Sebastian and said, "Sorry, Father. I didn't mean no harm. Just looking for something."

The priest nodded and said, "Well, we all search for things in life. It's one thing that brings many here. Perhaps I can help you?"

Byron shrugged and said, "Well, I went to confession before I left St. Helens, but my sister, who's writing her art history thesis on religious statuary, she came across a reference to a blackened statue of the Madonna in the St. Januarius Cathedral here, and since I was here on holiday, she asked if I would take a snap for her. I just can't find the church or the statue."

The priest scratched his left ear while thinking. After a moment he shook his head and replied, "Well, the St. Januarius Cathedral no longer stands, but you stand in the church build upon its ruins. As to this statue, I'm not the best person to ask, as I've only started serving here as a parochial vicar, but I've never seen such a statue. Father Alec is visiting the sick today, but I can give you his card. You may also want to check the library, because they may have information from the old church that I'm not aware of. I'm sorry."

Byron nodded. "I figured it was a long shot," he said. "Never heard of such things, so I'll admit I was hoping to see it. Thank you, Father."

He pocketed Father Alec's card and left the church. With the sun still peeking through gray winter clouds, he sighed. His breath floated before his eyes. Shoving his hands back into his hoodie's pockets, he walked through the Christmas market toward the town's library on the other side of the square.

The librarian on duty directed him to the Municipal Archives in the basement and helped Byron find the boxes containing the history of St. Rita of Cascia' Church, which he said would be the most likely place to find information on the old St. Januarius church. Byron spent two hours searching through church records. During his search, he found the lists of baptisms, marriages, and funerals performed in the church. He read the same accounts of the mob and fire that Sam read. But one sentence drew his attention. *After the fire, the mob looted the church, and the items not returned during penance were eventually delivered to St. Francis' Cathedral in Innsbruck.* He knew then he had a trip to make, but he had to complete at least part of his task here first.

* * *

Martin arrived at *Bean There a Latte* five minutes after Paul Byron entered the library. He helped Sam secure her package in the trunk. He then opened the door for her and helped her step from the curb into the car. She buckled her seat belt, and they drove into the mountains toward Castle Karnstein.

"You know, Miss Hain," Martin said as they left Karnsburg's southern edge, "a bouquet of flowers arrived for the Countess that appears to have been sent from you. Curious."

Sam looked away and fidgeted with her hair. She returned her gaze to the reflection of Martin's eyes in the rear-view mirror, batted her eyes, and asked, "Oh? Well, yeah, I sent her flowers. Just as a friend. Sometimes friends send each other flowers. I mean, with Lord Patriarchy watching over her, I thought she might appreciate a little encouragement gift."

Martin smiled into the rear-view mirror and chuckled. He nodded and said with a patronizing tone, "Of course that is your reason, Miss Hain. In all seriousness, I believe she will appreciate the gesture. She is not thrilled by his visit and the memories it evokes."

"Yeah, I gathered that from her emotional outburst last night," Sam said. "I've never seen her so enraged - except when anyone praises a cinematic or literary adaptation of *Dracula*. Do you know why it pissed her off so much?"

Martin pursed his lips and remained silent for a few moments. He checked on Sam through the rear-view mirror and saw her right hand tapping on the door rapidly. He nodded and then said, "The two are not unconnected. The Countess has a complicated history, and that history is for her to divulge in her own time. I know that she wants you to know her past, but she fears your reaction as her feelings for you are clearly more than mere friendship."

Sam looked at her lap and twirled her hair around her right index finger and said, "Yeah, mere friendship." She ignored his knowing wink and chuckle, adding, "Anything you can tell me about Lord Patriarchy that I should know?"

"Lord Volny is," Martin replied, "well, your mockery is not inaccurate. Prvan Volny has lived for over a millennium, and he has been the patriarch of Volny-Novikov clan for as long as Countess Karnstein has been alive. He is a varkolak, a warrior so fierce and covered in hair that many believe him able to transform into a wolf; although I know of none who have seen this feat of his. Make no mistake, he is a powerful, strong, charismatic, and well-connected vampire. And his clan is one of our few remaining allies."

Sam thought for a moment, her eyes staring at the mountains as the sun began its descent. She smiled at the scenery and then said, "Now that you mention it, she's never really talked about many vampires. I thought she just didn't want me to feel out-of-place."

Martin nodded. "That has always been part of it," he admitted. "However, there are other factors that have played into that."

Sam leaned forward, her eyes radiating love and concern. She then asked, "So, Martin, how should I, as her friend, approach this? Should I ask her what's up? Should I observe and comment?"

"As her friend," he held every sound of that word as he replied,

"I would advise you to let her take the lead both in handling this present inconvenience and in revealing her past. She wants you to know, but she has learned to be private and to be reserved." As they drove through the portcullis, he added, "Ah we have arrived. Prepare to be searched."

As Sam opened her mouth to ask what he meant, the car stopped about two hundred feet before the doors to the keep. Four dark-haired men in gray suits with nine-millimeter handguns clearly visible on their hips patrolled the courtyard. Two approached the car, hands raised to signal a stop. Martin stopped the car, and one moved to the door beside Sam. He hurriedly opened the door and barked an order for her to exit and stand against the vehicle. She complied, and he pushed her against the car and frisked her with a forceful, focused hand before rummaging through her purse. After the other man searched Martin and the bag containing Sam's gift for Destiny, the men allowed them to enter the keep through the servants' entrance in the garage.

As they walked through the keep, Martin repeatedly apologized, "Forgive me, Miss Hain, for this insult was not our intent. As an honored and beloved guest, you should enter through the main doors."

"It's fine, Martin," Sam waved her hand dismissively. "Honestly, it's no worse than the TSA on any flight. Like I said in the car, I'm more concerned for 'Milla's well-being than I am for any insult."

He nodded and said, "Yes, but you must understand that in both human and vampire aristocratic society, there are traditions for how guests are to be treated, and by forcing you to enter as a servant, Lord Volny's men, and by extension Lord Volny, are committing a grand faux pas. And, in the process, they are forcing Countess Karnstein to violate the ancient laws of hospitality, and it angers her that you are the victim of such an enforced violation."

"I'm not surprised," Sam said with a snort as they moved into the kitchen. Thralls who were neither human nor fully vampire busied themselves preparing cleaning and dinner. She added, "Lord Patriarchy seems more concerned with keeping some secret than any of the Watchers I've worked with or against in the past decade. I hope 'Milla's okay."

"I pray that as well," Martin said solemnly as he arranged a crystal decanter of wine, two crystal glasses, and a cheese board on a silver tray as he and Sam ascended to the drawing room.

As they passed Carmilla's office, Sam heard the two vampires arguing. Martin raised his index finger over his lips as his head motioned toward the closed office door. Sam signaled that she understood and placed her ear to the door. Shaking his head, Martin rolled his eyes. He raised five fingers and then pointed toward the drawing room. Sam nodded, and Martin silently took his leave.

"I see no reason in Vlad's name why Adolf Karnstein's daughter persists with managing investments for mortals," Prvan Volny said. "You waste your time and resources when you should devote them solely to your own kind and restoring the honor you have lost your clan."

"We do not live in a world populated solely by our own kind," Carmilla replied as she perused the most recent reports from her investment firm's branch managers. Without shifting her gaze toward him, she continued, "As I am certain you know, Lord Volny, we share our world with humans, and humans greatly outnumber our kind. Working with them, building rapport and goodwill, treating them as equals and not as playthings or merely food help to ensure our survival."

"What they prove," he raged, "are that you are as immature and uninterested in the actual performance of your duties as clan patriarch as you were two centuries ago. You were unready and unfit then, and nothing has changed. As this recent murder streak seems to be proving."

Carmilla clenched the muscles in her hands and jaw. She inhaled deeply, and then said, "I would gladly profess my innocence under any oath-mundane or magical. That you have not summarily shackled me and brought me to trial suggests you have no evidence beyond your own suspicions. And while we are on the subject," she spun her chair toward him and raised her voice to just beneath a seething yell, "I believe that moving my clan from the dark ages and into the current century where we will be engaged citizens in society and ethical stewards of our environments is the best way to ensure the survival and regrowth of the clan of which I am a *matriarch.*"

Sam clenched her fist in a supportive cheer as Carmilla's words earned her a lupine growl from Lord Volny. "While we are on the subject of your interactions with humans," he snarled, eyes narrowed and boring into her core, "I see that our previous punishment was too weak to rid you of your sapphic perversions. We shall not show you such mercy again."

Carmilla strangled the armrests of her hair as she rose to her feet. Though he stood nearly a foot taller than her, the rage in her eyes sucked enough heat from the room that even he took one step back. "Mercy? Mercy," she spat with a ferocity that caused Sam to retreat from the door before returning to hear Carmilla say, "If that is how you define mercy, then it is clear that the Council governing the vampires of Europe and the Levant has not ventured beyond the fifteenth century. My love is as beautiful and as natural as the quiet calm after a snowfall. I will also remind you that Samantha is a guest in my home. As such, your disrespectful treatment of her screams as both evidence of the Council's general disregard for women and as a gross violation of our customary hospitality."

As their discussion grew more heated, Sam crept toward the drawing room. She collapsed onto the chaise and said, "That man is one arrogant, misogynistic, bigoted, shit-headed fuckface."

"I think that covers most of it," Martin said dryly.

Martin poured the wine into the glasses, handed one to Sam, and set the other besides the bouquet of violets surrounding a single pink rose. She arranged the flowers so that the single rose shown clearly within the purple field. Martin walked to the door, turned, and said, "Be gentle with her. You are a light in her life."

Sam smiled gently as she asked, "You really care for her, don't you, Martin?"

"As do you, Miss Hain," he said. "I have had the privilege to watch her grow and adapt to the times better than many of greater age. Now, if you will excuse me."

As he bowed and left, Sam said, "I may have to pester you for stories of her youth, but I've got her back."

Sam heard Martin's chuckle echo down the hall. Half an hour later, Carmilla slammed the drawing room door behind her as she stalked toward her chair. She slumped into it, sinking into the plush velvet cushions. She reached for the glass of wine, and she drained it in one gulp. As she refilled the glass, this time to the rim, she noticed the flowers. The edges of her burgundy lips twitched and raised toward a smile, and when she read the accompanying card, she beamed. *'Milla, don't let the old bastard get you down. I've got your back. Sam.*

Tears of blood glistened at the corners of her eyes as she smiled at Sam and whispered through a choked voice, "Thank you."

Sam walked over and gave Carmilla's hand a gentle squeeze before saying, "You're not alone, 'Milla. I'm here, and I'm on your side. I heard the small bit of that little conversation and judging by the speed with which you emptied your glass, I figure the rest wasn't enjoyable."

She sipped from her glass and sighed. Scratching the side of her head above her left ear, she said, "No. Prvan Volny treats me as if I am still a fledgling being groomed to ascend to a place of prominence in my clan." She snorted and added, "preferably as an alliance-bride to some ancient patriarch of a former ally or even an enemy."

Sam wrinkled her nose and rolled her eyes. "Why," she asked, "does that not surprise me? I gathered from the dirty look that Lord Patriarchy shot me when he called me your midnight snack that this wasn't your fun uncle who shows up once a year with toys, candy, and a bottle of bourbon that he sneaks you a shot of every night. From what Martin told me, I don't see how the fuck he knew what was going on in Karnsburg before the police knew anything."

Carmilla lowered her eyes and placed her other hand atop Sam's, squeezing it. "He has always had one of his clan watching me since I became our matriarch," Carmilla said. Her voice trembled with a fear that shocked Sam as she continued, "but even before that, after the town burned and after Elisa was killed, his disdain for my father's choosing of me to ascend to a role of leadership and for my simple existence grew. I fear that if he turns on me, my clan will have no allies and will become vulnerable to hunting."

Sam leaned and hugged Carmilla as she sat. She felt the vampire tremble without breath but with a racing heartbeat granted by recent feeding. The Countess clenched and unclenched her fists. Her right foot bounced beneath her dress. Blood flowed from her lower lip as her fangs pierced it. Sam drew her finger across Carmilla's chin to wipe some of the blood away.

Sam's eyes welled as she felt a terror in Carmilla that she had never before felt. She whispered, "It's okay, 'Milla. I'm not going to abandon you. It's not the same, but I'll always be an ally and a friend."

"I... thank you," Carmilla said as she forced a smile onto her face. "It is just..."

"You don't have to say anything," Sam interrupted. "If you need to cry, I will hold you. If you just want to sit in silence, I'll be by your side."

Sam sat on the chair's armrest as Carmilla took a deep breath and said, "No, Sam. I... there is much I wish to tell you, but... no, I will tell you this tonight. The reason Prvan truly does not trust me is because I lost control while feeding."

"That must have been terrifying," Sam said.

Carmilla nodded and continued, "There had been a string of strange deaths in Karnsburg, all young girls. No one knew what happened, but I did not touch them. There was one young girl, a cobbler's daughter. Her name was Annalena Mayer. We were lovers, and she offered me her blood as we made love. I thought she was asleep and breathing when I left. I had been so careful, checking for signs of life with a hand mirror. I had to be, for we were no longer in a time when aristocratic negligence was tolerated. Well, the next morning, she was found dead. The villagers grew angry and formed a mob that burned buildings and homes on their way to our home. They demanded my death in revenge, and before I could wake from my daily slumber, my younger sister Elisa – who had begun the blood rites to elongate her life; although, she had another full year before she would be turned – volunteered to take my place."

Carmilla paused as crimson tears plummeted from her eyes. Sam grabbed a napkin and wiped her tears. "It's okay, 'Milla," Sam said. "Take your time, and if you want to stop, just stop. I'm still here, and I'll listen whenever you're comfortable sharing."

Her eyes closed, Carmilla nodded. "I thank you," she said. She breathed deeply and added, "I must continue. Well, I was exiled from my home by order of the leaders of the clans while we awaited Vlad Dracula to declare a time to hear the case and then judge my punishment. I was exiled to Ireland and there told my tale to that mystery story writer who adapted my story for his own purposes. When I returned, they too me to Romania where I was tried, found guilty, and punished."

"And that's why your sister's ghost remains," Sam said.

Carmilla nodded solemnly. "Yes," she said, tears returning to her eyes. "There is more to tell at a later night, but first, Samantha Hain of the Hain family and daughter of Arch Magus Donal Hain, there is something I must ask of you if you give me permission to do so."

The blending of her formality and fear stunned Sam. She took a deep breath. Her muscles tensed as she saw more tears forming in Carmilla's eyes and a tremble rattling her soft, pale hands. Sam swallowed hard and nodded, saying, "Ask me."

As she wept openly, Carmilla, in a cracking voice barely above a whisper, choked a simple request, "I ask for you to help prove my innocence. Please, Samantha, I am asking to hire you in a professional capacity to fix this for me. Please."

"'Milla, I don't think that's necessary," Sam replied.

Carmilla slid from her chair onto the floor. Sam's eyes widened as she saw the terror that darkened her friend's face. Kneeling before Sam, Carmilla sobbed and trembled as she pleaded, "Please, Sam. I beg of you. I do not want to suffer that punishment again or anything worse. Please help me. I will pay your price, and," she paused and inhaled sharply before saying, "I will cease any attempts to rekindle a romantic relationship with you."

Sam blinked, her private investigator training allowing her to keep her face neutral. For nearly five years, she declared that she wanted to be nothing but friends with Carmilla. She uttered those words almost daily. Those words rose from her stomach like acidic bile back into her throat. She forced herself to take slow, deep breaths as she heard every time she voiced that sentiment, and she hated hearing those words reverberate through her mind. Those words suffocated her, and her breathing grew rapid and shallow.

My feelings don't matter right now, she thought. *'Milla's terrified and needs me. Maybe...no, I have to focus on her needs. Yes, I love her, and I want her. But she needs this more.* Sam took one deep breath, nodded, and said, "Countess Carmilla Karnstein, I will help you."

5

Chapter 5

I stayed up with 'Milla as long as I could, but I guess she was right about thirty being the year age starts creaking up on me. She walked me to my room, and if I'm being honest, I got butterflies like when a date walked me to my front door. We stayed and talked at the door. It felt like time stopped. When we finally said good night and I closed the door behind me, I cursed myself for being so fucking silent. She gave me the out I've said I wanted for years, and I had the chance to tell her I've been all talk. I had the chance to tell her that I don't know how we'll work it out–maybe there's a therapist who specializes in human-vampire romantic difficulties–but that I wanted to move forward with her as more than a friend. I could have done that, but what did I do? I stood there and told myself that the best way to help her and ease her anxiety was to just agree to her terms. I was a fucking idiot.

I drifted to sleep after an hour of silently screaming at myself, only to find myself in another nightmare. This time, I was back in Butcher's Bend and sitting in my office alone. I went home to my apartment where I was alone and without Sandy

Paws. I lived my life alone. No one noticed me. No one spoke to me. I had no access to The Four Winds. Alone. A nightmare of my own making. I understood this message from my subconscious. Dream Sam scrolled repeatedly through her phone's contacts, anxiously looking for someone who wasn't there. And then a voice called to her–to me.

I groaned as I rolled over to see Elisa's ghost again, calling on me to follow her. Without waiting, she glided through the castle's halls. So I rushed to put on my pajamas and grab my phone and the jackknife lock pick set I always kept in my suitcase for those times I locked myself out of my hotel room. I followed her through the hallway, down the stairs, and to the lightless hall on the first floor where she passed through the double-locked door that led into the castle's dungeons. I paused at the door. 'Milla specifically told me this was the one area of the castle I was not allowed, but this was the second time her sister's ghost led me here. I had to choose between being a bad friend who broke a promise and a thorough investigator who followed any lead that might, in the end, help her client. I turned my back to the door, scanned the hallway for any sights or sounds that might show someone approaching, and then I spun around and picked the locks.

The stairs spiraled counterclockwise as they descended into the dungeon. I wished I had a sweater or a torch as the cold, damp air clawed at my core. My breath clouds were more dense than elsewhere in the castle. My nose wrinkled, and I pinched it to stifle the noise of a sneeze as I walked through the thick layers of dust and spiderweb that covered everything. Obviously, this part of the castle hadn't been used in a long time, which given what could be in a dungeon, that was probably a good sign.

I expected to find a torture chamber with a rack, an iron maiden, and maybe a Judas cradle here, but instead I found a crypt. Sadness weighed on the cold air. Odd, I thought, given that 'Milla showed me the family mausoleum door in the rear courtyard. I walked over to the glass coffin atop which rested an enormous bouquet of white lilies. I ran my fingers along the flower stems as I stared down at the sleeping, dead, form of Carmilla–no–this had to be Elisa's body. Why wasn't she buried with the rest of their family? The golden plate on the coffin read something like "Elisa Karnstein, Beloved Sister. Forgive me one day."

That's why she's buried here, and not with the rest of the family. Carmilla still held guilt over her sister's death. That was obvious from her confession earlier. But why did Elisa's ghost bring me down here? 'Milla just told me about her sister's death and how her actions contributed to it. There had to be something else going on here; otherwise, Elisa's ghost had no reason to bring me to the basement twice. I saw two archways that appeared to lead into different rooms. Following labyrinth rules, I chose the room on my left from that vantage point.

Passing through this archway, I found the torture chamber I sought. Two racks, a St. Andrew's cross, and a strappado stood against the walls, their metal bits rusted and their wood rotting from lack of use and care. An assortment of whips and pokers hung like billiards cues from a rack on the wall. A different sadness–one that reeked of anguish and betrayal–agitated the frigid air. I didn't see an iron maiden, and that caused a strange twinge of disappointment. Ignoring the archway that clearly led to the dungeon cells, I walked through the doorway through which I could see bookcases against the walls.

This room reeked of herbs and incenses like my father's

secret study always did. My jaw dropped at the sight of what were clearly ancient and, obviously, expertly crafted alchemical tools adorned with gold, silver, and diamonds. I stepped around a Goetic circle painted onto the floorboards. The bookcases held a vast library of what appeared to be medieval and maybe renaissance manuscripts. From a cursory scan of the revealed pages of the manuscripts that had lost their front boards, I deduced quite a few to be grimoires, possibly rare ones or those thought legendary by practitioners and historians, but they held less interest for me than the one leather-bound volume chained to a wooden desk that sat beside the bookshelves.

The bright maple brown leather still had a suppleness that suggested it has been regularly oiled. The intoxicating scent of old book blended with the faintest scent of violets and roses as I examined the exterior and construction. It had stitched binding, and the chain that bound the book to the desk went through the spine which told me the book was meant to be used but not removed. I opened the book and found a mix of pressed flowers, drawings, watercolors, and words, all arranged by date. I recognized Carmilla's handwriting, and then it hit me. This had to be a diary–'Milla's diary.

I knew I should put the book down and leave, but I thought there might be a clue that I was missing. She wrote in German throughout the book, so I knew I would only get an approximation of the meaning. I sighed as I skimmed the pages until I found the entries right before Elisa's death. Holding my phone in one hand so the flashlight could illuminate the pages and so I had access to my German-English dictionary app, I realized that if 'Milla didn't have handwriting as graceful and elegant as she did, I would not be able to read this.

When she mentioned the events leading up to Elisa's death, she wrote the same things she told me. She didn't lie; that was good to know. She really loved this Annalena. I startled myself when a growl rumbled through my lips. My heartbeat quickened. I wondered if she wrote about me in the same way, and yes, I became jealous of someone who's been dead for almost two centuries. I even offered to let 'Milla feed from me while we made love, but she always declined. Now I knew why.

I took a deep breath and refocused. The only thing that stuck out in the entries was a name she didn't mention. It seemed that this Hungarian named Yarono Bertalan arrived in Karnsburg right before everything started and presented himself to the Karnsteins as an emissary and diplomat for Vlad Dracula. Given 'Milla's hatred for Vlad, I'm surprised she didn't mention this guy to me.

Fuck! Just as I found an entry where 'Milla described what the local newspaper said about the body of one of the murdered girls when I heard footsteps and two people speaking in German. I closed 'Milla's diary and crept into the corner between two bookshelves and switched off my phone's flashlight. As I backed against the wall, I squeaked in surprise when the floorboard beneath my right foot sank. The click of an opening lock followed, and I felt a draft as the bookshelf to my left opened slightly. A secret passage just might have been the thing that saved me from discovery. So, with nothing to lose, I slid behind the bookshelf and closed it behind me, hearing it lock into place.

I switched my phone's flashlight back on, noting that its battery had dropped to under forty percent. The secret passage quickly became a secretly ascending staircase. I followed until

I found a dead end at the top with a lever against the wall. I chuckled and shook my head before pulling the lever. As stone ground against stone, the wall slid open, and I saw that the passage led to Carmilla's bedroom. I peeked my head from the passage and sighed with relief that she wasn't in her room. I stepped through the opening, and the passage closed behind me.

As I looked around her room, I heard her voice come from behind me, "Well, this certainly is an unexpected but desirable surprise."

I spun around with a sheepish grin on my face and a reactionary flush of my cheeks. Leaning against the door frame with her eyes shining like a cat's in the night, Countess Carmilla Karnstein smirked in my direction. She had already changed into her dressing gown, but a quick peek revealed that she actually wore something underneath. Likely because of Lord Patriarchy's undesirable presence. "Oh, hey, 'Milla," I said as I ran my fingers through my hair, "I didn't think you'd get here so early. Is it your bedtime already?"

With a raising of her left eyebrow, she set the candelabra on her nightstand. And then she folded her arms across her chest and stalked toward me. Her lips, tinted burgundy from the wine, curled into a smile. She methodically circled me and said, "Yes, and that begs the question, Samantha Blake Hain, of what your purpose is in my bedchamber."

My breathing stopped as she drew out the pronunciation of my name. A rush of heat spread through my body, and my breathing quickened. I tugged at my collar and replied, "Um, well, with all that's going on, I had this weird feeling that maybe someone had bugged your home. Since I figured you might have moved to your office to work, I crawled out of bed and came here to search. So far, nothing."

"Oh," she said, letting her warm breath brush the back of my neck. Her voice turned into that purr again as she added, "I am grateful. I am unaccustomed to having someone who is not a thrall or a bonded servant serve as a protector. I could, well, grow accustomed to having this feeling."

I spun around and looked into her eyes. Her chest seemed to heave as mine did, even though she doesn't breathe. I raised my gaze toward her eyes but stopped at her lips. She licked them, and I saw just the daintiest hint of a fang. And then she reached out and touched my chin with a single finger of her right hand and guided my eyes back to hers. I swallowed hard, causing her to chuckle.

"Sam," she said, "You know what they say, no? 'My eyes are up here.'"

I inhaled sharply and bit my lip as my eyes searched the floor for a brilliant verbal riposte. I stepped closer to her, my face inches from hers, and whispered, "But I like the rest of your body too."

Great. There went any pretense I had of no longer being interested in her. She slid her hand to the side of my face and brushed my cheek with the backs of her fingers. As she shrugged her shoulders, her dressing gown slid from her shoulders, revealing two slender straps of black satin curving over her porcelain shoulders. A sharp inhale shot through my lips. Carmilla sauntered to her wardrobe and as she opened the gown with her back toward me she turned her face so that I could see the right half of a knowing smile as she said, "Perhaps it is just me, but I find my chamber a bit warmer tonight than usual. No?"

"No," I said as I exhaled slowly while slipping behind her, "it is quite warm in here, 'Milla. Why don't you let me help you out of that dressing gown?"

I held the gown as she slid from inside it. I blinked rapidly as I felt my heart stop. Beneath that burgundy lace-trimmed dressing gown, 'Milla wore a racerback babydoll chemise whose rose-patterned lace left little to the imagination. I felt my cheeks flush, my heartbeat restart, and my breathing come in shallow rasps. She turned to face me, and the heat spread through my body. I dropped the dressing gown and instinctively wrapped my arms around her waist. She threw her arms around my neck, and I moaned as she ran her fingers through my hair.

"It has been some time since we embraced," She said, her face glowing in the candelabra's light she kept in the room.

"Yeah," I said breathily. "It's been a long time."

"It seems you have missed this as have I," she purred, bringing her face closer to my neck, and goosebumps rose as I felt the warm breath of each precisely intoned syllable.

"I never said I didn't," was all my brain managed to say.

She chuckled and whispered into my ear, "Good, because I have missed it greatly." I felt her lips brush against my neck, and I bit my lip and whimpered. She pulled away quickly and broke our embrace before adding, "But what am I doing? You have no desire to be anything but friends, and I promised to cease trying for anything beyond friendship if you agreed to help me during this time. And you agreed to do so. I am sorry."

God dammit! No, there was no god to blame for how this turned out. No one but Nick Scratch would have enjoyed the level of ironic suffering brought about by my earlier actions. I sighed and nodded. I said, "You're right. But as a private investigator, I have to be thorough, and as a 'fixer' as people seem to call it, my job is to ensure that those involved remain safe. And you're also a friend that I care about. So, I request permission to remain at your side until you fall asleep," and then I hastily added, "to protect you."

Carmilla shot me a searching eye. She drew her right index finger across her collarbone and said, "I do not know. You are aware that I sleep in the nude. It would be awkward after all these centuries to wear clothing while I slumber."

"Yeah, I'm aware." Those words squeaked from my lips. "I will remain awake, clothed, and vigilant. I promise you this."

"Very well," she said.

She opened her wardrobe before scooping up her dressing gown and placing it on a clothes hanger. Turning her back to me, she slid her babydoll over her head, folded it, and set it inside a drawer at the base of her wardrobe. She moved in such a way that I only saw only hints and shadows of anything that would suggest immodesty. As she sat at her vanity to brush her hair, I praised the mirror that allowed me to see a reflection of her body. As she moved to her bed, I saw her naked form and bit my lip to avoid drawing in a sharp breath at the sight. I'd forgotten how her black hair cascaded down over her breasts, covering her areolae. She nodded and smiled as she slid beneath the sheets. I followed and curled up next to her, remaining awake and trying to focus on how I could help her.

* * *

Two officers in their blue uniforms cordoned off the alley behind *Bean There a Latte*. The short, squat male with short gingerbread hair and a thick, bushy mustache photographed the scene, moving carefully around the scene to avoid disturbing his partner. His partner, a tall and slender blonde who kept her hair in a low bun, made notes in a small pocket notebook as she examined the corpse and the scene. A young woman with pale skin and ginger hair lay slumped against the wall by the dumpster. She wore a camel cashmere sweater with a pumpkin and brown plaid skirt and mahogany riding boots. Her purse remained by her side and appeared untouched. There appeared to be no bruising or lacerations, but the officer noticed two small puncture wounds on her neck. A small crowd gathered to watch as the ambulance removed the body. The officers reprimanded a few for taking pictures with their cell phones.

Two days later, *Kriminaloberkommissar* Benedikt Merkatz sat at his desk at the Saggen Polizeiinspektion station in Innsbruck, clicking his ballpoint pen mindlessly as he watched the clock on the wall tick down until his shift ended. A small brass-plated frame contained pictures of his wife, son, and the family spaniel. Using the pen's thrust device, he scratched his bald head behind his left ear. This middle-aged man had a scar on his wrinkled right cheek that he earned when a murderer attacked him during an arrest. He narrowed his blue eyes as he stared at his empty coffee mug. He returned his pen to its cup and limped to the Keurig to refill his mug.

He returned to his desk with a fresh mug of coffee, only to find another officer placing a case file in front of his chair. Through narrowed eyes, he searched the officer for intent before saying in his rich baritone voice, "And what's this now?"

"Murders in Karnsburg, Chief Detective," the officer said. "The municipals sent it over here."

"Well," he picked up the manila envelope containing the officer reports and photographs and said, "at least it's something to do. Quiet gets boring. Anything else?"

The officer nodded, "Yes, Sir. The Munies who wrote the report on the most recent victim are waiting for you in Interrogation Room 3. They said something about getting advice on how to report back to media given the peculiarities."

Detective Merkatz cocked a thick graying eyebrow and asked, "Which are?"

"I don't know, Sir," the officer said. "They didn't say."

"Damn," he said, sitting at his desk and spreading the packet's contents before him. "Tell them I'll read over their report and then go and talk to them."

"Yes, Sir," the officer said and walked away.

Chief Detective Merkatz read through the report, making notes of things that stood out, and placed the case materials and his notes in the manila folder before he refilled his coffee mug and walked to Interrogation Room 3. As they shook hands, the two Karnsburg officers introduced themselves. The short, stocky brown-haired man introduced himself as Arnold Sperling, and the taller, slender blonde stated that her name was Zarina Engelhardt. Chief Detective Merkatz offered them coffee and water. Officer Engelhardt requested and received a bottle of water. At Merkatz's direction, everyone sat at the interrogation room's table.

"So," Chief Detective Merkatz began, "your report seems straightforward, but I do have a few questions. Your report lists three victims, but you have only included photographs of Sophia Pichler and this Minna Bergen. What happened to the third? Or," he glanced at the report again and corrected himself, "the first victim's body?"

"Both are correct, Chief Detective," Officer Engelhardt

stated. "The first alleged victim did not die. We have several reports saying that an English woman was attacked while on holiday, but her boyfriend scared the assailant. She never went to the hospital and has returned home. Witnesses at the scene state her name was either Mathilda, Marjorie, or Janet. We have no other information about her."

Merkatz noted her answer and, nodding, said, "I see. And where did this alleged attack occur?"

"*Klub Abweichend*," Officer Sperling added. "It's the more popular of the two discotheques in Karnsburg."

"I see," he said. "And where is this discotheque in relation to the two murders?"

"Just over a kilometer," Officer Engelhardt said. "We assume that the killer met his victims in the club."

Without looking up from scribbling notes, Chief Detective Merkatz asked, "And what makes you assume male?"

"We have a few reasons, Sir," Officer Engelhardt said. "First, the last person the two deceased young women were seen speaking to was a man – reports say with blond hair and a 'not-unattractive-but-nondescript face'. Also, as you can see from the photographs, the bodies were found in locations where the snow, mud, and morning dew allowed us to get faint footprints in a size forty-seven. While not definitive proof, Sir, we believe this strongly suggests the assailant is male."

Merkatz nodded. He tapped his pen on the table as he looked into their eyes. "I agree," he said. "It's neither definitive proof, but it is suggestive. So, the cause of death is exsanguination?"

Officer Sperling scratched the back of his neck and sighed. Then he said, "Coroner reports indicate exsanguination increased their vulnerability to hypothermia. Reports indicate that the victims lost approximately nineteen hundred milliliters, causing them to lose consciousness and causing several organs to shut down."

"I see," the detective said. "And the more recent victim, this Minna Bergen, is she the only one with a business card for Karnstein Finanzberater?"

"Yes, Chief Detective," Officer Engelhardt stated. "We thought nothing of it. Do you think it something?"

He shrugged and shook his head, saying, "Likely nothing, but depending on the situation, this may shed light on a motive which, as you know, will help us find the killer, hopefully, before he kills again." He returned his notebook to the rear pocket on his trousers and said, "Those are my questions at present. They informed me that you had questions regarding handling the media?"

Both nodded in the affirmative, and then Sperling and Engelhardt looked at each other the way siblings did when neither wanted to tell their father what had happened. After a moment of silence, Officer Engelhardt said, "Well, Sir, the *Crier* is calling this the 'Karnsburg Vampire,' and we're not sure how to respond."

Chief Detective Merkatz chuckled and scratched the back of his neck. "Of course, they're calling him that," he said. "I would do the same thing. It's catchy. It'll sell papers–even to tourists who will want a souvenir of being in Karnsburg during a vampire craze. What you should tell them is that there is no vampire and that you have turned the investigation over to me. I will make arrangements and arrive tomorrow. I will answer all questions they have. Is that all?"

Engelhardt looked down and ran her fingers through her hair. Sperling sighed and rolled his eyes before saying, "The thing is, Chief Detective, and we hate mentioning this, but some older residents–including two municipal council members and the burgomaster's mother–are spreading rumors of a return of some Karnsburg vampire from two centuries ago. And it's causing crowds to follow all officers investigating anything and even stopping them at the grocery or at restaurants."

Merkatz tilted his head and asked, "The 'Karnsburg vampire?' What is that? Some local legend?"

"It is," Sperling continued. Shaking his head, he added, "And I wouldn't bring it up, Sir, but the legend names the vampire as Carmilla Karnstein, who was executed–and possibly by mistake–and well, that business card…"

"Is from the Karnstein Investments Firm," Chief Detective Merkatz said. "It's nothing more than a coincidence. Vampires do not exist. Local legends are marvellous stories to tell around campfires or to frighten naughty children into behaving. We solve cases with science and deduction. Not with superstition and hearsay. We exhaust all leads, but we do not give in to fears of things that do not now nor never have existed."

* * *

Sam woke with a start, blinked several times, and shook her head while yawning. Although the smoldering embers provided a small amount of light and warmth in this windowless room, Sam shivered. A complicated smile crossed her lips as the source of the chill revealed itself. She had spent the last three nights in Carmilla's bed, and as she woke each morning, she woke either embracing or being embraced by the vampire's icy, lifeless body. As her fingertips glided over Carmilla's soft, cold, sickly pale skin, skin which she had studied intimately many times, she drew her hand away only when the cold became physically painful. As she winced, she noted the lack of movement in Carmilla's chest and the lack of sound—either breathing or snoring—emanating from her bluish-pink lips.

Sam grabbed her phone, returned to her own chamber, and dressed for the day. She then descended to the kitchen where Martin supervised two servants cleaning. When he noticed Sam's arrival, he smiled and poured her a cup of coffee. As he busied himself making her breakfast, he said, "Nine forty-two. That is the longest you have spent in bed with her these past three nights. Is there something I should know, Miss Hain?"

Sam smiled as she inhaled the coffee's aroma before taking a sip. She then responded, "I'm simply doing my due diligence to watch over my client and ensure that nothing can link her to this crime."

His over-the-shoulder glance revealed a raised, questioning eyebrow as he said, "Of course, Miss Hain. By the way, what is your normal procedure in accepting a client and investigating their case?"

Sam smiled as the smoky aroma of bacon wafted through the air as Martin fried bacon, diced onions and peppers, and shredded potatoes. After a long, slow sip of coffee, she said, "Usually Destiny draws up a contract, we both sign it, and I take half my fee up front. Why?"

"Just a question," he said as he whisked a bowl of eggs. As he transferred them to a skillet, he added, "And how is this investigation proceeding?"

She shrugged. "I'm not sure," she said. "I spoke to someone whose fiancée was attacked but survived, and he claimed the assailant looked like a male but was pretty. After a bit of insult to those of us who love other women, he said it might have been a girl, but he seemed to think it was a blond man. Either way, 'Milla isn't blonde, and unless she has a wig or some magical spell, I doubt it was her. Plus, as soon as I saw the police blotter, I ran to check on her, and she was in her bed as pale and gaunt as she always was when she hasn't fed in a while. So, I'm sure that it's not her, but I don't yet know if either Lord Patriarchy or the Grimms agree."

"I don't think the Grimms are her primary fear," he said as he set a plate before her.

Sam blinked in surprised and then asked, "You don't think she fears a village mob, do you?

Martin poured himself a glass of blood wine and then sat in a chair opposite hers at the small table in the kitchen. He sipped the wine, and his face became solemn and stony as he said, "It is my understanding that the Countess has only spoken to you about the events surrounding Elisa's death. I will not elaborate on other events that she may fear; however, I will say Lord Volny's presence has opened a few wounds that, coupled with the increased activity of Elisa's ghost in recent weeks, have her quite concerned."

She ate a forkful of the farmer's breakfast Martin prepared, nodded, and said, "It won't happen again. I mean, I doubt it. Look, five years ago, I would have said the time of angry village mobs was over, but well, never predicted we'd all live through what we have in the last four years alone–especially back home."

"Yes," Martin nodded and said, "The last few years have seen a return to prejudices and actions that give those of us who have lived through them several times before a cause for concern. What has been pleasant is your presence, for since you are such a cherished *friend*, my Countess has radiated a calmness and happiness that has not been felt in these cold, empty halls in some time."

Sam smiled and brushed her hair behind her ear before replying, "Yeah, I was really looking forward to relaxing away from work and spending time with her. I didn't think I'd get tapped to fix a situation that feels like nothing more than a crime."

Martin drained half the wine from his glass before saying, "Then this should end quickly, allowing the two of you to resume your friendship, since the Countess has finally agreed to gift you that which you desire."

Sam focused her gaze on the table, avoiding his knowing look, as she ran her index finger along the rim of her coffee cup. "Yeah," she said, "she's giving me what I've been saying I want. Yeah."

She continued to avoid his gaze as he nodded, smiled, and said, "As you say, Miss Hain. Now, if you will excuse me, I must perform my regular duties."

Sam finished her breakfast and put her dishes in the sink, giving them a pre-wash. She refilled her mug and made her way to the drawing room and library. Next, she searched the shelves for something to read until she could call Destiny. She then skimmed a copy of the classic tales collected and altered by the Grimm brothers and then settled on a collection of tales by E.T.A. Hoffmann that included "The Nutcracker," "Vampirismus," and "The Lost Reflection." Sam read German better than she spoke it, so she spent the entire morning and much of the afternoon reading these dark fairy tales.

In the middle of the afternoon, after she finished the book, she called Destiny and asked, "So, how was meeting the parents?"

"They're still in town," Destiny replied flatly.

"You sound disappointed, Des," Sam replied. "What's wrong?"

She growled into the phone and then squeaked, saying, "Sandy, stop clawing at the sofa! It's as old as your mom."

"Hey," Sam interjected, "It's comfy. And you didn't answer my question."

Destiny sighed, saying, "Eh, nothing's wrong. They're nice enough people, and they seem to like me. It's just that they want to do *everything* as a family unit. We're doing brunch in an hour, and then they're all going to come watch the choir sing, which they did the past two nights. I haven't had a meal or an evening to myself since I got here. My guild has sent me so many messages asking me if I'm okay and even offering to 'raid Butcher's Bend' to save me." They both laughed, and then Destiny asked, "Then I'd have someone to watch the werewolf feud with me."

"The what?" Sam tilted her head as she continued, "How many S-T's are there? What werewolves? Are you okay?"

"Oh, I'm fine," Destiny said. "There's no violence. It's just the Johnsons and the Scartellis constantly trying to outdo the other on who has the bigger holiday display in their yard."

Sam laughed. The Johnsons and the Scartellis were large families of werewolves who lived on the same street in the Veiled Heights. So far, they have feuded over who can have the largest "litter" of children, whose lemon bars made the most at PTA bake sales, whose picket fence could remain whiter, whose haunted house was scarier, and whose kids were better at anything in which they could compete. Now, they added Christmas decorations to that list. Sam rolled her eyes and asked, "Is Rayna fanning the flames?"

113

"You bet she is," Destiny said. "That witch loves to stir that cauldron. Anyway, so how are things in the Alpine love nest?"

Sam rolled her eyes before she sighed and responded, "Oh, you know, just dealing with a vampire murdering young girls, a patriarchal asshat, waking up in 'Milla's bed for three days in a row, and then her promising that, if I fix this situation for her, she'll never even flirt with me again. All in a day's…"

"Shit! I lost the pool money," Destiny interrupted and then said, "but I mean, three days in her bed, huh? So, I guess you're about to be Facebook official and all that?"

"Hold up," Sam said. "What's this about pool money?"

"Oh, nothing really," Destiny said as she scooped Sandy's litter box. "It's just that, well, some of us Karnhain shippers set up a betting pool on when the two of you would get back together. Oh wow, Sandy, you pooped a lot last night. Ew. And I've got the 28th as the day you'll finally admit the truth to her. So, that's the pool."

Sam narrowed her eyes and sighed. She leaned back on the chaise and scratched an itch on her right leg before saying, "I knew about the pool. But what I want to know is how much money? And why did you pick the day I leave to come home?"

Sam heard the crinkling thud of a plastic grocery bag being dropped in a dumpster. As Destiny threw the litter into the garbage, she said, "Last I checked, it was almost three hundred, and I promise that if you help me win, I'll buy you a really nice bottle of bourbon and a present. And I chose the 28th because you're stubborn. I wouldn't expect you to profess your love on Christmas in a romantic gesture when you could spend the entire holiday debating internally whether you want to be honest with her and yourself or continue being stubborn. And then, at the last minute, you would sheepishly apologize for everything and say that you really do want a relationship. We all love you, Sam, but you're not a Hallmark Holiday Movie."

"And why isn't it 'Hainstein' instead," Sam asked.

Destiny's guffaw caused Sam to hold her phone arm's length from her ear. When she calmed enough to speak, Destiny said, "Oh like anyone would believe that you're a top."

Sam glowered at the phone and growled. "Well, none of you will win," she said, "since the only way to continue having a chance is to throw the investigation and endanger her."

"Wait! Let me put you on speaker," Destiny said as she plopped onto Sam's sofa and patted her lap. Sandy Paws, Sam's calico cat, leapt onto Destiny's lap and received scratches behind her ears. "Sandy," Destiny continued, "your mom said something really stupid, which she's going to explain to us right now. So, what do you mean you'd have to endanger her to flirt awkwardly?"

Sam sighed and twirled her hair around her finger. "Everything that's going on has 'Milla spooked," she said, "and she begged me to fix this situation before it gets out of hand. She promised, as part of my payment, to end all attempts to rekindle things. And…"

"You said 'no,' right?" Destiny interrupted. "You told her this was pro bono, right?"

Sam lowered her head and scratched behind her left ear. Destiny strained to hear Sam's response, as her voice was a hush above a whisper when she said, "No. I just promised to help."

Sandy meowed plaintively, and Destiny slammed her palm into her face. Her shoulders slumped forward as she said, "Sam, both Sandy and I want you to know that we still love you, but you need to fix this before you fix the murdering vampire."

"I know," Sam whined as she buried her face in her left hand. "I wasn't thinking, Des. 'Milla started confessing something from her past that she still feels guilt over, and I've never seen her so terrified. She was crying blood, and then she knelt and begged me to fix things. I just wanted to help her, so I agreed."

At this point, Martin entered the drawing room and said, "I apologize for the interruption, Miss Hain, but a police detective is waiting in the entertaining chamber. I think you would be best suited to attend to his questions."

Sam nodded and said, "Alright, Des. Seems I'm needed for a quick fix. I'll text you later."

* * *

"So, what's this all about," Sam asked Martin as they walked toward the entertaining chamber.

"A police detective has arrived from Innsbruck to investigate the murders, Miss Hain," he said.

"Murders? I was only aware of one death," she said, shooting him a concerned look as they descended the spiral staircase.

"Apparently, Miss Hain," Martin said, "There was another three nights prior, and this victim carried a business card of the Countess' investment agency."

"That's circumstantial," Sam said. "I bet he's just trying to find a motive."

"Likely, Miss Hain," Martin said. "However, with the Countess indisposed as she is currently, I told him that she was unavailable due to meeting with a client in Vienna but that her *fiancée* would speak to him if he so desired. And he desired to speak with someone."

Sam froze. Her jaw slammed against her collarbone as she

processed his words. "Hold the fucking phone," she stammered. "Martin, I'm not her fian... I'm not–we're not a–I'm..."

"I am aware," Martin said with a sly grin and a wink, "that you are just a friend who happens to flirt constantly and who has spent the past three mornings in her bed. Forgive me for thinking there might be desires you seek to avoid telling yourself. Besides that, Miss Hain, naming you as her romantic partner will hopefully give your statements more weight with him."

Sam's mind drifted to thoughts of a wedding, of her vintage-inspired, lace gown, of Carmilla in an elegant and tailored power ensemble, and of a seven-tiered wedding cake with raspberry jam between the layers and a lemon-rosewater buttercream frosting. Leaning against the wall and twirling her hair around her finger, she sighed wistfully. Martin's laughter snapped her back to the pressing issue. She blushed. He shot a cocked an eyebrow as he smiled, causing her eyes to narrow. She harrumphed and continued down the stairs.

Chief Detective Merkatz sat in one of the mahogany throne-style chairs with burgundy velvet cushions embroidered with golden badgers. Instead of the navy uniform, he wore a charcoal suit with a pale blue pinstripe. The fire blazed and crackled in the hearth, and electric lights set in wall sconces provided illumination. Oil paintings depicting the patriarchs and now the first matriarch of the Karnstein-Bertholt clan lined the walls. Merkatz stood when they entered and with a nodding bow, he offered his hand. Sam's firm handshake took him by surprise. Martin introduced them and excused himself to procure refreshments.

As they took seats opposite a small wooden table, Sam raised an eyebrow and asked, "So, Chief Detective, Martin tells me you're investigating those murders I've read about in the newspaper?"

He nodded and said, "Yes, Miss, er, Hain, but I must wish you congratulations on your upcoming nuptials."

Sam inhaled sharply and blushed. She smiled wistfully and said, "Thank you. It has been a journey. But that is not why you are here."

Martin arrived with a tray of grapes, spiced nuts, and coffee, as Merkatz refused the offer of anything stronger while working. He opened his blazer and produced his notebook and pen from the interior lapel pocket. With a click, he said, "No. I would not be here, but the second victim had a business card for the Countess' investment brokerage firm in her wallet. I was hoping to learn something about her and perhaps find a motive."

Sam nodded. "I understand," she said. "And I'll do all I can to help. Had we known you were on your way here, perhaps 'Milla would have postponed traveling to Vienna to meet with a client. I'm not sure I can offer you much information. I don't get involved in the specifics of her business transactions, and I would not feel comfortable opening a stranger's, albeit a dead one's, financial information." She turned to look at Martin and then asked, "Do you mind if Martin stays, Chief Detective? I'm better at reading German than speaking it right now."

Chief Detective Merkatz, in a heavily accented English, said, "I can switch to English. Your German is elementary, but not bad. I take it you have not been learning long?"

Sam smiled and looked at Carmilla's stern portrait before answering, "Once I realized we were becoming serious, I started learning. I grew up with English at home. My father tried to teach me Irish, as that was his native tongue, but when speaking in it, like German, I can converse with young children and school textbooks."

He laughed and nodded, saying, "If I need help to find either the library or the train station, I'll ask you. Then I take it that you wouldn't know much about Miss Bergen and her accounts."

Sipping her coffee, Sam shrugged and shook her head. "I'm afraid not," she said. "I don't ask specifics about any client, and I've only met a handful of those who have large accounts. And to be honest, I don't know if 'Milla would know either. She has an amazing memory, but most of the individual accounts are handled by one of her brokerage agents. I'd call the office on the card and talk to the agents there. If you leave your card, I'll have 'Milla call tomorrow after she returns."

"I thought you mentioned she would return today," Chief Detective Merkatz inquired.

Sam blushed and giggled, saying, "She will return this evening, but can you blame me for wanting to have a bit of fun when she returns? I see a ring on your finger, Chief Detective, so I'm sure you understand."

He nodded, made a few notes, and then asked, "Yes, and would you humor me? Good. Can you tell me where Countess Karnstein was on the nights of the murders?"

"I most certainly can," Sam said. "We spent the early part of the evening dining in the dining hall, then we retired to the drawing room with wine, and then we ended the night in bed. Is that all?"

"Just one minor thing," Chief Detective Merkatz said as he twirled his pen in his hand. "Countess Carmilla Karnstein, it's strange that she shares a name with someone whose name I'm hearing thrown about whenever people—including local

politicians—start rambling about the Karnsburg vampire, so…
"

Sam interrupted him with a deep laugh. She said, "You're not suggesting that she's a vampire, are you?"

"No, no, no," he said, waving his hand and shaking his head. "I only ask, because as this legend gets thrown around, I find the name a curious connection."

Sam narrowed her eyes. She believed he told her the truth, but she also knew that police detectives knew more than they told. She sipped her coffee silently for a moment before saying, "From what she's told me and from what I've read in her library, it is a family name."

"That's what I thought," he said as he stood. "I'll leave you my card. When she returns and has a night of rest, have her call me. Thank you."

Sam and Martin escorted Chief Detective Merkatz to the keep's door. There, Lord Volny's men searched him again and then walked him to his car. Sam exhaled, stretched, and unclenched the muscles in her shoulders. She returned to the library and collapsed into one of the chairs. Martin followed a few moments later, carrying two crystal glasses and a decanter partially filled with bourbon. He handed her one glass, sat in the chair on the opposite side of the hearth, and raised the glass in a toast.

Sam moaned happily as the smoky, caramel flavor of the bourbon warmed her throat. She looked toward Martin and said, "The cop doesn't worry me, but something he said about the rumors in town does."

Martin nodded as he lowered the glass from his lips. "Quite right, Miss Hain," he said. "We know of her innocence this time around, but we must be prepared for the twin demons of fear and ignorance to possess the mortals once again."

Sam laughed darkly and shook her head. She sighed and, as she gazed into the amber liquid, said, "That was nearly two hundred years ago, Martin. I mean, I suppose given all that's happened in the last few years, people may be likely to attack a wealthy woman believed to be connected to a series of murders."

He nodded and refilled their glasses. He chuckled in a way that sounded almost like a giggle, smiled at Sam, and said, "And you performed the role of the Countess' fiancée quite convincingly."

Sam smiled, realized he saw, blushed, and glanced away. "You don't think," she asked, "she'll be upset when he tells her he spoke to her fiancée? Do you?"

He chuckled and said, "Well, perhaps you may need to renegotiate the payment that you have *accepted*, but I do not think she would be opposed to the idea. Of course, one of you would need to cease being stubborn."

Sam shot him a glare, which he returned with a knowing wink. The fire crackled and popped. Sam opened her mouth to respond, but gunfire caused her to jerk her head toward the wall. She and Martin leapt from their seats and raced to the window. Gazing into the courtyard, they saw Lord Volny's men in a firefight with several armed attackers. Sam winced as three of the four men in the front courtyard fell. She looked at Martin and said, "I need a gun."

"Come with me," Martin said as he raced from the library with a speed unexpected for someone of his age. As they ran, an alarm sounded, and an artificial voice directed all thralls and human servants to report to the armory.

She followed him to the castle's armory, where she previously marveled at the rapiers and long swords as well as the ceremonial and ancestral armors. Martin produced his key ring and used one of the longer keys to unlock the black steel gun safe. The door opened to a storage closet larger than Sam's college apartment. Martin handed rifles and handguns to the servants and thralls, directing them to fan out on the lower floors and to watch the doors and windows. Martin grabbed a nine-millimeter handgun and an HK G36 assault rifle.

As Sam grabbed two HK USP handguns and a short-barreled shotgun, she said, "I guess we have this floor?"

"No," he said. "All of our windows are made of the highest level of bullet resistance glass, and I have already activated the riot shutters for increased protection and alerted the police. We do a quick sweep on the hallway where both the Countess and Lord Volny rest, lock the door to that hallway, and then descend to help with the defense."

"Gotcha," Sam shouted as she raced from the armory.

Bullets cracked and snapped in the early evening air. Sam and Martin stalked the keep's third floor. Glass shattered. Sam pushed into Carmilla's chamber. Martin continued to Lord Volny's. They secured both vampires, locked the hallway's entrance door, and raced down the stairs.

As soon as they reached the first floor, Martin charged into the chaos of gunfire, broken furniture, and shattered glass. The attackers wore helmets and Kevlar vests. Sam stood at the base of the stairs and blinked. She heard an owl hoot, and as she opened her eyes, Old Tom's Hill loomed before her. Her nose wrinkled at the smell of burning flesh. Her heart rate increased. She winced and breathed deeply. After another blink, the interior of Castle Karnstein returned.

A bullet from one of the attackers ricocheted off a stone

wall next to Sam. She dove behind an upturned chair. Her heart raced. Quick, shallow breaths burst through her lips. She fired, grazing the attacker in the shoulder. The attacker turned toward her. She fired again, sending a round through the attacker's lower jaw. With a burst of blood staining the floor, he slumped and fell.

Martin kept to the walls, his pace methodical. His undead lungs evoked no chest movement. He kept his eyes wide as he moved through the shutter-darkened floor. As one of the armored attackers fired three rounds into the chest of one of Lord Volny's men, Martin slipped behind him and slammed the rifle's buttstock into his helmet. The attacker staggered forward. He spun around, and Martin fired six rounds into his face. The attacker fell. Martin stepped over his corpse and continued.

Sam's lungs pushed breath after breath through her mouth. Sweat soaked her forehead and rappelled down her cheeks. Her eyes darted from side to side. Her nose wrinkled as she smelled the reek of burning flesh. She killed another attacker with a single shot. Gritting her teeth, she forced her mind to think about protecting Carmilla as she fought. Sam tripped over the body of a slain thrall. She screamed. Her muscles quaked.

An attacker snuck up behind her and slammed his pistol's grip into the back of her head. She grunted. He slid his arms forward, pinning her in a full nelson. She slammed her boot heel into his foot and thrust her elbows back into his sides. He twisted and slammed her to the floor, his body weight pinning her down. Blood dripped from her nose. She groaned. Her jaw trembled. Her shallow breaths came in triplets. As he rose to his feet, she spun around and shot his knee. He grimaced and yelled, and as he grabbed his knee, her next shot landed between his eyes.

Martin fired twice more, killing two of three attackers who neared one of the two ascending staircases. The third spun and fired. Martin's preternatural speed allowed him to dodge. He pulled the trigger and heard the faint click of an empty magazine. As the attacker fired twice more, missing once, and then piercing through his abdomen. He dropped his rifle and sped forward, pinning the attacker to the wall by his throat. With a hungry growl, Martin plunged his fangs into the attacker's unprotected neck.

As the chaos ended, Sam rose to her feet. Her body shook as she saw corpses strewn around her. She smelled burning flesh. She gritted her teeth as the glassy film on her eyes turned into mist. She tasted iron on her lips. Her heart thundered inside her; her chest heaved as she rasped her breaths. Through the tear and sweat induced haze, she saw a figure descend the stairs. Shaking her head, she sighed, dropped her guns, and slumped to her knees. The figure rushed toward her. She whispered the word, "Zozo," and then fell unconscious.

When she regained consciousness, Carmilla cradled her, wiping sweat, blood, and tears from her face with a lace-trimmed handkerchief. Directed by Martin, the thralls and servants busied themselves cleaning. Sam smiled as her eyes met Carmilla's and through a tired, small voice, said, "You're safe. Good."

"I am," Carmilla said. "Thanks, in a large part, to you and Martin. Come, let me get you to someplace more comfortable and less cold than my floor."

Sam tried to stand, but before she got her footing, Carmilla scooped her up and carried her toward the stairs. As she wrapped her arms around the Countess' neck, Sam chuckled and said, "I forgot just how strong you can be." And then she rested her head on the vampire's shoulders.

A few moments later, they arrived in Carmilla's personal chambers. While Sam undressed, the Countess drew her a hot bath, bathed her, toweled her dry, and helped her to bed.

6

Chapter 6

The attacker slammed me to the floor as he used his body weight to pin me down. I think the fucker broke my nose. I felt my jaw tremble. My heart tried to break my ribs as it thundered in my chest. As tears welled up in my eyes, my breaths came in quick, trembling triplets. He moved his feet, and I spun around, shooting him in his kneecap. Black clothing, Kevlar vests, helmets, and military grade weapons. These guys weren't a village mob, but I had no clue who they were. He yelled and grabbed his knee.

Then I saw him, and I smelled the burning flesh. I saw my father grabbing his knee after I shot him on Old Tom's Hill. I fired again, hitting my father right between his fucking lying eyes. As he slumped and fell forward, he wasn't my father anymore. I wasn't at Old Tom's Hill. I was in Austria, tasting my own blood as it dripped from my nose, and this man I just shot wasn't my father. He was someone I didn't know. I still smelled the fire. Bullets cracked. Bones broke. Humans screamed and died. I curled into a fetal position and clenched every muscle I had to stop the tears.

All fell quiet. I rose to my feet. And then a solitary pair of boots descended the stairs. I saw the figure looming in the shadows. Four horns curled from its head. As that black goat fur and those six-fingered claws came into focus, I shook my head. My shoulders slumped. I couldn't fight him right now. I had no chance. I dropped the guns, and he rushed me. And all went black.

When I came to, I found Carmilla cradling me in her arms, wiping away the blood and sweat. Our lips moved, but I don't remember what we said. I remember her carrying me up the stairs to her personal chamber, helping me bathe, and then tucking me into bed. As Martin approached with glasses of water and bourbon for me and wine for 'Milla, I managed to say, "You're strong. And you're pretty. And you're safe."

"I would say the same things of you," She said with a smile. "And I am only safe now because you and Martin led the defense of my home."

I turned to Martin, who looked unphased and unhurt. Lucky fucking vampire. I sat up, sipped my bourbon, and then said, "That can't have been a village mob. I don't think it was the Grimms. So, who the fuck attacked us?"

"When we examined the bodies, we found one in possession of a wax seal bearing the insignia of the Order of the Dragon. I assume they are either foot soldiers or mercenaries."

"Order of the Dragon," I said. My voice trailed into memories of Old Tom's Hill and the night I learned that my father and his precious Astrum Argentum had aligned with the Dragons and some fucking fae noble for some, as of yet unknown, purpose.

"Yes," Martin said. "Well, I must depart. The local police may be here soon, and someone must speak to them."

As he walked out, I turned toward Carmilla, but she refused to meet my eyes. She sat on the edge of the bed with her eyes downcast. I placed my hand atop hers, gave it a gentle squeeze, and asked, "What's wrong? I mean, aside from my enemies crashing your home. Sorry about that."

She shook her head. Still refusing to look at me, she said, "I do not think it is your recent actions that have brought them here."

"What do you mean?" I grew concerned, because I could see the bloody tears forming at the edge of her eyes.

She wiped them away, turned to me, and with a weak smile, said, "I will tell you tomorrow night. I swear this promise upon the blood within me and the honor of my family. But tonight, you need rest."

At that moment, Lord Patriarchy entered the room. That hooked nose made looking down on me easier. His eyes scanned the length of the bed, and he cocked a thick, bushy gray eyebrow before saying, "Ah, you have calmed down. Such an outburst is unfitting for a soldier."

Sam narrowed her eyes as she rolled them. "Well," she said, "I suppose it's a good thing I'm just a midnight snack that bites back. I'm sorry for the loss of your men."

He snorted. "They were weak," he grumbled with a chortle. "Do you think I would waste my best soldiers on something like this?"

I slammed my right fist onto the bed as I glared at him, saying, "Well fuck you. They had lives, families, people who cared about them. They were people. They deserve better from their lord than to be dismissed because they were ambushed by the fucking Order of the goddamned Dragon. You..."

"How dare you insult my honor as their lord," Volny interrupted, punching the bedpost as his eyes bulged and as his nostrils flared. "A mortal like you has neither the right nor the knowledge to speak on such matters."

"A mortal like me," I shot back, side eying him as I sipped my bourbon, "who has made a reputation and a career of fixing issues your kind have with adapting to the recognition that you actually have to share this world with us mortals. And with only one exception early in my career, I've never failed. Also, I didn't see you get involved in the firefight."

He growled. I sipped my bourbon. His meaty hand tore the canopy as he screamed, "Were it not for the eternally honored tradition of aristocratic hospitality, I would rip your head from your neck for such statements, little mortal. It would be in your best interests to learn how to speak properly to your betters."

"Threaten me all you want, o noble Lord Volny," I said with a mocking, overdramatic seated bow. "But be warned that should you act upon your threats, the outcome could be quite Grimm for you."

He stormed from the room. Carmilla breathed a sigh of relief as he left. I shrugged and finished my bourbon. Carmilla stayed at my side until sleep overcame me. We reminisced about some of our happier moments together and then told each other stories from our childhoods. She then sang a lullaby that has been passed down through her family. It was in an older dialect, so I only understood a few words to the song about giving eggs to children and spears to Odin. The last thing I remember is her kissing my forehead.

That beautiful and unknown but familiar face fell to the stone floor and shattered. As the jagged fangs of its true face opened for a howl, the creature's black hair that I once thought to be 'Milla's twisted into strange appendages that turned what I thought was a human into a spider-like creature that slithered and crawled on four hair legs while its human legs kicked the air and its arms reached forward to grab and rend. Dressed in a white, lace-trimmed nightgown, I raced through the halls of Castle Karnstein as that thing chased me.

I called for Carmilla as I passed her empty bedchamber. No response came. Crawling on the ceiling, that thing chased me. I passed the library, and the thing leaped into the open doorway, preventing my entry. I screamed for Carmilla as I raced down the stairs, tripping when I felt the creature's saliva drip onto my head. My heart pounded in my chest as I ran. Breathing heavily, I screamed for Carmilla as I raced toward the keep's doors. The only response came from the creature's growl as it leaped over me and blocked my escape. I cursed and spun around, racing down a different hallway.

Tears streamed down my cheeks as I ran, calling for Carmilla, Martin and even Destiny. No one answered. That creature gained on me. I felt and smelled its hot, rancid breath as its jaws snapped at my heels. It shot one of its hair legs forward. The rough, stringy hair whipped my back. I screamed as I felt barbs rend my flesh and tear the nightgown. As I raced down the corridor, I saw that damned door to the dungeon ahead of me. Pushing hard, I reached the door and found it locked. Screaming, I turned as the creature rushed me, its rancid, toothy jaws open wide as it screamed and howled in hunger. Those rotting, yellow-black fangs closed around my throat, and I shot awake.

Cold sweat drenched my body as I sat up in the bed. My chest heaved as my heart pounded against my ribs. I rubbed my temples and sighed. I looked at the window and saw the blue morning sky. After three days of waking up next to 'Milla, this felt lonelier than waking up next to her cold, lifeless body. And then, between Elisa's ghost and these nightmares, there had to be something in the dungeon I needed to find. I winced as my fingers caught on knots as I ran them through my hair.

I sped through my morning routine and then walked to Carmilla's bed chamber. I sat on her bed as she lay on her back, cold and lifeless. I reached out and held her hand. I leaned down and kissed her cheek and said, "I'm sorry, 'Milla. I know you'll tell me the truth in your time, but I have to use all the time I have to find that one thing that will help me protect you. Pro bono."

I rose from her bed and searched the bookshelves for the level that would open the secret passage to the dungeon. After a few moments of searching, I found this mismatched set of bookends that didn't want to move when I pushed them. The one on the right was bolted in place, but the one on the left concealed a hidden lever. I switched my cell phone flashlight and descended the stairs. When I returned to that alchemist's room, I went straight to 'Milla's diary that was bound to the desk. I took a deep breath, grabbed my small notebook, and opened the diary again.

* * *

27 September 1827

Both of them are gone, and it is my fault. Annalena was so full of life, so young and vibrant, everything I was at her age. We embraced throughout the night, and it was only before I left she tilted her soft, pale neck toward me and offer herself in the most intimate of ways. I felt her heartbeat as I fed, and I felt her heartbeat as I finished.

131

I know I did, because, as I transformed into a mist and departed through her bed chamber's window, she opened her blue eyes to gaze upon me and say, "I will see you tomorrow night, my love."

I do not know what happened, but she died. Rumors reached the castle that her parents saw her at breakfast, but they later found her lifeless body in her bedchamber. An apothecary of some renown – a man visiting from Budapest named Yarono Bertalan, I heard – examined her and said she had been dead for some time. He then pointed to the bite marks on her neck. And then they found her diary, and she detailed our relationship. Then the mob formed.

We saw the fires from our castle, and I think they will haunt me for the rest of my immortality. In its anger, the mob hurled torches onto every building that they found as if they were part of Florian's black band. Thick clouds of smoke blackened the evening sky. It made waking as early as we did easier. Ash rained upon us as we watched the torch-wielding mob raze the homes of innocent people in their lust for revenge. The enhanced senses we possess provide great assistance in hunting for prey, but now I know I will never not hear their chants for my death.

Father did not yell at me as he always had before. Instead, he apologized. He blamed himself for granting me the liberties that I had enjoyed without teaching me the responsibilities that accompanied them. He knew I would succeed him, but he now realized that I could only truly succeed him if I produced an heir. And that would not happen because of my sapphic perversions, as he called them. He then lectured me on how a woman loving another woman was acceptable as a dalliance, but it was not the proper way to spend even a human lifetime.

When the mob reached our portcullis, none could hear anything beyond their screams for my death. As Father, Martin, and the other men debated on a plan of attack, I knew that they would kill the entire village, and I could not stand such an injustice. The village already burned from the villagers' rage. Adding our own indignant ire would solve nothing. I said nothing, but I left the war room and made my way toward the keep's main entrance. When I reached the portcullis, Elisa had already given herself to the mob.

She glided through the portcullis and said, "I am Carmilla Karnstein, heir to House Karnstein-Bertholt. I have heard your cries of anger, and I give myself to you so they may be sated."

I called out to her, begging her to come back. As they bound her in chains and draped crucifixes around her neck, she turned and smiled. She shook her head and said, "Elisa, do not worry for me. I will always be with you, my beloved sister"

Our guards dragged me back to our keep as I drained myself, crying and screaming. I have never had much love for the Christian god and his followers, but the travesty that they called my sister's trial—my trial—transformed my indifference into hatred. One hour is all they took to decide to kill her by staking her on their own altar. I loved seeing lightning strike the church, reducing it to rubble and burning all the buildings beside it. But Father ended my joy by decreeing that, since I had endangered our entire clan, I would be exiled until the Elder Council decided my punishment.

21 February 1851

Escorted by several members of the Bertalan clan, we traveled to Brasov where I was to be judged at Bran Castle. The Council of Elders, the Patriarchs of all the vampire clans of Europe and the Levant, gathered to decide how to proceed with any issue that impacted or threatened our kind. Today, I was such an issue. The Patriarchs postured as they always do, giving speeches that praised our noble king, Vlad Dracula Tepes, for his courage, wisdom, and mercy; listed the glorious achievements of their own clans since the last Council was called; and then offered their opinions on the morals of the younger vampires, especially me. For a group of men who denounced the immorality and unnaturalness of my "sapphic lusts," they routinely broke from their monologues to demand that I provide specific details of my time in Annalena and any other "perverse dalliances." When Dracula called an end to deliberations, they sent me to the oubliette to await their decision.

When they summoned me for my judgment, my father glared at me as I entered the chamber. I stood before the assembled body of Patriarchs and our King. Dracula leaned forward on his throne and leered at me, his tongue licking his lips. He was an unattractive man: short and squat with ruddy skin, unwashed and knotted black hair, and a thick mustache. I shuddered as his eyes devoured my body as if I were a meal. Though my heart pounded, I raised my chin, holding my head high. He seemed to laugh at my false courage.

My father stood and said, "I, Count Adolf Karnstein, Patriarch of House Karnstein-Bertholt, wish to thank the assembled Council of Elders for providing the wisdom of your collective millennia to the problem caused by my elder daughter's indiscretions. I also wish to thank our noble King, Vlad Dracula Tepes, for the mercy and wisdom he displayed in mitigating the punishment decreed by this esteemed and noble Council.

"Carmilla Karnstein, my beloved first-born daughter, for your indiscretions and unnatural lusts that have caused the death of your sister Elisa and caused untold devastation in the town of Karnsburg, this noble Council has decreed your death and our lands and titles stripped from us in both mortal and vampire society. However, our noble King has offered a compromise. We will keep our lands and titles, and you will continue to live. You will, of course, be given to King Dracula as his newest bride, and you will bear him a son. That son will take your place as my heir. Through the acceptance of this decree, you will atone for your crimes."

20 March 1859

I have not written for some time and keeping my thoughts here is the one pleasure I am allowed. If any god exists in any heaven, I pray now they grant me respite in eternal death. For eight years, my husband, if you can call him that, has kept me prisoner in our bedchamber in his castle. Naked and chained to his bed with my legs splayed like a mortal whore, he granted me permission to feed only after he fucked me to the point where his filthy seed dripped from me. He has permitted me to be in the presence of others only when he desires to have them watch as he flogs me with his barbed whip, thrusts hot pokers into my skin and even my holes, or forces me to pleasure myself on the Judas cradle as his three other brides, whom he calls my "sisters," tease and torment my sensitive flesh. I suppose I am to be thankful that King Dracula has decreed that my "training" will not truly begin until after I have produced his heir.

Yesterday, a Roma midwife declared I was with child. For now, my torture is lessened. I am permitted to wear clothing again; although, what he permits me to wear is little more than a cross between a nightgown and a shroud. As long as I wear this iron collar, I may move freely about the castle. The servants look at me with pity and speak to me only when they must. And my "sisters" look upon me with disgust and derision, their words mocking and haunting. And when he has visitors, he parades me around on a leash and forces me to kneel at his feet, chained to whatever chair he sits in.

Why do I not flee and return home? I know that I deserve this for what I have done. I have dishonored my family and my clan – the clan I am to one day lead – and caused the deaths of my sister and lover. I have had no communication with my family since I have come to live with King Dracula. He claims that he writes them on my behalf, but I never see any return letters. I have seen my father when he comes for official visits, but he will no longer look me in the eye.

13 December 1859

I have been too distraught and drained for the past two weeks to write, but now I feel I must commit this to the page. After the midwife told him I would give birth within a week, he demanded I observe some tradition of the vampires who turned him. To that end, he forbade any from providing me sustenance until after I have survived the birth. I ripped the heads off three servants who came to bathe me as my hunger grew worse. Does this man know nothing of my people? A rage that could topple Rome fills us when we go hungry.

After five days of starvation, I gave birth to a handsome boy. I know that every mother says their child is an angel, but he looked so much like Elisa that I could not help but believe she had returned in his body. As I kissed him for the first time, I whispered his name, Ellison Aleksander Karnstein, into his little ear.

He did not come to see our son or me until the next evening. As he held Ellison in his rough, dirty hands, he asked if I still hungered. Stupid man. Of course, I was still starving. No woman ceases to be hungry simply because she pushed out a baby. I told him that I was. He nodded; ripped Ellison's head from the neck; and threw his bleeding, lifeless body into my chest. As my eyes and mouth opened as wide as they could, he simply shrugged and said, "You will eat what you are given, or you will starve. Never will you produce a worthy heir."

Before I could react, he was on me, mounting me with his knee on my stomach. His shit-covered left hand held my mouth open as his right hand squeezed Ellison's blood into my throat. Bloody tears poured from my throat as quickly as he squeezed it from my child's body. He laughed in that brittle, hollow, mocking laugh that echoed throughout the cold, dark halls of this lonely castle. When he had drained Ellison of blood, he hurled his little body on the floor, crushed his chest with the heel of his boot, and departed.

6 November 1889

I am free! As I write this, I am sitting on a train heading toward Innsbruck. That said, when word of my deeds reaches my people, I doubt my return will be met with open arms. But tonight, for the first night in nearly a century, I woke before darkness and watched the moon rise. As the sun descended, it bathed the sky in beautiful swathes of red, orange, and gold that faded into purple. As the stars pierced the royal hue, the sky darkened, and the waxing moon neared its fullness, I smiled. I smiled for the first time since I was forced into marriage.

I know that I should both recount what happened and prepare the portion of the truth that I shall tell. Since early May, that monster has been distracted with a Mister Harker who is helping him acquire land in London. From what I overheard in this castle, he planned to extend his empire into the New World, using England as a launching point for his movement. I doubted the young solicitor knew his true plans, but I can recall his horror when his mind began opening to the truth of what was around him.

I have already recorded my few interactions with this young Englishman. He was handsome enough if one were into men. My sisters seemed into him; perhaps they enjoyed tormenting him, as he was less of a man and more of a puppy. But when the time came to sail to England, I learned I was to be left behind, bound to that crumbling, empty ruin by Dracula's devil-taught magic. My jailor informed me that I would have my fill of rats and stray animals until my body expired and that his Hungarians would be watching me.

In the middle of August, I recalled the Prince of Holland

mentioning something about a physician and philosopher who had been researching our kind at the last Council of Elders meeting before my abandonment. I searched the pages of my diary, and I had recorded his name—Van Helsing. I wrote to him, in Latin for safety, and convinced one of the Hungarians to post the letter for me. I told him that I knew of what he sought. I told him of Dracula's arrogance and monstrosity, of his powers, and of his weaknesses. I warned him of Dracula's plans. I begged him to release me.

I heard nothing from him until two days after October's moon turned dark. He said that he and a Mrs. Harker were at the Borgo Pass on their journey to end the world of Dracula's evil. I met them at the door and opened it as Van Helsing's hammer smashed through the wood. He raised his crucifix and screamed for me to retreat, calling me a hell-spawned monstrosity. When I began speaking to him, he charged me, knocking me to the ground and raising a stake in the air. As my tears streamed from my eyes, I remember only Mrs. Harker saying, "No, Abraham. Not her."

He turned and questioned her, demanding to know if her resolve had wavered in this unholy place. She simply pushed him off me and helped me to stand. As I stood there, jaw agape, as she turned to the old professor and said, "She is not our enemy. Look at her stringy hair, sunken cheeks, and skin sallower than even Lucy's after her death. She has suffered as well."

Van Helsing then eyed me closely and said, "What is it you want, demon?"

I sighed and said, "I want to return home so that I can mourn the death of my sister in the proper manner. That is all that I want.

"Then why do you remain here?" He asked.

I walked deeper into the castle and said, "He has bound me here with magic he learned from the Devil himself. I cannot leave while he continues to live. If you help me, I will show you where his three brides sleep and where he sleeps; though he has not yet returned."

He did not trust me, but that Mrs. Harker, her expressions and words told me she did not pity me but that she felt a compassion for me. There was a beauty to her spirit, a strength and love that transcended the mortality of her form. I desired to embrace her, but it is not proper to take someone against their will. It hurts. But it seemed that Professor Van Helsing trusted her, and so he tolerated me. I kept to my word. I showed them where my sisters slept and watched as he killed each of them. And then I watched as he purified Dracula's own coffin and then burned his library.

As the sun descended, I began crying and shaking. Van Helsing screamed at me to be silent, and Mrs. Harker winced and told him that Dracula neared. When I asked how she knew, she revealed the bite marks on her neck. I understood then that she, in a small way, understood what I have endured. We raced to the keep's main entrance and saw his servants racing toward the castle with riders pursuing them. Four men, including Mr. Harker, stopped them before they reached the castle. When they ripped the lid from the box, I screamed as Dracula sat up, his eyes open. And then Mr. Harker and another man ended his vile life.

As the sky darkened, I sank to my knees and cried. As one of the men raised a rifle in my direction, Mrs. Harker moved between us. She ignored the men's protests, even those of her husband, and helped me to my feet. I thanked her and Professor Van Helsing and then staggered toward home. A nice innkeeper near the Borgo Pass took pity on me, cleaned me up, and gave me the clothes I now wear. I only pray that I can return home before the servants spread word to others of my kind about what has happened.

Sam pushed the chair away from the desk and exhaled slowly, her eyes welling with tears. She knew Carmilla hated Dracula, but she did not know why that hatred ran so deep. Sam had always assumed the movies and even the book were not accurate depictions of the vampire experience, but the truth proved to be far darker and more powerful. She licked her lips and tasted the salt from the slowly falling tears. She closed the diary and ascended through the secret passage.

* * *

Sam crept from Carmilla's bed chamber. As she walked toward her room, she halted when she heard Martin say in a matter-of-fact voice, "Getting a peek of your *fiancée*, I see, Miss Hain?"

Hoping her face and voice did not resemble a child being caught with her hand in the cookie jar before supper, Sam turned, smiled, and said in her best Southern belle voice, "Now, Martin, I don't have the faintest idea what you could imply. I was simply checking in on my friend who believes herself to be the focus of last night's attack."

His lips curled into a smirk, and he raised a single eyebrow. He ceased his performative use of a feather duster on the wall and said, "After last night, it became clear that you needed rest. One could argue that unless the Countess is by your side, rest does not come to you."

"I just wanted to make sure she's okay. She seemed distant when I asked her what she meant about being the target," Sam said, running her right hand up and down her left arm. She added, "You wouldn't happen to know why, would you?"

Martin sighed and nodded. "It is a very personal memory," he said. "I can promise you that if she said she would tell you, then she will do so. In some ways, it changed her."

"What do you mean," Sam asked, taking a step closer to Martin, and lowering her voice.

He started walking toward the stairs and said, "Come with me."

They walked into the drawing room, and Martin closed the door behind them. His eyes flashed red and then returned to their natural oak brown before he said, "What I say here does not leave this room."

Sam folded her arms across her chest and narrowed her eyes at him. "Martin," she said, "I don't need the vampire tricks and threats. I will always keep 'Milla's secrets. And I make that promise to you now, knowing full well the importance your people place on sworn oaths."

He nodded and said, "The Countess was an impulsive and open child. Yes, I know it is difficult to imagine that now, but she was once a true free spirit who never met a stranger. And she was charming…"

"She still is," Sam interjected with a smile.

He chuckled and busied himself dusting the mantle. "True," he conceded, "but you did not know the eight-year-old child who would invite village girls to the rear courtyard and host tea parties, which I had to cater."

His smile drifted wistfully as nostalgia illuminated his face. Sam smiled and said, "I would have loved to have seen that. I would love to have known her before what happened to her happened."

Martin sighed and nodded. He covertly added two figurines to Carmilla's winter village. One was a brunette in a vintage dress, and the other was a woman in a burgundy gown. He placed them beside each other near the mistletoe that hung from the small Christmas tree in the village. He turned and laughed. Then he said, "Her father, Count Adolf, did not approve, but he tolerated her childish impulsiveness, believing it to be a phase. It was not. Well, it would not have been a phase, had events not transpired as they did."

Sam nodded, worry darkening her face. "I've always loved how focused, driven, and methodical she is. I mean, I talk about going in with a plan, but I spend most of my life doing whatever seems like a good idea at the time. If I were more of a planner, maybe…"

"And that is one thing that drew her to you, Miss Hain," he said. "And no, it was not so much that you reminded her of who she used to be, but she sees in you a balance of energy in which she finds comfort."

Sam beamed and bounced before she said, "She always said that I brightened her dark immortality. I always assumed it was just the whole nocturnal life for centuries thing. No offense."

"None taken," he said. Then he shook his head and sat in one of the chairs and said, "No, the Countess was a free spirit who fell in love easily. We kept a platoon stationed throughout Karnsburg, because she regularly snuck out of the castle, with my full knowledge, to engage in various romantic liaisons. That was a logistical nightmare at times."

Sam scratched behind her ear. Twisting at the waist, she lowered her face but kept her eyes on Martin as she asked, "So, after the events or event, how many lovers did she have before me?"

"There was that one nocturnal liaison in August of 1932," Martin said, observing Sam's surprise before continuing, "Yes, she had options, but she feared intimacy. And so, I cannot stress how terrified she is about revealing this event to you. Also, that is why she and I are both adamant that you rest today."

"I appreciate the concern, Martin," Sam said, "but I'm fine. I pushed through things. Just had a little trouble at the end."

Martin's tone became gentle as he said, "You pushed through when it was needed; however, I have seen the same thing happen countless times in countless wars. And you need rest." He rose and walked to the door. When he opened it, he said, "Return to your chamber, Miss Hain. I will bring you coffee and food to you, and the Countess will spend the evening with you when she awakens."

Sam returned to her room and scrolled mindlessly through her social media, her attention focused on everything she learned about Carmilla. She assumed that her friend and former lover had a secret or two in her past, but the combination of her sister's sacrifice and a force marriage to an abusive husband who humiliated her, isolated her from her family, raped her, and forced her to drink the blood of her own child was not the dark secret Sam expected. The more she thought about what happened in the events leading up to that and their parallels in current events, Carmilla's breakdown the other night started to make sense. And with what Sam learned from Destiny in October, Carmilla knew that the Order of the Dragon had obtained the Tepes signet ring, which meant they were closer to being able to resurrect Vlad Dracula.

She's terrified it'll happen again, or it'll be worse this time, Sam thought. She sighed. Sam closed her laptop and drew herself a hot bath. She tied her hair up in a bun and dropped an oudh and jasmine bath bomb into the steaming water. The water transformed into a glittery, translucent purple color. Sam disrobed, hanging her clothes neatly on one of the iron hooks on the castle wall. As she sank into the water, her muscles relaxed, and a soft moan escaped her lips. Her breaths came slow and deep, and she imagined the stress and worry leaving her body.

Some time later, Sam heard Martin's voice emerge from her bedchamber, "I have your lunch, Miss... Hain where are you?"

"Sorry, Martin," she called out. "I'm in the bath. Can you just leave it on the nightstand?"

"Yes, Ma'am," he said. "Enjoy your bath, but it will get cold." And then he closed the door with a performative thud, communicating to her that he had left the room.

Sam relaxed for a few more minutes before her phone alerted her to a text from Destiny, suggesting a three-way Zoom call with Destiny's father. Sam stretched her neck and rolled her shoulders before stepping from the bath, toweling herself, and then sending a response asking for twenty minutes to dress before the call. She brushed her hair and then slipped into a forest green swing dress. She moved her laptop to the vanity and then grabbed the full plate of sauerbraten, roasted carrots, and mashed potatoes.

Sam joined Destiny's call as she ate. Destiny's gray cable knit beanie with a "Don't Panic" pin affixed to it covered most of her blonde ringlets. She wore circle-framed blue-light glasses that slipped off the bridge of her nose. They smiled and waved to each other, exchanging pleasantries as Sam ate her lunch. A few minutes later, Werther Grimm joined. His short blond hair had begun to silver, and the lines on his face had deepened since the last time Sam saw him. As they exchanged pleasantries, he casually noted that Sam had gained weight. She brushed it off and said, "It's good to see both of you, and Des, I know it's early for you. Thanks."

"Hey," Destiny said in a chipper voice that suggested she had chugged four Red Bulls, "if I can't see my best friend in person because she's spending most of December in an Austrian castle owned by a sexy vampire countess who happens to be *just a friend*, then I'll take a Zoom call."

Werther chuckled. Sam rolled her eyes and said, "Yeah, well, that's likely all we'll be because..."

"You were stupidly stubborn and didn't speak up?" Destiny asked.

Sam sighed and stabbed a roasted carrot with her fork. She nodded and said, "Yeah. But I'll be damned if I can't help her stay safe during all this. After last night's attack on the castle; though, I'm not sure I'm good enough."

"What? What attack?" Destiny screamed her questions, causing both Werther and Sam to wince and cover their ears. She continued, "Dad, did you know anything about that?"

The elder Grimm shook his head. "No," he said, "We have not authorized such an action."

"It wasn't the Grimms," Sam said as she drank her water from a crystal glass. She closed her eyes and sighed, continuing, "It was the Order of the Dragon."

"The Order of the Dragon," Werther asked, scratching his cheek. "Are you certain? That would be a bold action on their part."

"Yes, Sir," Sam nodded. "Martin found that one of them had the order's insignia among his possessions. They attacked before sunset, killed most of Lord Volny's men stationed to help watch 'Milla's actions, and died on the keep's first floor. We're not certain of their motives. I thought they were targeting me, but 'Milla thinks she was the target."

Destiny's face screamed confusion. She tilted her head to the side and asked, "Why would she think that? I mean, you seem the most logical target after what happened in Ireland."

Sam nodded and swallowed a forkful of mashed potatoes. "I know, but," she paused for a sigh, "that does lead to a question, Mister Werther. If you were to learn of a Veil Piercing that happened over a century ago, how would you proceed?"

The elder Watcher's eyes rose to his ceiling as he thought. He tilted his head and asked, "Do you mean if we uncovered a Piercing that we had not investigated?"

"Yeah," Sam said. "Like say if something happened almost one hundred and thirty years ago, but no action was taken then. Would you correct it?"

"One hundred and thirty years," He mused as he leaned back in his chair. His head bobbed as he continued, "None of our hunters who were active then would still be alive today. What have you found?"

"I don't know if it's anything," Sam said, looking away from the screen as she spoke. "I just came across a diary entry that references a rumor or something about one vampire contacting a vampire hunter to kill another vampire. Would you investigate? How?"

Werther eyed her through the webcam and stroked his chin. "I don't know," he said, shrugging his shoulders. "Honestly, at this point, we would be so far removed from the incident that unless there were irrefutable evidence of the event, I do not believe there would be anything we could do."

Sam appeared relieved to hear that. They talked for a few more moments about lighter subjects. After Destiny lamented her choir's last performance at the Whimpering Willow Retirement Community where a handful of residents' snores drowned out their singing, Martin entered and said, "Pardon the intrusion, Miss Hain, but Chief Detective Merkatz and another officer have arrived to ask some questions about the events of last night."

"Shit," Sam said, turning back to the laptop screen, "I've got to go. I promise to talk to both of you later."

7

Chapter 7

I looked up from my phone and smiled when Carmilla sauntered into the drawing room that evening. She embraced me in one of the longest hugs we've shared. I trembled as my body relaxed, allowing my tears to fall. So many emotions burst through my eyes. I worried for 'Milla's own mental health, given that I secretly learned why she's so terrified now. My exhaustion from helping defend the castle and the realization that I'm not mentally strong enough to keep fighting and protecting her. I cried for the general stress of the murder investigation and my professional involvement with the "Karnsburg Vampire" case, as the local press had dubbed it. And I cried because being in Carmilla's arms felt like being home.

As we broke the embrace, I smiled again and said, "Hey, I have some good news."

"Oh," She said, with an unexpected musicality in her voice. "And what might that be?"

"Well," I said, "that detective visited us again this afternoon along with another officer who photographed the damage, examined the bodies of the fallen humans, and examined the front courtyard and first floor of the keep. And while they have no clue who attacked or why they attacked, the fact that the 'Karnsburg Vampire' killed another last night while we dealt with being attacked means that you are no longer a person of interest. So, that's one thing we can cross off our list of worries."

Her smile was less enthusiastic than I had hoped to see, and she nodded, saying, "I am glad for our sakes, but I am unhappy for this newest victim and her family. I know that losing someone whom you love hurts greatly."

"Yeah," I said, squeezing Carmilla's hand, "it does. I just hope the detective's faith in his theory that this is a human and not a vampire, which he refuses to believe exists, is justified. Of course, he did wish us success in our future wedded life."

We shared a nervous laugh at Martin's justification of why Chief Detective Merkatz should talk to me about the investigation. I never knew a detective who needed a reason to talk to anyone, but Martin suggested that I had a level of authority in the house, which seemed to satisfy the detective. Yet, that laugh suggested that we both wanted that future for ourselves. Or so I hoped. I just knew it wouldn't work unless I could figure out a way to get used to waking up to her lifeless body.

We moved to our usual seats by the roaring fire, scented with rosemary and sage. I poured each of us a glass of the Sanguinovese that Martin left for us. We sat in silence for some time, Carmilla's eyes bored through the wine in her glass as if she expected a sign to emerge from its dark cherry depths. I sensed 'Milla's nervousness, knowing that she dreaded my reaction to what she needed to share. I understood that fear.

I wanted to assure her I would neither betray nor abandon her. I wanted to comfort her. But I knew that if I showed any certainty, she would either grow suspicious or retreat into her own darkness.

After a few more minutes of silence, I leaned toward her and said, "Hey, drink doesn't have the prophetic qualities mortals assign to it. What's up, 'Milla?"

She looked at me, smiled weakly, and offered a single chuckle. She turned her gaze to stare into the crackling, dancing flames in the hearth. Her chest heaved once, and then she said, "I offered you similar words before your trip to Ireland, knowing that many other concerns affixed their heavy weights on your soul."

"And you admitted that you didn't care about the details but that you cared about me," I said. "I want to return the sentiment. No matter what troubles you, I care about you, and I'm going to be by your side."

She smiled. Her eyes shifted to look toward me while her face remained turned toward the fire. She sipped her wine and said, "You are so certain of that. I pray you are correct, but you will please forgive me of my fear. It has been many years since I have been this close to anyone and have trusted anyone as much as I have trusted you."

I crouched in front of her, resting my hand on hers as I said, "I know I haven't lived as long as you have, but I feel the same way about you. And I know you feel you need to share something with me, but you don't have to do it now. If not on this trip, then I'll make my way back here to listen to you when you are ready to talk."

I squeezed her hand and moved closer. My eyes flitted down, and I realized that I was maybe two inches from her knees.

Not that I haven't been there before, but this wasn't the time for that. Bloody tears trembled at the edges of her eyes, and I saw her swallow hard. Her chest started heaving as if her lungs pushed her breaths in quick, shallow rasps. My heart started beating at the same rhythm I imagined hers to beat.

She shook her head, sighed, and said, "No, it is better to stake the heart now and accept the consequences." She gestured to the chair nearest her and said, "Please sit. I wish to discuss this as equals, both in actuality and in position."

I nodded and sat in the chair beside her. We turned our chairs to face each other, and I watched as she fired a panicked glance toward the heavens. I asked, "Do you want me to close the door?"

She shook her head, saying, "No. I thank you for your discretion, but you are the only soul in this castle who does not know what I am about to say."

I nodded with a concerned smile. We raised our glasses to our lips simultaneously, but 'Milla gulped more than I did. She set the glass on the table, dabbed her burgundy-painted lips with her handkerchief, and closed her eyes for a moment. Then, with her eyes still closed, she whispered, "The shortened form of the story is that, as you may or may not know, I do not have many friends and allies—even among my own kind—because I am a traitor to vampire kind."

"A traitor," I said with an upward inflection. "I thought that earned true death, and you're here."

"Were I convicted by the Council of Elders," she said, "I would be dead. There is, fortunately, I suppose, a lack of evidence beyond the circumstantial."

"What happened," I asked.

She forced a deep breath, likely from memory of her time

151

as a mortal, and then her voice trembled as she said, "It is a long story. It began with Elisa's death. I was exiled to Ireland and befriended the La Fanu family. You know the liberties they took with my story, but that is the price I willingly paid for their friendship and aid. When I returned several years later, I learned that I was to be escorted to Brasov in Romania where the Council of Elders would meet under the watchful eye of the King of the Vampires of Europe and the Levant, Vlad Dracula Tepes."

Her voice spat his name, her hatred for him contorting each sound into a hiss. Her clenched fists dug into the armrests on the chair. 'Milla's body shook with rage and sorrow as bloody tears fell. I grabbed her handkerchief and wiped her cheeks clean, smiling and reassuring her that she was safe here, surrounded by those who love her. She nodded.

"There," she continued, "the Council decreed that my actions had endangered both my clan and all vampire-kind. They demanded my death. Then *he* intervened with the option of an arranged marriage and forced impregnation to cure me of my embarrassing and dangerous 'sapphic perversions' as he called them. Once I bore him a son, a proper heir, my clan's honor would be restored. My father, ever conscious of our honor, readily accepted. And that night, I was wed. I became one of the many brides of Dracula.

"But that was not the end of my punishment. His servants bound me to my bed, naked and splayed like a whore, available for him to use until such a time as I became pregnant. For three weeks, he allowed me to eat only after he emptied himself into me, and I never had a full meal. He released me from that prison only when he desired to torture me in front of others for his and their amusement. He thrashed me with a barbed whip, shoved hot pokers into my sensitive areas, spat on me, slapped me, and kicked me. When visitors arrived, including my father, he paraded me before them, naked and on a chain leash; he would then attach the leash to his chair, forcing me to kneel beside it as if I were his dog."

She cried. Her body quaked. Her sorrow choked the words as they exited her throat, "At least... at least once the midwife declared me to be with child, the beatings stopped. He allowed me to wear a shroud, but nothing more. I still found myself treated like an animal, but while I carried his child, I gained a small amount of value in his vile eyes. As the birth neared, he bound me to my bed once more and starved me, claiming it a *family tradition*."

It was lucky for Dracula that he bound her. I've seen 'Milla hangry, and unless she were... oh fuck! That's what it was. She... that fucking bastard... that fucking bastard broke her. My heart thundered with a growing rage.

She exhaled slowly and continued, "Well, I gave birth to a beautiful boy. I am sure you have had many friends say that their baby looked like an angel, but mine looked so much like my Elisa that I named him Ellison Aleksander Karnstein in her honor. My joy was short-lived, however, when *he* returned."

She hid her face in her hands as she sobbed. I walked over and wrapped my arm around her shoulders. Her cries became wails, and I said, "It's okay. Take your time. Do you need to take a break?"

She shook her head. She smiled at me while wiping the tears from her eyes with her fingers. "No," she said, "it is hard, Sam, but I want you to know the truth of my shame and why the Order of the Dragon is targeting me here and not you."

"Okay," I said, refilling her wineglass. "But at least take a break to—well, you don't breathe—but to un-breathe? At least that got a chuckle from you. And then have a drink. I don't want you getting dehydrated, or is it desanguinated?"

She smiled and took a slow gulp of her wine. "You are truly a light–the light of all lights–in my life," she said. "Well, as I was saying, *he* entered. When I showed *him* my son, he held little Ellison and asked if I were hungry. When I said that I was," she paused, and I held her tightly as she trembled and sobbed. "He then ripped my son's head from his neck and hurled his body at me. When I did not immediately drink, he forced my mouth open and squeezed the blood from my son into my throat. And then he mocked me and left."

I brushed her hair from her face and cupped her cheek with my hand. "Hey," I said, "I don't have words to express either my sympathy or just how shitty that was, but 'Milla, surviving such horrific abuse does not make you a traitor. It makes you a survivor. It shouldn't have fucking happened, but I'm happy that you survived."

"My treason," her voice rattled at just above a whisper as she said, "came later. At one point, he decided to move to England. You have read the Irishman's novel, so you know most of the story. Well, my role came after he left, after he abandoned me to his Hungarian servants who remained in the castle. I convinced one to deliver a letter to a physician in Amsterdam, an Abraham Van Helsing who the Council of Elders had watched for his inquiries into our existence during his research on blood transfusions. I told him everything about Dracula and begged him to free me. Months passed in silence until I received word that he and a Mrs. Harker were less than a day away. I met them at the door and offered them entry into that prison, but he wanted to kill me. And to be honest, I do not blame him. It was the kindness of one who did not know me, this Mrs. Harker, that saved my life. I then showed him where the other brides slept so he could kill them. I showed him where Dracula slept so that he could destroy that bastard's place of safety. Then Dracula returned, but Van Helsing's associates slew him before he reached the castle right at the setting of the sun. And under the protection of Mrs. Harker, I walked to my freedom.

"The kindness of a human," she mused, "is a powerful magic that so few recognize. I swore that night to honor her by adapting to the changing world. I knew that if my clan–if all of us–were to survive, we needed to learn the new technologies and adapt our lifestyle to be more synchronized with the mortal world. You are the day. We are the night. Mirrored reflections connected by blood and hunger."

"Is that when you began your investment brokerage firm," I asked.

"Not immediately," she said. "I had to return home, explain my arrival, and rejoin my clan. That took several decades, and we lost many allies as rumors spread of my involvement with the mortals who slew Dracula. And that is why the attack last night, by an order of knights who have sworn loyalty to him, targeted me and not you."

Crimson tears plummeted from her eyes, and she fell silent. I wanted to say so many things to her. I wanted to comfort her as she recounted abuse that I would never truly understand. I wanted to tell her how proud I am of her for holding her head high, walking out, and building a new life for herself and her clan. I wanted to tell her all those things human women tell each other for encouragement and support, but everything I thought to say rang hollow in my own mind.

155

I sighed and clasped her. "I'm sorry," I said, "I have so many things to say, but none seem powerful enough to convey the meaning I need them to convey. If anything, just know that none of this lessens my opinion of you. You have endured and survived and thrived through so much, and I am honored to know you and to call you my friend. I'm still here, and I'm not abandoning you. I just wish you weren't attacked on your son's birthday."

Carmilla nodded as I held her. Then she froze. She pulled away and searched me with her bloody, tear-stained eyes that looked like a horror movie killer had carved them out with a glass shard. She shook her head, and my lungs stopped. She narrowed her eyes, and she said, "Yes, but I did not say his birthday. How did you know that?"

Shit! I closed my eyes and pulled at my dress' collar as I said, "After Elisa led me to your dungeon three times, I thought maybe the key to fixing the issue lay down there. So, I picked the lock and found your diary. I'm sorry."

Her face flushed as she flared her nostrils and said, "You did what? You, Sam, after I asked one thing of you. Everything of mine was yours, but I asked only that you leave my secrets to me to reveal in my own time. And you promised me. How?"

"I'm sorry, 'Milla,'" I apologized. "You asked me to take you on as a client, so I did what I thought was best to help me fix the situation." I shrugged. "I had no idea it would resolve itself as it had."

"You gave me your word, Samantha Hain," She said, her voice taking on the air of a disappointed parent. That fucking hurt. My cheeks burned with shame at the thought of disappointing her. I just fucked up. And then she continued, "And in my world, one's word is everything. I trusted you."

"Yeah, I know I fucked up," I said, "but you have to believe that I took what I thought was the advice of your sister's ghost. I'm trying to help keep you safe because…"

"Yes," she interrupted with a sharp finality. "And I'm sure resolving whatever else you feel you need to resolve for this will be easy for you since it is clear that I am nothing more to you than another client."

She stormed from the drawing room, and I heard a door slam from the hallway. I dropped to the floor and slammed my face into my right palm. I trembled and wept. Yeah, I fucked up any chance I had of getting back together with 'Milla. Worse than that, I disappointed and hurt one of my dearest friends and the woman I love. Fuck.

* * *

Sam returned to her chamber and fell onto the bed. Her breaths slouched from her lungs in tortured rasps. As her mascara ran down her cheeks, she called Destiny, opening the conversation with, "So I have some bad news."

"Did Carmilla use ancient vampire magic to impregnate you with identical twins before the wedding?" She asked, adding, "Because that would mean no one wins the pool."

Sam shook her head and offered a single chuckle. "What? No," she said, "but no one's going to win the pool for a different reason."

"Oh no," Destiny said, "What did you do?"

Sam rolled onto her stomach, contorted her face in confusion, and asked, "Why'd you assume it was me?"

Destiny rolled her eyes and said, "You're stubborn, but I don't know what happened. So, what happened?"

157

Sam recounted the conversation in minimal detail. She purposefully did not divulge Carmilla's secret. Sam trusted Destiny, but she had already breached Carmilla's trust once. She did not want to do that again, and she did not want to take the chance that her information would lead to the Grimms investigating Carmilla's role in Dracula's death. She explained her reasoning for doing what she did and explained how the repeated visits by Elisa's ghost that led her to the dungeon's door caused her to suspect that the double-locked door hid a key piece of information. And then she said, "And I only did for her what I would do for any other client, Des. I don't get why she can't see that."

"I think she saw that," Destiny said, "and that's the problem. Sam, she's not just another client to you. She's a friend, a former lover, and the one woman you want to spend the rest of your life with. It's you who didn't see why what you did was so important. By keeping this one promise, you validated her desire to be open about something in her past that she has felt the need to, well, *literally*, keep hidden and locked away. And you know how important promise-keeping is to vampires, right?"

"Yeah. Yeah," Sam sighed as she closed her eyes and lowered her head. "I know that they view promises as almost as binding as a devil's contract. So I... fuck... basically just lost my soul."

Destiny exhaled in frustration before saying, "Let's not go all forlorn gothic heroine who mopes herself to death. Give her time to calm down and then talk to her. I love you, Sam, but you're a stubborn bitch. That's what got you into this, so do something you don't enjoy doing. Admit you were wrong and tell her the whole truth–especially your feelings. That's your best chance at salvaging this."

Sam sat up and rubbed her temples while sighing. "I know. I know," she said, "and I'll get to that, I promise, but I have a feeling that there's something everyone's missing. If I can find that, I can show 'Milla that I did the right thing for her. I have a weird feeling that this apothecary, this Yarono Bertalan, is the key to all this. I just don't know where to look. Anything you could do to help with that?"

Destiny rolled her eyes and said, "Yeah, I'll see what I can dig up. You work on your apology."

Sam ended the call and opened the Uber app. She knew that the Karnsburg Vampire found all his victims at *Klub Abweichend*, so since she wanted to see if a connection existed between this seemingly random serial killer and the attack on Castle Karnstein and since she had been hired by Matthew Walpole to fix the situation and protect his fiancée, she decided to make herself a target to lure this vampire out of the shadows. She changed into something that lacked bloodstains, grabbed her overcoat, and headed to meet her ride. When Martin inquired as to her actions, she told him that she needed a drink to blow off steam and that he should check on Carmilla.

While Sam chatted with Destiny, Paul Byron sat in his hotel room and initiated his own Zoom call to Knight-Commander Bertalan. As he waited for his superior's audio to connect, Byron ran his thick fingers through his unkempt red hair. The elder man rubbed his temples, allowing his thick, black curls to bounce. They exchanged formal greetings, which ended when Bertalan, in his thick Hungarian bass voice, said, "Status report now, Squire."

Byron nodded once and then said, "Three victims down and the bobbies are on the case. I'll do one more and be done with it. I've also started talking up the old vampire legends around town, but that's not getting the traction I hoped. Haven't heard anything from Miss Hain since yesterday morning, so I assume the attack on the castle went off without trouble."

Bertalan glowered and shook his head, saying, "It did not. Prvan Volny's men proved little threat, as we had observed their security movements and prepared our tactics accordingly. We had intelligence that suggested that the traitor's estate steward Martin had military training; however, we assumed him trained in more archaic tactics. And then there was the presence of Samantha Hain. The Arch Magus appears to have been correct about her intuitiveness and her skill with a handgun. She will need to be dealt with. But the traitor still walks the earth."

"Should I change tactics, Knight-Commander?" Byron asked. "I do have a hunter's kit. I could easily stake the old bitch through a window using my crossbow."

Bertalan held up one open hand and said, "Keep that as a fallback. You will need to gain personal surveillance on the castle for your new task, which you will complete after you choose your next victim. Hunt tonight."

"Yes, Knight-Commander, Sir," Byron said. "Might I ask my next task?"

Bertalan nodded, ran his fingers through his thick curls, and said, "Given her recent actions, it appears that Samantha Hain will be more of a liability than an asset even if we break her. We will now terminate two problems with one mission. Once you have your latest victim, kill Countess Carmilla Karnstein. Frame Samantha Hain for her death so that the Karnstein-Bertholt clan removes her as a threat for us."

Byron smiled. With a chuckle, he said, "Good thing I paid that bitch using your money. I'd hate to not be able to get it back."

"Yes, well," Bertalan said. "Oh! Are you progressing on that personal matter you have embroiled yourself in?"

"No, Sir," Byron shook his head. Throwing his hands into the air, he said, "None of the records here seem to mention that bloody black statue. I figure, after this next kill, I'll piss off to Innsbruck for a few days to see if there's anything in the diocese's archives or a larger library. Can't believe I made that bloody deal."

"Yes," his superior said through narrowed eyes. "It was a rookie's blunder, and we pray that it does not cost anyone beyond you anything. Do not endanger our work. Over and out."

* * *

The lime Jetta dropped Sam off at the entrance to *Klub Abweichend* as the clock atop the town's administrative hall tolled ten o'clock. Freezing rain and hail pelted her as she walked toward the discotheque. As the music pulsed, the rhythmic lights danced from blue to green to orange to red in time to the music. Sam joined the line seeking entrance and passed through the Corinthian-style columns beneath the triangular piedmont. The bouncer nodded and let her pass into the neon-lit darkness beyond.

Sam rolled her eyes as she surveyed the crowded dance floor where a crowd composed of dozens of people younger than her gyrated rhythmically to the electronica's pulsing bass lines beneath the mirrored ceiling. The wall panels pulsed with the music, but Sam found her eyes drawn to one brown-haired young man who danced to a beat only he could hear. She laughed and shook her head. She walked to the black light lit bar and sat at the corner farthest from the entrance. One of the three bartenders, a blond man with a thick handlebar mustache connected to his pointed goatee, strolled toward her, took her order, and made her a whiskey sour.

Sam inhaled the lemony scent as she took her first sip, wincing from the cocktail's bitterness. On any other night, she would have enjoyed this beverage. On this night, she tasted only the bitterness that burned in the back of her throat. Turning her back toward the revelry of the human throng, she swirled the yellow liquid in her glass. Her mind drifted to the south, to Castle Karnstein, and to the matriarch of the Karnstein-Bertholt vampire clan.

It's both a blessing and a curse, she thought, *that we don't have a psychic connection like Stoker wrote of Dracula and Mina. If we did, she'd know I was thinking about her, about how much I love her, and about absolutely fucking stupid I am. I know I'm right about there being something down there. That's why Elisa's ghost kept leading me there. I know it. But I also know how important promises are to vampires. That whole 'must be invited in' thing is really just a part of that; an invitation is a promise of hospitality. Oh, fuck! I accepted a promise of hospitality, and then I violated its tenets. I didn't just break a little promise. Fuck! I violated a key tenet of a social relationship with a vampire. Ugh.*

Sam downed her drink and requested another. The bitterness remained as she drank, but this time, she tasted the bitterness and felt the burn in her throat with less intensity. She turned in her chair, keeping her back toward the growing crowd at the bar. The bartender checked to see if everything was fine, and she smiled and told him that her mind was focused on planning an apology for upsetting someone she cared about. He nodded and left her to think. A wistful smile decorated her face as her mind drifted to the night she met Carmilla.

"It was my second time at The Four Winds. I went to make a deal with Nick Scratch in order to spend time with my mother. I traded him a favor of his choosing 'at a later date' for the last hour of my birthday each year. Nick took the contract and walked off to fuck his gorgeous wife, and I sat at the bar to finish my drink.

"And that's when she approached me in that perfectly fitted burgundy maxi dress with a high slit that exposed her right thigh and a demure sweetheart neckline. Her black hair cascaded down to the middle of her back and hid most of the exposed skin on her chest. Without a word, she sat beside me and said, 'An open favor as part of a bargain with Samael? You have courage. I like that.' We talked until she had to return home due to the impending sunrise. As she turned to leave, she simply and matter-of-factly said, 'I will see you here in one week.' And I returned.

"She was always so confident and assertive, but she was also gentle and kind. I wanted to speed things along, but she kept the pace of our developing romance slow. Given the headspace I was in at the time, I'm grateful that she is who she is. I fell in love fast, and I fell hard. And I'm still madly in love with her." She sighed, downed her drink, and ordered another. "I fucked up. I've got to fix this."

Lost in her thoughts, Sam did not see the man who slid into the seat next to her. Aside from the waves that framed his face, he had pulled his long blond hair into a ponytail and tied it with a white ribbon. He wore a purple velveteen frock coat with bronze-plated buttons, an open shirt of white gauze,

163

and black trousers and pointed-toe ankle boots. He ordered a glass of red wine, and as he sipped, he extended his little finger in affectation. The bartender rolled his eyes and tried to convince him to leave Sam alone, but he refused.

"Drink," he began in an accent that would have passed for Romanian for an old Universal horror film, "offers no answers to those who seek them in its burning depths."

Sam sipped her drink without offering any indication that she heard him. So, he leaned in closer and said, "I said, 'Drink offers no answers to those who seek them in its burning depths.'"

Sam growled and rolled her eyes. She glared at him and said, "I heard you the first time. I didn't answer because I didn't want to talk." She turned back to her glass and sipped.

He released his hair from the ponytail and shook it into a wild mane. He sipped his wine while keeping his eyes on her, smiled, and said, "Then forgive me, but you are nothing if not the most beautiful creature upon which my weary eyes have ever laid."

Sam offered a dismissive hand wave while she sipped her cocktail. Undaunted, he slid his stool closer and said, "I have walked this land for many a moonlit night, and never have I laid eyes upon one so exquisitely ravishing as yourself. Please, I simply must speak to you."

Sam again rolled her eyes. Her instincts told her to tell this stranger to leave her alone. She turned and narrowed her eyes. As she glared at his hazel eyes, she paused and observed his demeanor and outfit. She realized that this might be the Karnsburg Vampire.

She rolled her eyes again and then flashed a dark smile, saying, "Well, I suppose that in the spirit of giving, I shouldn't be such a bitch and give you a chance." She extended her hand and said, "I'm Samantha."

The man extended his hand with the affectation of a noble desiring his hand to be kissed. Sam shook it, noticing that it was rough and calloused. "My name," he said, "is Varney Von Schreck. And it is truly a pleasure to make your acquaintance, Samantha."

Really? Sam thought, *'Varney Von Schreck?' That explains why your dialogue sounds like a bad penny dreadful. I'm still too sober for this bullshit. Alright, let's take this fucking trip.*

They talked for an hour, and Varney volunteered to pay for Sam's drinks, and Sam allowed him to do so. She paid little attention to the conversation, as she neither cared for nor believed his stories of his exploits and wanderings around the lands that once comprised the Austro-Hungarian Empire. Sam, pretending this "Vampire" was Carmilla, forced herself to touch his arms and hand as they conversed.

After a few more rounds, Sam said, "Well, it's been fun, but I need to get back to my friend's house. Thank you. It's been lovely."

He stood and bowed as she rose from her stool. She walked away, and he grabbed her wrist, saying, "I will bid you farewell, but I would be a poor companion if I allowed you to walk into the winter night alone. Please allow me to accompany you to your destination. I may know a shortcut."

Sam rolled her eyes but nodded in assent. Varney escorted her from the discotheque and into the town square. Clouds filled the winter sky. Sam smirked as she saw a white cloud form from his breath. As they walked through the icy slickness covering the square, Varney held onto Sam to keep her from falling. He guided her into the dark and empty Christmas

Market, explaining its history and significance to her. She bit her lip to avoid laughing at his overdramatic descriptions.

As they moved into the Lovers' Grove, Sam observed, "I don't think this is the way to her house."

"Oh, I think you will find this dalliance to be quite pleasurable to your senses," he said, pushing her against a fir tree in the deepest part of the grove.

She slapped his hands away, saying, "No, I don't think I will. Fuck off, Dorkula."

She pushed past him, jamming her shoulder into his as she walked. His cheeks flushed, and he glared at her. "You come back here," he said. "I spent my hunting time on you, you ungrateful bitch."

She responded by raising her right middle finger as she continued walking. Varney Von Schreck growled and reached a hand into his coat pocket. He produced that syringe with two needle points attached and charged after her. He grabbed her left arm and yanked her toward him. She cried out in surprise. He swung his syringe at her neck. She turned to face him, grimacing as the two needles scraped her skin. Her heart quickened.

Her breathing became rapid. She kicked his stomach, pushed off, and punched. Her right fist slammed into his cheek. He jabbed her stomach. She grunted. He swung his syringe like a haymaker. She blocked and riposted by thrusting her palm into his nose. As blood dripped from his nostrils, she reached with both hands and grabbed his hair. He spun and ran away as the wig lifted from his head. As her breathing and heart rate returned to normal, Sam exited the grove and Christmas Market and then called the police.

*** *

Chief Detective Merkatz wore a baby blue button-down shirt, opened two buttons below the collar, and a pair of dark blue trousers as he walked through the municipal police station in Karnsburg late at night. He carried two cups of black coffee in his left hand so he could open the door to the interrogation room where Sam Hain sat. She smiled and thanked him as he handed her a cup. He sat in a chair opposite her.

"Good morning, Miss Hain," he said as he flipped open his notebook. "I wasn't expecting this, but here we are."

Sam remained silent for almost a minute as she drank her coffee. Then she nodded and said, "Yeah, you're telling me."

He chuckled, looked at his notes, and said, "Seems you told the municipal officer that you were out for a drink at *Klub Abweichend*. Couldn't you get the drink you wanted at your fiancée's castle?"

She sighed. "Trust me," she said, "the drinks at 'Milla's castle are far superior to the ones there. We had a fight. I said something stupid. And I wanted to mull things over where nobody knew me. I took an Uber, and I planned to take one back after two rounds."

He nodded as he took notes. He clicked his pen on the table once, searched her with his eyes, and then asked, "So why did you stay longer in conversation with your assailant?"

"I tried to avoid it," she said. She paused and sipped her coffee. As she inhaled its rich, earthy aroma, she smiled and said. "I ignored him for about fifteen minutes, but he wouldn't shut up. And then when I did talk to him, to be honest, I thought his bullshit would be entertaining."

Chief Detective Merkatz tilted his head and asked, "What

do you mean by that?"

Sam laughed and said, "Oh, that's right! I'm the first person he's attacked that you've been able to speak to. Anyway, he gave me a fake name, called himself Varney Von Schreck." She guffawed for a moment before continuing, "He was dressed like a cross between a bad Hot Topic clearance rack version of the vampire Lestat and a historical romance novel cover model. And he spouted these lines that wouldn't have even made it past a penny dreadful's editor."

"I see," Merkatz nodded. "And then you decided to leave with him for what reason?"

Sam shrugged. "It was stupid," she said, "but I didn't think there would be any danger. Your *vampire*, who happens to be mortal by the way, has only killed local women. I'm not local, so I thought I was safe. Also, as cheaply made as his costume was, I really didn't suspect him to be a dangerous killer."

"Oh, I see," Merkatz said, scribbling notes with one hand while sipping his coffee with the other. Using the pen, he scratched the back of his neck before asking, "Well, can you describe him physically?"

"Not as well as I would like to," Sam said. "It was pretty dark, but he was tall with broad shoulders. Probably just over six feet tall. Sorry, I don't know the metric conversion. He had fair skin that he must've tried to even out with foundation, but he didn't set it. It wasn't evenly applied, and I could see some ruddiness underneath. Green or hazel eyes. I guess he was handsome, but his face came across as 'Generic White Male Face Number 5.' Very square jaw. And after the wig came off, I got a quick glimpse of short, light hair. Maybe a strawberry blonde or a pale red."

"Did you get a good look at the weapon," he asked.

She shook her head and replied, "Not really." She leaned back in her chair and exhaled. "It looked sort of like a pair of brass knuckles with only two little points that were on the inside of the hand. That explains why he tried to slam it into me. He's strong, but he's slow."

"I see," Merkatz said, leaning forward and resting his elbows on the table. "Now, Miss Hain, you said with certainty that our vampire was a mortal. What gives you that confidence?"

She leaned forward, eying him suspiciously. "Why, Chief Detective," she said, "I thought you would recognize that we live in a world explained by science and not superstition. Besides, when we walked outside, I could see his breath clouds. Vampires, being undead, do not breathe. If he breathed, he had to be alive; therefore, he could not be a vampire. Logic."

She smiled. He shook his head and laughed. "You are not a normal witness to question," he said.

With a triumphant expression and tone, Sam replied, "No, I'm not. In case you've forgotten from our previous conversations, I am a private investigator. Even tipsy, I've got a trained eye and a pretty good memory. He's also a little coward, running when someone stands up to him. Oh, and he had rough hands with callouses, like someone who works out a lot or does construction or something similar. Is there anything else? Can I call an Uber?"

"No," he admitted, shaking his head. "If I have any other questions, I know where to find you. And I will bring you back to the castle."

8

Chapter 8

I watched the sun rise over the Alps as Chief Detective Merkatz drove me back to Castle Karnstein. Before I met Carmilla, I always imagined living with my lover, waking up, and watching the sun rise while we sip coffee and cuddle. Now, my thoughts turned to watching the moon rise while drinking wine with 'Milla. We chatted idly, mostly about family and work, on the hour-long drive. As we pulled into the front courtyard, hired workers toiled to repair the damage from the attack. Martin paced at the foot of the stairs before the main entrance. When Merkatz stopped the car, Martin walked over and opened my door.

"Good morning, Miss Hain," he said. "We're glad you're well. It seems you had a rather eventful night."

"Yeah, I did, Martin," I said. "I'll tell you about it in the kitchen. I need carbs."

He laughed and followed me. Martin pulled a chair out at the small table and then set two glasses before me. He walked to the refrigerator and grabbed water and orange juice. He poured me a glass of each, set the bottles on the table, and then busied himself frying bacon and potatoes. As the bacon sizzled in the iron cast-iron skillet, he asked, "So, is there anything you wish to say?"

I chugged my water and then refilled it, saying, "I'm a fucking idiot. That sums things up."

He removed the bacon to drain and then dumped the potatoes into the bacon grease. As he pushed the potatoes around in the pan, he said, "Yes, you were. The Countess was quite angry last night."

"Yeah," I said, lowering my head. "I broke my promise to her, and I knew how important keeping promises is among vampires. And, in the process, I violated her privacy. I thought I was doing the right thing for the investigation, but I should have–no–I *did* know better. I can justify my actions, but I was wrong. At the end of the day, I fucked up. And I owe her an apology."

"You do," he said as he brought my plate of bacon and sausage. "You will have to wait because she has much work to accomplish tonight. And I would give her time to calm down before you speak with her. But more importantly, are you well?"

I stabbed the potatoes with my fork and said, "Yeah, being attacked by a fake vampire helped sober me up. I took a couple of hits, but I gave as good as I got."

He smiled and said, "I have no doubt. We both worried when the police called to say you were being questioned after being attacked. The Countess stayed awake as long as she could, but when the first ray of light rose over the mountains, I sent her to bed for her own protection. I would suggest you get some rest as well."

I agreed and finished my breakfast. I ascended the stairs

171

to the third floor and walked down the corridor. I passed by Carmilla's room and peeked inside. Bloody tears stained her face, and my eyes glassed over with tears. Did she cry herself to sleep over our fight? I grabbed a makeup removing wipe from her vanity and wiped the blood from her face before it dried too much. Then I made my way to my own chamber. Carmilla left a note on my bed that simply said, *We need to talk.* Shit. Those words were never good. I needed a bath, but that could wait.

It was still early, but I still had another job to do. I called Matthew Walpole. His voice sounded surprised but chipper, so I said, "Are you still in Karnsburg? I have some good news for you."

"Nah," he said. "I'm going to be in Innsbruck for a few days researching this strange piece of architecture I saw in town. Should be back in three or four days. What's the news?"

"Well," I said as a yawn escaped my lips. When he returned the yawn, I continued, "I ran into the guy who attacked Mathilda and killed the other women last night. Turns out, he's not a vampire."

"Are you sure?" He asked, which surprised me. I thought he'd be ecstatic at that bit of information.

"Yeah," I said. "Vampires don't breathe, and white clouds formed in front of his face as he breathed. I'm not saying he's not dangerous, but your fiancée won't turn into a vampire. And that means you're safe from the Grimms."

"Oh, yeah," he said in a surprisingly unenthusiastic tone. "Well, that's good news, I suppose. Thank you."

He ended the call. I shrugged, removed my clothing, and went to sleep. I dreamed I wore black cat print pajama pants and a gray tank top, my normal lounging clothes, as

I raced through the hallways of a castle. Zozo's bleating growl reverberated through the halls, and I heard that fiend's cackle echo in my mind. My heart pounded as I ran through this long corridor lined with doors. Each one slammed as I drew near. The clopping of hooves thundered from behind me. I felt hot breath on my neck. I screamed.

The hallway felt infinite as door after door slammed in my face as I approached. Zozo's laughter turned hollow and mocking. He punctuated his laughs and bleating growls with mocking words that I heard in my mind, *Why do you run, little lamb? Give in and accept the inevitable.* I called for help, begging for Carmilla, Martin, Destiny, Werther Grimm, High Bard Murphy, anyone to get me out of there. Silence. No one came. No one spoke.

I continued running, and I finally saw an open door at the end of the hallway. It had an ending! Either I would be safe, or I would die trapped and alone. I took a deep breath and rushed toward the door. Zozo's furious hoof beats slammed into the ground. He moved faster than I did. My breathing became swift and ragged. I saw someone, a figure in red, beyond the door. I decided that figure had to be better than another fight with Zozo, so I pushed harder.

I crossed the threshold and spun around to the empty, silent hallway behind me. I saw no doors along the walls and no evidence that anyone other than myself had run through that passage. I clutched my thundering chest and started slowing my breathing. And then I heard something metallic rattle behind me. I tried to swallow the lump in my throat and my heart sank.

My muscles tensed as I turned toward the sound of the rattling. Struggling against heavy black iron chains around her wrists and neck that forced her to her knees, was Carmilla in a red dress. Her hair was knotted, stringy, and greasy. Bloody tears streaked down her face. The pooled blood blackened her eyes. I raced over and held her. Her lips moved, but no sound emerged. Her fangs had broken.

With my arms wrapped around her, I kept telling her that things would be fine, that I was there, and that she would not be alone. I felt her body tremble and the warmth of bloody tears on my shoulder and chest. Something unseen hurled me against a wall as flames leaped from the floor and circled 'Milla. I closed my eyes from the sudden explosion of light. When I opened them, that creature, that shadowy creature with its bloated stomach, gangly arms, and overstretched mouth filled with rotting and jagged fangs appeared inches from my face. One arm pinned me to the wall. It crawled over me; my body trembled, and my breathing and heart rate quickened. A putrid, three-pronged tongue slithered out from its mouth toward me, dripping spit and bile. It breathed on my neck, licking my skin with the tips of its tongue. I closed my eyes. I felt its face lunge toward me. And I screamed.

I shot awake and sat upright. When I regained focus, I found myself in the bedchamber in Carmilla's castle. I saw snow falling onto the windowsill. Wrapping the blankets around my body, I shivered. No one lit the hearth last night. I woke cold and lonely.

* * *

Paul Byron sat at a box-covered mahogany table in the unheated basement of the Tyrol State Archives in Innsbruck. The librarian left a book cart beside his table to make returning the boxes easier. Old parchment and leather perfumed the air. The archivist, a stern-faced man with a graying comb-over and thick gray mutton chops, sat behind a tall mahogany desk. He dipped a green fountain pen into an inkpot to refill it before he continued updating the catalog of manuscripts contained in the collection he oversaw.

After four hours of research, Byron had learned more than he cared to know about Karnsburg's history from its reestablishment after the death of one Carmilla Karnstein to the dawn of the twentieth century. He laughed, mentally mocking the folly of those ignorant to the true nature of the world around them. He pushed box after box aside, throwing the contents back into them with no regard for organization. Land transactions, elections, festival dates, establishment of businesses, and police reports were plentiful, but he found no records on the black Madonna of St. Januarius' Cathedral. As he dug through the final box on his table, he found a single sheet of parchment from St. Rita of Cascia Catholic Church stating that all records for St. Rita of Cascia Catholic Church were housed within the church itself and that all records from St. Januarius' Cathedral were located in the Tyrol State Archives under the "Old Karnsburg" record section.

"Shit," Byron thought, shaking his head. "Now I have to talk to that bloody asshole again."

He grunted and then loaded the dozen banker boxes onto the cart. He winced at the shrill squeak of the cart's wheels as he pushed it along the oak floor. The archivist glowered from behind his half-moon glasses at the noise. Byron approached the desk and pushed the cart in front of the return box.

"Alright, old man," he said in this thick Scouse accent, "I'm bringing your boxes back."

175

The archivist counted the boxes while keeping an eye on Byron. He then nodded and asked, "Are you finished?

"Nope," Byron shot back. "Didn't get what I needed. I need the records for Old Karnsburg. Specifically, I need the boxes on St. Januarius' Cathedral. So, hurry up. I ain't got all month."

The archivist growled as he wheeled the box-laden cart behind the desk. Before he brought Byron the records he sought, he spent his time inspecting the boxes, reorganizing their contents, and then returning them to their shelves. As he searched the Old Karnsburg Records section for the items requested, Paul Byron's cell phone rang as Chief Detective Merkatz called him.

"Take it outside," the archivist shouted.

Byron power walked to the stairs. As soon as he reached the ground floor, he answered in hushed tones, "Hello. What do you need?"

"Hello, Mr. Walpole," Chief Detective Merkatz said, "Is something wrong? Why the whisper?"

"Sorry," Byron said. "I'm walking out of the State Archives in Innsbruck. I figured it best to be quieter than usual."

"Ah, very true," Merkatz said. "I called because there has been a development in the case regarding the attack on your fiancée."

"Case? I didn't talk to no detective," Paul Byron said.

"No," Merkatz stated. "However, the Karnsburg Municipal Police turned the case over to me after the first murder. And there have been a few other developments since then, but I would like you to come to the police station in Karnsburg to answer a few more questions."

"Can't we just do it over the phone?" Byron asked. His words came swiftly, making them nearly unintelligible. He began panting.

Merkatz shook his head as he replied, "I'm afraid not, Mr. Walpole. Standard policy. You're not in any trouble, but we do need you here. How soon can you return from Innsbruck?"

"Tomorrow afternoon at the earliest," he said.

"Good," Merkatz stated. "I will expect you at three o'clock and no later. Good day."

"Shit! Fuck!" Paul Byron exclaimed, stomping and pounding his fist into his empty hand in anger as he returned to the State Archives.

When he returned to the basement, the archivist had pulled the four boxes of records they possessed for St. Januarius' Cathedral. Paul Byron's eyes widened in surprise, and the archivist explained that many records were lost to the fire of 1827 that destroyed most of the village. And of what was not destroyed, much was looted with only a portion returned. Byron grumbled but accepted the box-laden cart and returned to his table and continued his search.

The first box contained records of church membership, births, baptisms, weddings, and deaths. The second and third contained homily notes in Lain, none of which helped Byron find any information on the black Madonna. Sweat beaded on his forehead as his heart trembled. He wiped his sweaty palms on his jeans before he opened the fourth box. When he opened the fourth box, he found a series of church ledgers, detailing all the financial transactions of the cathedral. He learned the black Madonna statue was brought back by Crusaders returning from Acre, and it remained in the cathedral's chapel behind the high altar. Unfortunately, no records of the statue existed after the year 1817. Cursing this last complication, Byron slammed the ledger onto the table and stormed from the State

Archives without returning his boxes.

While Byron searched the Tyrol State Archives, Sam received another Zoom call request from Destiny Grimm. After Sam's audio connected, Destiny waved and asked, "Hey, so, have you apologized yet?"

Sam shook her head. "No," she said. "When the detective brought me home this morning, 'Milla was already asleep. Seems she cried herself to sleep."

"The police? Sam, what did you do?" Destiny looked concerned. She leaned forward and cuddled a plush Snivy.

"I needed to clear my head," Sam said, "so I went out for a drink. Ran into Count Dorkula the non-Vampire Killer of Karnsburg. He attacked me. I fought back. He ran away. I spoke to the police."

Destiny's eyes shot wide, and she shouted, "Are you okay? What happened?"

Sam grimaced from Destiny's volume. She explained what happened after she left the castle in as much detail as she could remember. Destiny mimicked the act of vomiting when Sam described the vampire's opening lines, and she cheered when Sam described snatching the assailant's wig. As Sam concluded recounting her conversation with Chief Detective Merkatz, Werther Grimm, dressed in a charcoal suit, joined the conversation.

"Hi, dad," Destiny said.

"Mister Grimm, how are you?" Sam asked.

"Quite well, Samantha," he said, "and I hope the same can be said of you after last night."

Taken aback, Sam asked, "How did you know?"

He folded his arms across his chest as he said, "Our agent concluded his report this morning. It did include your visit to and questioning by the police. So, are you well?"

"Yes, Sir," she said. "I was attacked by the not-vampire and scared him off. As a result of that and the attack on us, 'Milla is no longer a person of interest.'"

He laughed. "Oh, I needed that laugh," he said. "But we are aware that there is no non-human mythical being activity in Karnsburg beyond the Countess, and she has been careful to abide by the laws and customs regarding her interactions with mortals. As such, neither of you should feel threatened by our agents."

Sam sighed and relaxed her shoulders. "That's such good news," she said. "I know she was worried about that."

"Yes," Werther Grimm said. "However, the Order of the Dragon remains a threat with which you must contend. And this murderer is still at large, but I would stay out of that, Samantha. Let the police do their work."

* * *

"*Folge mir,*" called the voice of an Austrian woman.

Sam turned from the voice, pulling the blankets over her face. In her sleep, she mumbled, "I don't speak sleep in my German."

"Follow me," the voice repeated. This time, its words echoed, in English, inside Sam's mind.

"I'm tired. Go away," came Sam's indistinct and grumbled response. She curled into a tighter ball and drifted back into her dreamless sleep.

"Follow me! And help my sister," the voice screamed in her mind.

Sam groaned, throwing the blankets to the side. She rolled

over. Her eyes blinked three times. She groaned again as she sat up and stared at the translucent, spectral body of Elisa Karnstein. The ghost's hair floated wildly. She held a candelabra in one hand while she extended the other toward Sam. Sam let her feet hang over the side of the bed. Her toes curled in the frigid pre-dawn air.

Sam shook the sleepiness from her head, blinked again, massaged her temples with her right hand while muttering, "I'm not going into the dungeon again. I've already fucked things up enough."

"If you are still here, then there is time to make it right, for both of you," Elisa said. She turned and glided into the hallway.

"This better not be some fucked up Christmas ghost thing," Sam said as she slid her feet into a pair of slippers and hurried after the ghost.

As they walked through the keep's halls, Sam heard Carmilla and Martin conversing in the Countess' office. Elisa moved at a rapid pace that was manageable for Sam to follow. They descended the stairs, the ghost's illumination providing minimal light for Sam to keep her footing. Sam tensed, her heartbeat increasing as they reached the ground floor. She sighed with relief as they passed the unlit hall that led to the dungeon and continued their movement.

They exited through the rear doors and descended the stairs into the castle garden. A thin layer of snow blanketed the ground as tiny flakes descended from the sky. As they walked, the candles placed throughout the area burst to life with pale blue flames. Sam shivered as her breath clouds mixed with the falling snow. Elisa led Sam through the hedge labyrinth with practiced skill. They passed the central fountain whose waterspouts strained to push the dragon's blood through the icy scabs that had formed over its stony scales. Elisa walked to the edge of the Karnstein-Bertholt family mausoleum and passed through the iron door. Sam heard the click of a lock being unlocked and the grind of a large bolt being moved. The door slid open a few inches.

Sam clutched her own shoulders. Her teeth chattered. The white breath from her sigh wafted through the air with a melancholic languor. She opened the door and entered. She walked through the cold, damp hall of worked stone. Blue flames burned silently from wall sconces. Sam passed through the square chamber filled with funerary urns and then walked into a chamber that resembled more of medieval catacomb than a modern mausoleum. Corpses, resting in elegant marble caskets, lay in carved recesses in the walls. Each recess had a bronze nameplate beneath it stating the name, birth and death dates, and major achievements of the vampire interred within.

The flames allowed Sam to see that Elisa sat on a stone bench in a chamber deep within the mountain. Sam approached this chamber, noting that intricate scroll work adorned the archway with a capstone depicting two ravens flanking a single eye on a throne. This chamber's walls had no recesses. Instead, a rune-etched sarcophagus sat between two braziers atop a raised dais.

Elisa patted the bench, and Sam sat beside her. When Sam did so, Elisa said, "Welcome to the resting place of the eternal glory of the Karnstein-Bertholt clan. I am certain that you have many questions. I will answer what I may."

Sam yawned through chattering teeth before saying, "I really just want to know why you keep waking me up at night. You guide me to the dungeon, which led to 'Milla getting pissed off, and now you bring me to the family crypt. Why?"

"So that you can help my sister regain her light," Elisa said solemnly. "Let me tell you the story of our family. I am certain that you already know that we are one of the oldest noble houses of European and Levantine vampires."

"Destiny mentioned that when 'Milla and I started getting serious," Sam said.

Elisa nodded. She ascended the dais and rested her spectral hand atop the sarcophagus. "Here," she said, "rests the first of our line, Ziegwulf the Bloody-handed of Thracia. Ziegwulf was warlord over a dozen clans who, following the sacking of Rome, moved into the land where we now stand. He was the eldest of three brothers, and his younger siblings, Radu the Fire Starter and Rigal Red Spear, like him led great war bands who ravaged what is now Europe and the Levant. Their exploits have even inspired legends of terrifying monsters as far away as Siberia and Northern India. And this all transpired during their mortal days."

She returned to the bench and sat beside Sam. Elisa looked her over and then smiled. "Our history records that one night, before a great battle, she said. "according to tradition, they held council with a wise man—one of the Solomonari—who was to use his magic to influence the outcome of the next morning's raid. He promised them victory if they paid him one quarter of their lands, one quarter of their grains, and one quarter of their children. Obviously, they refused. And so, the wise man cursed them to forever feast upon their own and to never again taste the wine of victory under the light of the sun."

Sam chuckled and said, "Let me guess. They lost the battle?"

Elisa shook her head. "No," she said. "Their war bands emerged victorious, but the three brothers did not return home with their warriors. They fell in battle when a spear pierced each of their hearts. However, as the sun set, they slowly opened their eyes and rose again. As the sky darkened, they found their vision improved. They woke hungry and with new appetites. Each followed the scent that appealed to them most, which, as I am certain you will deduce, was the first and most favored of each of their wives.

"To simplify, they had become vampires. When they realized what had happened, they returned to their warriors, claiming that Wodan had blessed them to be the great feeders of his ravens. They convinced their warriors to drink the blood of enemies and even offered the worthiest their own blood to drink. Those who partook of this ritual returned from the grave, changed as their lords were changed. And yes, according to our history, they first fed and produced offspring as their lords had first done. Such is how we learned how to procreate until the power in our blood became powerful enough that even fully turned members of our clans could bring forth children."

"I can see that, and it's an interesting story," Sam said. She shrugged and sighed, "But I don't see how that helps me understand 'Milla or what's going on any better."

Elisa shook her head and raised her index finger to Sam's lips. Sam narrowed her eyes as Elisa said, "Be patient. You know the line of Ziegwulf. The line of Radu is the line that gave birth to Vlad Dracula. Rigal's line, it is believed, has ended."

"Nobles are all related, they say," Sam shook her head. "I see that's the same for vampire nobility. So, I guess her forced marriage to Dracula was..."

"A punishment for her," Elisa said, "and his only chance at a legitimately worthy heir, despite his other brides whose blood was of questionable purity and provenance."

Sam scratched her head and shifted to sit cross-legged. "I get the punishment," she said, "but if he needed an heir, then why in nine hells worth of fuckery did he kill their son and make her drink his blood?"

"You must understand two things," Elisa said, leaning closer to Sam and whispering. "The first is that the punishments imposed upon her had nothing to do with the murders of mortal peasants. Such things were beneath the notice of even mortal aristocracy in most cases. They sought to punish her so that she would cease to be one of Sappho's daughters, if you will."

Sam exhaled while running her fingers through her hair. "Fuck," she exclaimed as her eyes welled, "And I thought modern conversion therapy was shitty. I just want to hug 'Milla and tell her how happy it makes me she's still here. She's so strong."

"She is," Elisa said, beaming. "But the second, and likely more pertinent, thing you must understand is that all the young girls who were found murdered before Annalena were examined by the town's physician – not this apothecary. And his reports, if one is to believe the local newspaper, mentioned trembles, pains, and spasms but not bite marks or blood loss."

"So, what you're saying," Sam asked, "is…"

"Bring light to my sister," Elisa said before she faded into nothingness.

Sam sighed. The flames in the sconces died as Elisa departed. Sam sat in the darkness of Ziegwulf's burial chamber for a moment with her head bowed and her arms folded across her chest. She turned her attention toward the sarcophagus and asked, "Don't suppose you have enough power left to protect your heir while I search for some way to bring her light, do you?" After a moment of silence, she rose and returned to her bedchamber.

* * *

While Sam spent the evening with Elisa's ghost, Countess Carmilla Karnstein sat in her office typing furiously at the wireless keyboard for her computer. The crystal glass filled with Sanguinovese that sat on a cloth napkin atop her desk trembled, spilling some of its contents on her furniture. Her eyes blazed with unnatural and unholy fire, and her chest heaved with the memory of how to display rage. She growled. Martin entered and wiped the spilled wine from her desk.

"I take it that you are still upset over last night's fight with Miss Hain," he asked as he moved one of the small wooden side tables closer to her chair and placed the wine glass atop it.

"No, Martin. I haven't thought about that all night. I am simply checking my email," she said. "Why would you suggest such a thing?"

"You have not ceased typing since I entered, my Countess," he said. "However, you are at the computer's desktop. There is no browser open, and so, there is no window displaying your email."

She pursed her lips and glared at him from the corners of her eyes. He smirked and began dusting the bookcases on the far wall. She sighed, throwing her hands into the air, and saying, "How am I supposed to feel, Martin? She broke a promise to me, acted as if she were justified, and then—and then—she," the corners of her eyes welled with blood as she said, "and then she nearly gets herself killed by that thing pretending to be

185

one of us."

"No one is saying that you should not feel hurt," he replied. "But your silence and your being *in meetings all night* after you left her a note saying that you needed to talk is neither productive nor mature."

She threw her hands up in frustration, asking, "Then what would you have me do?"

Martin glanced over his left shoulder and said, "Talk to her adult to adult, woman to woman, lover to lover."

Carmilla turned her gaze toward the framed photograph of her and Sam that she kept on her desk. Taking it in her left hand, she traced the frame with her right while, in a calmer but mournful tone, said, "We are not lovers. We are..."

"Actresses," he interrupted. He sat in one of the two chairs on the opposite side of the desk from her, folded his arms across his chest, and said, "I have observed the way the two of you behave together, and there is no one who would see that and say that you are merely friends, my Countess."

Carmilla slumped in her chair and then drained her wine-glass. "It's not that I don't want to be her lover again, Martin," she conceded. "I do not believe that she desires the same thing."

Martin massaged the bridge of his nose. A human would have mistaken his sigh for a growl. He leaned forward, placing his right elbow on Carmilla's desk. He then rested his chin in his hand, looked her in the eyes, and asked, "Have we been in the same castle these past few weeks?"

Carmilla grumbled as she refilled her own glass, "Besides, she is treating this like one of her normal cases, and..."

"That is exactly what you asked her to do," Martin interrupted. "My Countess, you requested that she perform one of her fixes. And it appears that she has provided the investigating detective with enough information to clear you of any suspicion."

"Yes," Carmilla groaned, "but she broke her promise, snuck into the basement, and read my diary. She knows the importance of these things to us, and she acted as if the *case* was all that mattered. And after that, she even..." Carmilla's hands shook, and crimson tears fell from her eyes. She continued, "And then she went out and got attacked by that monster. Martin, she could've been killed."

"You are correct," Martin conceded, straightening the piles of paperwork on her desk. "I would like you to consider the night of the attack. I saw the look in her eyes the moment she saw the carnage. She fought through a flashback and breakdown over whatever horrors she experienced in Ireland. I have seen that look on countless warriors throughout my many centuries of service to this clan. She fought through and only broke down when she had visual confirmation that you were safe. It was not the case. It was not the castle. It certainly was not Lord Volny or his men. It was you. She fought a battle within and a battle without in order to protect you."

A brief smile caused Carmilla to blush. She released her hair from its bun, ran her fingers through her lustrous black hair, and said, "She could have died, Martin. After Annalena and Elisa, I cannot lose Samantha! Her actions were impetuous, impulsive, thoughtless..."

Carmilla's eyes burst wide. She covered her mouth with her hand. She and Martin locked eyes, and he offered a sympathetic smile. With a nod, he said, "The same charges your father and the Council of Elders leveled against you." Carmilla lowered her gaze and nodded. Martin clasped her hands and increased the sincerity and compassion in his tone as he continued, "You are both strong, intelligent women. You are alike in so many ways, but one of the worst traits you both share is a fatal case of stubbornness."

Carmilla covered her eyes with her hand and sighed. "I can't do anything now, Martin," she said. "I have given her what she wants. I have promised never to attempt to rekindle our romance. She has rendered the service for which I hired her, and as matriarch of the Karnstein-Bertholt clan, I must keep my word. And if the Order of the Dragon has decided it is my time to die, I would rather her not be a casualty of my final punishment."

Martin nodded and said, "Given what transpired in Ireland, I do not believe that she will be safer if you are separated; however, that is your decision."

Martin rose to his feet. He refilled Carmilla's wine glass, left the decanter on the side table he placed beside her chair. While he finished cleaning her office, she continued justifying why she had to accept that any chance at a rekindled romance with Sam Hain had passed. He remained silent. He finished his cleaning and walked toward the door. As he stepped through the door, he stopped. Without turning around he said, "The woman who risked everything to gain her freedom from Vlad Dracula, who bared her soul and risked death through honesty with Abraham Van Helsing, fears openness and honesty with the woman she loves."

9

Chapter 9

I have now realized that I should have taken a course in archival research when my advisor suggested it as an elective, but my know-it-all, twenty-year-old ass decided to take History of Film Noir instead. Of course, those were the days when I planned on becoming the "cool" English teacher. Here I was, private investigator and supernatural fixer, again poring through the records in the basement of the Karnsburg City Library where they housed the Municipal Archives, or as I have learned, the records that have not been transferred to the Tyrol State Archives in Innsbruck. I had to find whatever Elisa wanted me to find, and I had to mend things with Carmilla.

What brought this to mind was the fact that I spent most of the morning going back through the records on the fire that destroyed the old town. If I were better trained at combing through archives, I could have avoided a lot of digging through the same files and boxes again. Maybe I had missed something. Elisa's ghost seemed to think I had.

After lightning struck St. Januarius' Cathedral, it spread to the half-timber-framed buildings nearest it, but I didn't see anything significant in the spread pattern. There may have been a moral lesson, but I didn't care. As soon as the fire spread, people started looting. I understood that after a flood or hurricane people could start looting, but by all indications, the church was still burning when these dumbasses charged in to steal cash, statuary, and anything else they thought valuable. Seems they repeated this for any other burning home or building they believed housed valuable objects. Nothing seemed important in any of these records.

I returned this box to the archivist, who then brought me a small cart containing four more boxes. My eyes widened in shock, and the archival librarian, an elderly man who dressed like Mister Rogers, smiled warmly and said, "It's easier for both of us if you take a few boxes at a time. I'm hoping these have what you need."

"So do I," I said. "I just wish I knew what I needed to solve this conundrum. Would any of these boxes have medical records from the town doctor at the time?"

He paused and stroked the collar of his sweater as he thought. A few moments passed before he shook his head and said, "I don't think they do, and I don't know if we turned those over to the State Archives in Innsbruck. You get back to searching, and I'll go see if we still have those."

I spent another few hours going through these boxes. I skimmed a lot of business ledgers, which may have been interesting for someone else. However, that changed when I found a series of books bundled together by a leather cord with an identification tag that read "Mayer Cobblers."

Carmilla's deceased lover's name was Annalena Mayer, so this seemed like my best shot to get a lead. Most of the documents were financial records for the business, and I pored over those ledgers and contracts. The only notable finds there happened to be two large donations of twenty thousand kroner to help ease the family's debt from business expansion. The earlier donation, which cleared the family's debts, came from someone identified only as "C.K." This had to be 'Milla offering to help her lover's family. The second, which was delivered to the family by Yarono Bertalan, arrived two days before Annalena's death, and was "on the behalf of an unnamed benefactor." I made a note of that because 'Milla mentioned his name in her diary.

The last document in the bindings was a partially-burned journal that belonged to Annalena. From what I gathered, she was only sixteen at the time. 'Milla liked them young back then, but she still looked to be twenty-two. My face flushed as read some of the later entries, and I growled upon reading how this child claimed no one could love 'Milla as much as she could. And then I came to the last entry, which I presumed to be the day she died.

26 September 1827

My love departed before dawn this morning. I pray that God in heaven shows mercy and allows us to be together for all eternity without the damnation that was thrust upon her. The daylight hours are when God displays the beauty of His handiwork, and it saddens me that my beloved Carmilla can no longer experience such glories.

For breakfast, Mister Yarono Bertalan, an apothecary visiting from Budapest, joined us as Father needed to measure his feet one more time for the custom boots he ordered. I was not especially hungry, but I ate toasted bread and an egg topped with a salad of white parsley and dandelion. I helped Mother wash the breakfast dishes, and then I began to feel weak and suffered from a burning in my bowels and a trembling in my arms. I retired to my room to...

Someone had burned the rest of the page, so I don't know if Annalena Mayer ever returned to her journal. I skimmed through my notes and found that Bertalan examined her and claimed he saw bite marks. A vampire's bite does drain blood, so the weakness fit. Those burning bowels and trembles didn't fit the profile of Post-Bite Sickness. Something didn't add up. An apothecary comes to town, pays the family a visit, she gets some strange symptoms and dies, and he declares it a vampire bite. Destiny's name and number appeared on my phone screen, so I excused myself from both the Archives and the library to take the call.

"I haven't apologized yet, Des," I said. "What's up?"

"Well, that was my first question," she said, "but Miss Sandy Paws and I were hanging out on the sofa and watching *Avatar: the Last Airbender* on your Netflix account, and we reached the episode where Zuko apologized to his Uncle Iroh for betraying him. And then it hit me. Maybe, just maybe, Carmilla isn't as pissed off at you as you think. Maybe she's hurt, because you lost your way—you lost sight of what was really important. So, we decided to call you. What're you doing?"

I laughed, but I knew Destiny was right. "I'm at the Municipal Archives," I said. "I had a conversation with Elisa's ghost last night, and so I'm doing some research. Things aren't adding up."

I explained most of what I knew to Destiny. I told her about the fire and the murders that led to 'Milla's exile. I explained how a Hungarian apothecary examined Annalena's body and declared her the victim of a vampire attack. I explained how the newspaper report said and Carmilla believed her former lover died in the night, but Annalena's own diary revealed she was awake the next morning and told what she ate for breakfast. I then told Destiny how the people who escorted 'Milla to trial had the same last name as the apothecary who determined a vampire caused Annalena's death. I didn't tell her about 'Milla being forced into an abusive marriage with Dracula.

"What I don't know," I said, "is what caused those symptoms. I have a suspicion that this apothecary guy is a poisoner, but I don't know what poison was used. Dandelion isn't poisonous, but I've never heard of white parsley. But parsley's just one step above eating grass, so I doubt that's anything."

"Hmm," Destiny replied. "I don't know. Do you, Sandy Paws?" My cat meowed into the phone, prompting praise from her mommy. "I'd Google it, but it's probably nothing. Or you could visit the local library."

"I might do that," I said. "The Municipal Archives are in the library's basement."

"There you go," Destiny said. "Oh! And don't forget to make copies of any evidence. If you can find enough to prove Carmilla's innocence, the copies will help you convince her. Anyway, Sandy and I have to finish *Avatar*, so we're going to let you get back to your research. Don't forget: apologize! Bye."

I returned to the Archives, and the archivist handed me a single leather-bound volume whose ragged spine needed help to hold on to the pages. Apparently, the great-great-grandson of Karnsburg's only physician before the burning handed over the doctor's personal observation journal, which appeared in chronological order by month only. I skipped to the month closest to Annalena's death to see if anything stood out. Yes, I kept my phone on silent so I could have my German dictionary app handy to help translate the many words I didn't know.

I found the murder victims in the doctor's records, but the doctor's reports for their deaths did not mention vampire bites. And since modern toxicology didn't exist, there were no reports detailing the presence or absence of poison in their blood. He did interview families who were with them before they disappeared. Some mentioned pain, increased drooling, muscle spasms, and convulsions. All reports mentioned complaints of weakness and some kind of "lower intestinal distress" as he termed it. He said that taken together, these pointed to some kind of poison, and he believed it to be hemlock.

I made copies of all the relevant pages, returned this volume and the other boxes to the archivist, thanked him, and ascended to the library. I searched the database for any book on local flora, and I searched for the first book listed, *Leopold's Ledger of Local Flora*. I took the book to a vinyl chair and searched. My heart raced as I read through the entry for hemlock, and I beamed upon seeing that white parsley was another name for hemlock. I photocopied the pages and called Martin to tell him I needed a ride back to the castle and that I had evidence that 'Milla had been set up.

* * *

"What the fuck do you want?" Paul Byron blurted as he answered a call on his cell phone as he sped from Innsbruck to Karnsburg.

"That is no way to address your superior, Squire," responded Knight-Commander Bertalan.

"Sorry, Sir," Byron corrected, slowing the silver Miata's speed, and exhaling slowly. "I'm a mite stressed right now.

What do you need, Sir?"

"Apparently I need to assign all Squires a course in manners," he replied. Byron straightened his posture and swallowed hard. Bertalan continued, "However, that is not the purpose of my call. We need to discuss your progress on the mission."

"Right. The mission. About that," Byron said, grabbing a handful of his thick mop of ginger hair. "I've got everything under control, Sir."

The Knight-Commander snorted. He asked, "Do you really? I'm beginning to doubt that. And why does it sound tinny? Where are you?"

"I'm on the road, Sir," Byron said. "I was in Innsbruck for a couple of days looking for a black Madonna statue."

"Ah," Bertalan said with an air of annoyed disdain. "Your little dalliance. I trust you have found this precious statue?"

Byron changed lanes as he said, "I found that it existed, so that fucker didn't lie to me on that bit. I've got to fucking find it."

"For your sake," Bertalan said, "I hope not. I have not heard of another death in Karnsburg. Have you forgotten about that aspect of your mission?"

"No, Sir," Byron said, shaking his head as he avoided a fallen box on the highway. "I almost had one, but I got my ass beat by Sam Hain in a bloody fight instead. And now that bald detective wants to ask me a few questions."

"You engaged Samantha Hain before you slew your final innocent and assassinated the traitor?" Knight-Commander Bertalan growled into his phone, causing Byron's head to slam against the seat's headrest. "Why? You had orders. Why did you not follow them?"

Byron breathed slowly as his hands choked the steering

wheel. "I didn't plan on it," he said. "I was hunting for the last one, and she walked in and sat in a dark corner by herself. By the time I got to her, she'd already had a couple of cocktails, so I thought she'd be easy picking to get a two-for-one deal."

"And now the police want to speak to you." Bertalan said flatly while massaging his temples with his index finger and thumb. "You disobeyed orders. You endangered the mission. I should have your head for this."

"No. No. No, Sir. Shit…" Paul Byron stammered as he swerved to avoid traffic. "Give me one more chance, Sir. After tonight, neither the traitor nor the thorn will trouble us."

"Fine," Bertalan sighed. "You have tonight. Should you fail, death will come for you. Over and out."

Paul Byron sped through the remaining distance between himself and his hotel, ignoring Chief Detective Merkatz's request for further questioning. He opened his suitcase and pulled out a briefcase, which he opened. Inside, protected by foam padding, rested a hand crossbow, five slender wooden stakes, a crucifix, and a vial of holy water. He closed and latched the case.

The sun's setting brought an increase in activity within Castle Karnstein. Martin supervised the kitchen thralls who prepared the night's meal. While one thrall pureed parsnips, Martin hovered over the thrall searing the filet. He moved like a battlefield commander, shouting orders and reviewing performance. The air in the castle trembled with anxiety and anticipation. After the thralls prepared the beef wellington, the parsnip puree, the fingerling potatoes sauteed in garlic and rosemary, and the serving cups of the chanterelle mushroom gravy, Martin prepared the serving plates for the table, placed an 1819 Sanguinovese in a decanter to aerate, and selected the perfect glasses. He checked the diners' silent progress on the security camera and then headed to the dining hall.

Tonight, Carmilla and Sam dined in the formal dining hall on the castle's second floor. Tall, arched windows of stained glass lined the northern wall. Electric lights shone from modified wall sconces. Per family tradition, a three-pronged candelabra stood atop the long mahogany table near each occupied seat. Their flames danced with dissonance as the two diners sat on opposite ends of the table. As the servants cleared the empty bowls from the silent soup course, Martin, his eyes narrowed in frustration, served the main course.

As he placed her meal before her, Sam smiled and said, "Thank you, Martin. This looks lovely."

"Yes." Carmilla snipped as he set the gold-trimmed porcelain plate before her. "As always."

Martin excused himself and left the dining hall. As with the soup course, the sounds of silverware clanking against porcelain and the errant smack while chewing provided the only sounds to penetrate the tense air. From a distance, it appeared that the two women stared at each other while eating; however, their eyes never met. Each shifted her gaze slightly to avoid direct eye contact with the other. Knives slashed through rare filet with a torturer's precision as the juices and gravy bled onto the plates.

Carmilla dabbed the corner of her mouth twice with her cloth napkin before asking, "So, Martin says you performed research today?"

"Yes," Sam said. "I found some things that bring light to the situation."

"Good," Carmilla said curtly.

Martin slammed his palm into his face and slid it down to

his chin. Watching from the kitchen's security camera, Martin surveyed the silent supper with growing frustration. He shook his head and massaged his temples while the thralls monitored the apples, walnuts, and brie baking in the oven. During the forty-seven minutes they took to eat the main course, the two women said three sentences to each other. He prepared each serving plate and then wrote a note that he set at the edge of each plate. He then sliced and toasted baguette rounds, arranged the silverware, and then plated the brie rounds.

As the thralls removed the main course plates from the table, Martin smiled. "It seems you both enjoyed the wellington," he said."

"I did," Sam said with a smile. "It was delicious."

"I did. It was excellent, Martin," Carmilla said.

A drop of blood slid from Martin's lip as he bit hard. He nodded his head and accepted the compliments. He set the cheese plates on the table, refilled their wineglasses and Sam's water glass, and then he excused himself. As they looked at their plates, both Sam and Carmilla saw their notes, which both read, *Stop being miserable and talk to her.*

They ate in physical silence that screamed into the voids within their souls. Sam's planned apology looped into her mind, but every time she opened her mouth to speak, Carmilla's gaze turned away, stifling her voice. Carmilla wanted to vocalize the depth of her feelings, which she assumed Sam already knew. As her lips parted to speak, she glimpsed Sam's eyes, silenced herself, and averted her gaze.

Viewing from the kitchen, Martin crushed a crystal snifter with his hand. Ignoring the injury, he growled, "They deserve each other. Damned to spend eternity together in silence."

And he switched off the camera feed as he left the kitchen with the parfait glasses filled with a sweet cream zabaione topped with iced blueberries and crushed amaretti.

Shattering glass broke the silence in the dining hall. Carmilla inhaled sharply as a stake plunged into her chest. Sam leaped to her feet and raced toward the vampire, calling her name. Dressed in black with a mask hiding his face and a beanie covering all but a few wisps of his hair, Paul Byron crashed through the window. He brandished the two-needle syringe and charged Sam.

Eyes wide, Sam grabbed a chair and slammed it into his gut. He grunted and staggered back. She dropped the chair. He tackled her, knocking her into Carmilla. The stake scratched her cheek. Sam groaned. Her chest heaved as her breathing came hard and fast. He mounted her and punched; she blocked him and then kicked him off her.

As she stood, Martin opened the dining hall's door. He dropped the desserts as he saw the scene before him. Sam punched Byron's kidney. He grunted and doubled over. Sam called out, "Martin! Get blood bags." He nodded and sped from the doorway.

Byron slammed the fanged syringe into Sam's left shoulder, piercing through a scar from her first investigation. She winced. Sweat beaded on her forehead. She pushed him away. He charged, jabbed her kidney, and slammed his fanged syringe into her cheek. He raked it across her face. Sam screamed. Her heart thundered. He shoved his combat boot into her ribs, kicking her against the table.

Sweat stung Sam's eyes. Her vision blurred. He leaped upon her and slammed her head into the table. She cried out. She swung a candelabra, wincing as the candle wax dripped onto her skin. The flames scratched at Byron's eyes. He screamed. Sam thrust her foot into his groin. He doubled over, sweat staining his black clothing. He punched. Sam rolled to her side. His fist slammed into the mahogany table. She shoved her elbow into his chest, spun, and punched his face. He staggered back. Sam slammed a chair over his head. He dropped to a knee. The wooden chair broke as she slammed it into the side of his head. Byron collapsed onto the floor.

Sam raced to Carmilla, cradling her head in her lap. Blood seeped into Sam's dress as Carmilla's jaw trembled. Her eyes wide and stained by crimson tears, she barely noticed Sam holding her. Sam pulled the stake from the Countess' chest. Carmilla screamed. Tears fell from Sam's eyes as she said, "Hey, 'Milla. It's me. I'm here."

"Samantha," Carmilla said, her raspy voice barely above a whisper. "I am glad…"

"Shh," Sam whispered. "It's okay. Martin's bringing you blood. You're going to be safe. Just hold on."

Carmilla shook her head and smiled. "No," she said. "I am glad… at the end… to see…"

As Carmilla's words faded, Sam looked around the room and grabbed a shard of broken glass. She breathed deeply, staring at the jagged glass in her hand. She bit her lip, closed her eyes, and slashed across her left arm, wincing at the pain. Sam brought her wrist to Carmilla's mouth and said, "Drink. Please. Take as much as you need. I give it to you."

Carmilla's tongue licked the blood. Sam inhaled sharply. The vampire lapped the blood, savoring the taste. Sam whispered encouragement as she watched the wound slowly close. Carmilla lapped faster, moaning as her desire to fully sate her hunger waxed. Sam's breathing came quick and shallow. Her cheeks flushed. Carmilla's eyes opened, and she plunged her fangs into Sam's flesh. Sam threw her head back and moaned.

"Oh, fuck yeah," Sam moaned. Her vision blurred. As Carmilla fed, Sam held her close. From the corner of her eye, she saw Martin and Lord Volny enter, and then she lost consciousness.

* * *

Vampires dreamed more frequently during their fledgling century, but the frequency of dreams entering their death-sleep plummeted after that period. The Van Helsing Institute for Nosferatic Studies has long theorized that this occurs due to the increased loss of humanity that occurs after centuries of inhuman, monstrous behavior. However, the Rice-Elrod Center for Studies on Vampiric Ethnography put forward the theory that, as vampires age, their bodies drain of blood faster during death-sleep than they did as fledglings, and as such, their organs direct the remaining blood to the organs necessary to keep their undead body in a functional state. A newer postulation emerged from the Cushing-Polidori Institute for Un-dead Medicine that hypothesized that, since vampires can die of old age, they cease dreaming when their animating soul has left their body. Regardless of the reason, for the first time in over a century, Countess Carmilla Yosefine Karnstein dreamed.

Wearing the black pencil dress that she wore that evening, Carmilla walked through the damp, dark, drafty halls of a ruined castle. The narrow halls gave her a vertigo-like dizziness as she moved along the gray stones. She steadied herself by resting her hand on the frigid wall as she called out for anyone to answer. Only the clicking of her stilettos on the stone, the howling of the winter wind, and the echo of her voice returned to her ears. Windows and missing, crumbled wall sections revealed the cloudless night where a lone bat flew before the shining full moon.

She staggered through the narrow halls, feeling a strange familiarity to these ruins, and calling for anyone to attend her. No one returned her calls. She descended along a counterclockwise-turning staircase and into an even narrower hall. Then she heard a cacophony of hollow, mocking laughter from ahead. The laughter grew louder, and Carmilla noticed that a woman's cries and screams punctuated the hollow, sardonic merriment . She crept toward the sound and saw a red curtain with a frayed right edge hung in the doorway to the chamber ahead.

She pushed aside the curtain and watched as two dark-skinned men with thick black curls and bushy mustaches laughing at a naked woman bound atop the pyramidal seat of the Judas cradle. Her arms and legs, bound at the wrists and ankles, trembled in exhaustion as she struggled to balance herself. Bloody tears plummeted from her eyes, and she cried in pain, begging for mercy as their rough hands slapped her face, yanked her matted and knotted black hair, and spat in her face.

"Stop it," Carmilla screamed as she pushed the men away only to find that she moved through them.

Her eyes shot wide as she stared at her hands. Her feet felt the floor beneath her. She remembered feeling the walls as she moved. She shook her head. Carmilla approached the woman and tried to free her. Her hands slid through the cradle and the woman's hips, and as she turned and saw the woman's face, she leaped back.

"It's me," she whispered, "but the castle was not ruined as this even after he abandoned me for London. Where am I?"

"You are where you refuse to leave, 'Millie," Elisa's voice emerged from behind her.

Carmilla spun around to see her sister's ghost floating beside her. "So, this is it," she sighed, "I am damned, and this is where I will remain."

Elisa shook her head and placed her hand on her sister's shoulder. She asked, "Have you not damned yourself since your exile into Ireland?"

"I did not die then, my sister," Carmilla said as her gaze returned to the image of her own torture. Then she added, "I thought I escaped."

"And what did you do when you left Castle Bran," Elisa asked. Her face showed no emotion as her gaze rested on Carmilla.

"I returned home," the Countess said with a shrug. "I rejoined my clan after telling Father that mortals had slain Dracula. I added lying to my treason. He did not truly believe me, but no evidence emerged that proved my involvement. You know this, Elisa, for I told you all of these things upon our first encounter after my return."

"I do not think that we saw the same things," Elisa said. "You returned home," she added, "but you did not leave Castle Bran."

Elisa turned and floated away. Carmilla's lip trembled as she asked, "So you are going to leave me to my damnation? I did not think I was reckless, Elisa. I am sorry that you died because of me."

Elisa walked through a doorway, leaving it open. Carmilla's gaze fell. She sighed and turned her gaze back to the scene of her own torture. The men kicked the Judas cradle away, causing her to drop as far as the ropes allowed. Her bones cracked, and the men laughed. They cut ankles and wrists free, but left the rope affixed to her collar, leashing her to the room's center. They laughed as they threw rat carcasses toward her, causing her to crawl and scramble for the smallest scrap of food. Carmilla heard the door close, but she did not notice it disappear.

Carmilla slumped onto the cold stone floor. Her body trembled. She buried her face in her hands as crimson tears flowed.

"Stay there, if you so desire," Elisa's voice snapped from within Carmilla's mind. "Or you could move beyond. It is your choice."

A door clicked as it unlocked. Carmilla's head jerked up. She scanned the room but saw no one. She heard the leashed woman, herself, crying and slurping the last drops of blood from the rats. Carmilla shook her head as her shoulders slumped forward. She sat for a moment, staring at the scene before her as the men returned and the torture began again.

She scratched her head and said, "No. This is not correct. His mortal servants did not torture me without his presence. Do I remember it wrong?"

A door opened. Carmilla turned to see a sliver of light emerge from the crack. *So, this is my damnation,* she thought. Chuckling, her mind continued, *It felt so warm. As a child, I thought death would be cold. I suppose it is different for us than for mortals.*

The door creaked as it started to close. Half as much light shone through the narrowed opening. She knew this was neither how Vlad Dracula abused her nor how the Hungarian servants mocked and tormented her after he abandoned her for England. *Nick Scratch is a great liar,* she thought. She clenched trembling fists as her thoughts flowed like her bloody tears, *convincing us all that Hell is a place of ironic punishment. No, Hell is knowing the truth but being forced to spend eternity surrounded by the lies. Elisa...after all these years, she has her revenge.*

The door creaked as it moved again. Only the faintest sliver of light remained. Carmilla's vision dimmed. Her heart slowed. She nodded, knowing what this meant. She thought, *It is over. I wonder what death looks like.*

As her thought trailed into silence, she felt something cold on her lips. Instinctively, she licked them. It was blood, and it had a familiar spicy and sweet taste. Its taste provided a comfort that she had not felt in years. Her eyes brightened, and her sight slowly returned. She whispered into the chamber, "What was it that Elisa said? Is it possible?"

She rose to her feet and observed the scene. She shook her head as she said, "I survived those decades. I survived. I walked out."

The door screamed as it opened. Carmilla turned toward the warm, golden light that emerged from beyond the door. She turned back toward the image of herself being tortured, smiled gently, and said, "You'll survive. Stay strong." And then she walked through the door.

Carmilla watched herself siting behind the desk in her office, poring over reports and records. The phone rang. She acknowledged the time and opened the custom video conferencing software that her investment brokerage firm used for administrative meetings. This conference call included the officers of the Non-Human Mythic Investment Division, and she laid out their mission to help their clients navigate life in the changing modern world of mortals while keeping true to the tenets of the Old Ways.

Carmilla smiled and said, "And we have helped so many."

"You should be proud," Elisa's ghost said as she appeared beside her sister. "For too long, our people and many like us have opposed change. Many have suffered greatly. But you, 'Millie, you have helped more than you may know."

"I have learned how bitter the taste of suffering is," Carmilla said, her eyes focused on the floor. "I do not want others to taste that."

She smacked her lips, noticing the pleasant taste had disappeared. Her shoulders slumped forward, and her chin rested upon her collar. She sighed and shook her head. As her gaze returned to the confident Carmilla in the scene, Elisa squeezed her sister's arm and asked, "What troubles you?"

"It all feels hollow," Carmilla said. "I remember those early decades of my endeavor. The allies of our clan abandoned us. Two wars ravaged our lands. And that vile little colonel who arrogantly named himself *Fuhrer* nearly exposed and destroyed so many of us as he mechanized the cruelty of Vlad and his ilk. I have been lonely."

"And yet," Elisa said, "you have not been alone. Martin has always been at your side, even before your exile. You smiled, sister. I know you have fond memories of sneaking out as he pretended to not see you. I have been here, after a fashion. And now, this Samantha Hain joins your triangle of support."

That taste returned, and Carmilla smiled. She closed her eyes and savored the spicy and then sweet taste on her tongue as if she were drinking cherished blood. She licked her lips as she emitted a soft moan. Elisa smiled.

And then Carmilla sighed. Her face darkened, and blood

pooled in the corners of her eyes. She said, "How can you not hate me? What they did to you because I was reckless and undisciplined was unconscionable. You could have lived and ascended to my place. Our clan would not have lost so much of its honor amongst our own kind. I am the reason you died, Elisa. I am the reason you are bound and unable to rest."

"Walk with me," Elisa said as she floated from the room.

Carmilla followed as Elisa led her into their castle's rear courtyard. They walked through the hedge maze until they reached the central fountain. Elisa sat on the stone bench, and Carmilla sat beside her. "Tell me," Elisa asked, "do you recall the origin of our family crest?"

Carmilla nodded. "I do," she said. "Ziegwulf the Bloody-Handed is said to have slain a man in dragon scale armor with his bare hands. The poets claimed he fought as tenaciously and savagely as an angered badger."

Elisa smiled and said, "A badger slaying a dragon. Many would say that an impossible feat, but you have, in your own way, accomplished it. Yet, I fear that I am not the one bound, dear sister, but you are. At the time, I offered myself to protect the one destined to become our matriarch. You have done more than I could have done, and I have been able to bear witness to it. Though I have minimal contact with those I love and with their loved ones, I have seen and learned a great many things to which you have refused to see."

Carmilla wept. Elisa slid her arm around her sister's shoulder. They sat for a few moments in silence until Carmilla, her face drained and pale as the blood poured from her eyes, said, "Please, tell me what I can do to earn your forgiveness. Please rest. I am so sorry for my actions. I am sorry for being impulsive and reckless. I am sorry for being headstrong.

Please, Elisa, I love you, and I meant nothing to happen to you. I…"

"If forgiveness you seek," Elisa interrupted her older sister and said, "then you must ask the person who has suffered for your actions."

Elisa's ghost disappeared. Carmilla found herself alone in a room with only a gold-framed circular mirror. As she gazed into the mirror, she saw herself. She closed her eyes and took one deep breath. She exhaled.

When her eyes opened, she lay in her bed. Martin, assault rifle in hand, guarded the door. A middle-aged man with salt and pepper hair, pale blue eyes, and a thick handlebar mustache examined her body. Lord Prvan Volny stood in the opposite corner, his arms folded across his chest. She groaned as pain shot through her stiff and sore muscles. She looked around the room and said, "Martin, where is Samantha? Is she alive?"

Martin turned toward her and smiled. "She is," he said, "and thanks to her for her quick and selfless actions, so are you. She is in the dining hall with the detective explaining what happened."

Carmilla saw the bloodied bandages on her chest. Her examiner, Doctor Emil Bertholt, was a physician employed by her clan who had proven capable of keeping their secret. He shone a light in her eyes, and she flinched, glaring at him. He nodded and then said in his squeaky baritone, "Do not worry, Countess. The bandages are for show. Your wound has already healed, but they shall be removed once the detective leaves."

Lord Volny approached and bowed. Carmilla nodded. "Well," he said, "in light of the evening's events, it appears that the Council of Elders' fears regarding your actions have proven...unfounded. I shall depart for Budapest at sunset tomorrow. You, Countess Karnstein, are cleared of all suspicion."

She sighed in relief as he left the room. A few moments later, Samantha Hain entered the room, a glass filled with bourbon in her hand. She beamed when she saw Carmilla sitting in bed, raced toward her, and embraced her. Both cried. As they pulled part, Carmilla saw the scar on Sam's cheek and placed her hand over it. Her gaze shifted to the bandage on Sam's wrist and asked, "Samantha, what happened to you? You did not try to... *you know*, did you?"

Sam swigged her bourbon and shook her head. "No, 'Milla," she said, "Fucker staked you with a crossbow, started a fight, did pretty well. I mean, he was Order of the Dragon, after all. Speaking of, sorry about breaking one of your chairs on his head, but that did knock him out."

"A chair can be replaced," Carmilla said. "You cannot."

Sam blushed into her bourbon and said, "I feel the same, so since you were bleeding out and Martin hadn't arrived with your blood yet, I did what I had to do. I gave you as much of my blood as you needed."

"You... you fed me?" Carmilla's voice came in a sharp whisper. Sam nodded. Carmilla's gaze darkened. She closed her eyes, swallowed hard, and said, "I could have killed you. I've done it before."

Sam shook her head and brushed Carmilla's cheek, saying, "When you were a fledgling, maybe, but you're a bit too old for that now."

Carmilla shook her head, laying it upon Sam's chest and throwing her arms around her. "No," she said through guilt-choked words, "It was not that long ago in terms of my life.

I…"

Sam raised Carmilla's chin with her thumb and index finger. She smiled warmly and lovingly as she said, "We've got a lot to talk about, 'Milla. But both of us need rest. How do I say this in your way? Countess Carmilla Karnstein, Matriarch of the Karnstein-Bertholt clan, let us make a pact to speak tomorrow night, openly and honestly."

Carmilla blinked and said, "You know the wording of our oaths?"

Sam winked, "I asked Martin to teach me. I want to do this right by you."

Carmilla smiled and said, "Well then, in that case, Samantha Blake Hain of the Hain family of humans, I agree to your pact. We shall speak openly and honestly tomorrow night in the drawing room."

10

Chapter 10

The next evening, I walked into the kitchen as Martin uncorked a bottle of wine and poured its deep, almost black, purple contents into a crystal decanter. No servants milled about the kitchen tonight. I smiled as I grabbed two glasses from the mahogany china cabinet. As I set them on the serving tray, he looked over and smiled, "Thank you, Miss Hain, but you are a guest here. It is tradition that you do not lift a finger to work."

"Is it tradition for guests here to fight off an attacker who stakes the Countess," I replied. I cocked an eyebrow, taking the decanter and placing it on the serving tray.

He paused and thought before responding, "It has been a few centuries, but it is not an unheard-of occurrence. My only personal regret is that you did not kill that bastard."

"I understand," I said, "but I don't like killing. I've had my fill of killing. And Werther Grimm advised me to focus on protecting 'Milla and to let the police handle any criminality."

"Yes, Ma'am," he said with a sigh. "I simply worry that the money and power of the Order of the Dragon will render our police and justice system impotent. That said, you offered Countess Karnstein a sizeable portion of your blood. I must say that I am quite surprised to see you doing as well as you are."

"Well," I said, shrugging my shoulders, "I have this thing about keeping those who procure my professional services alive. I had no intention—hey, don't give me that eye, Martin. Fuck! You're almost as bad as Destiny on that front. Fine, fine. I didn't want her to die. After all," I winked, "she is my *fiancée*."

"I do believe," he said, "that you will need to discuss that with her. The wine should help, as should the information you've uncovered."

I smiled and nodded. "I hope so," I said. "I know I fucked things up by going into the basement and reading her diary. Even without the importance vampires place on oral promises and oaths, I should've known just how important that privacy is. I got blinded by work. I want *us* to work out. I really do, Martin. I may have blown it permanently, but at least I can let her know that she did not kill Annalena and that it appears that she was set up."

Martin sighed and shook his head. "I cannot believe that we overlooked that," he said. "That our agents did not see those connections. That *I* did not see those connections."

I walked over and patted his back. "It's not your fault," I said. "It's easy to miss this type of conspiracy if you're not looking for it. I mean, had Elisa's ghost not guided me, I wouldn't have found the clues I needed to figure out where to look."

He smiled and chuckled. Shaking his head, he said, "After all these decades, Elisa still seeks to protect her older sister. And it seems she realizes that you have a role to play in her life as well."

I nodded. As I picked up the serving tray, I said, "Well, let me head to the drawing room. I want to be ready for when 'Milla wakes up."

I set the serving tray on the small table and poured wine in our glasses, taking a sip from mine. As soon as I lit the fire in the heart, Carmilla sauntered into the room wearing nothing but her burgundy dressing gown. I covered my sharp inhale with a wide smile. Her messy hair told me she just awoke and came to the drawing room. She had no meetings. She took no time. This meant a lot to her, and my heart sped up. We embraced, and she again ran her hand along the scar on my cheek.

"I hope I have not kept you long," she said with a playfulness I haven't heard in her voice since my birthday. "I came as soon as I woke."

I smiled and shook my head. "No," I said. "Martin and I bid farewell to Lord Patriarchy, and then I slept for most of the day. I just finished setting up in here when you walked in."

I handed her a glass of wine, which she sipped, and then said, "Well, you seem to have taken quite well to your role as my *fiancée*, as Martin named you."

Sadness darkened her voice. It was a sadness I fully understood. We were still entwined in each other's arms. I smelled her natural spiced honey scent, and I blushed, biting my lip to avoid leaning into her neck and kissing her. I sighed.

"We do need to talk, 'Milla," I said.

We broke the embrace and sat in the chairs. Carmilla nodded. She sipped her wine again and said, "We do. First, I wish to thank you again for saving my life last night. Your actions exceeded any expectations I could have had."

I shrugged and offered a sheepish smile. "You're welcome," I said. "You called me your protector after the first attack, so I had to live up to that. But you know that I would do that for you in half a heartbeat."

She blushed. I saw it. I made Countess Carmilla Karnstein blush. I almost wished Martin were in the room so that I'd have a witness. She nodded and then said, "I am grateful. After our last interaction before dinner, we knew nothing of your whereabouts until that detective called to say you were attacked and being escorted home." Bloody tears rained from her eyes as she continued, "I was so worried. And I had thought perhaps…"

"I would never abandon you," I said, leaning toward her. "We've fought before, 'Milla. I think that having a day to cool down helped both of us." I shrugged and continued, "I know it helped me think of what I both need and want to say to you."

"Ah," she said, "Martin mentioned that you uncovered something important in your research for my… case." Her voice faltered as she spoke. I heard the fear choke her.

"That can wait until later," I said. I gulped my wine, took the deepest breath of my life, and said, "My first night here, I made a promise to you. I promised I would respect your privacy and allow you to tell me your story in your own time. I made that promise willingly, as a guest and as a friend. I thought it would be an easy promise to keep. I really did. Things happened as they did, and I got a bit cocky. I was blinded to that cockiness. I thought I could treat this like any other case–any normal case–separating the work from my feelings. I let the work blind me to how my actions affected you. In my efforts to protect you and to prove your innocence, I broke my promise and violated your privacy. I was wrong for violating your privacy, for breaking my promise, and for thinking I could do this with only my head and not my heart. I'm sorry."

I gulped the rest of the wine in my glass. Carmilla's silence lasted for what felt like an eternity. She nodded, and I saw her chest heave as if she took a deep breath, and then she said, "In the few years I have known you, Samantha, this is the first time you have apologized." She chuckled and added, "It is the first time either of us has ever apologized to the other. I accept your apology. And I too must apologize for my outburst and the silence with which I met you for the next two nights. I was wounded, but my actions were befitting neither of our history nor of my status. Please forgive me."

"Of course, I forgive you," I said. I chuckled and shook my head. I refilled my wineglass and said, "We are both cursed with a fatal case of stubbornness."

She sipped her wine and shot me and curious glance. "I see Martin has lectured you as well," she said.

"Martin, Destiny," I said. "Oh, and your sister's ghost. She actually proved to be invaluable during my investigation. She loves you." As do I. Dammit, Samantha Blake, just fucking tell her!

"She always has," Carmilla mused, her voice gaining a nostalgic lilt. "So, what did you uncover in your investigation?"

The moment arrived. 'Milla listened as I provided a step-by-step breakdown of my investigation. I started with how, from her diary, I learned of the presence of the apothecary Yarono Bertalan who was an emissary from Vlad Dracula. Then I showed her Annalena's diary, slowing my speech to keep any jealousy hidden, and focusing on how the young girl woke up the morning after her rendezvous with 'Milla. I highlighted the white salad she had in her breakfast and the symptoms she recorded before she died.

215

"But we never heard of this," Carmilla interjected. "Why did no one bring this to our attention?"

"I don't know, 'Milla," I said. "I've got two guesses. First, most people don't look for this type of conspiracy unless they have to. Second, from all the other records, the mob formed and marched quickly. There likely wasn't time to gather evidence."

I continued narrating my research and findings. I told her how Elisa directed me to look for the medical records of the murdered girls, since, according to Yarono Bertalan, Annalena and the murder victims shared symptoms. I showed her the town physician's reports on two of the victims, illuminating the similarities with the symptoms Annalena reported, and adding that none of the common symptoms suggested a vampire's bite. Her eyes lit with joy as I mentioned that the common symptoms suggested hemlock, or white parsley, poisoning. I concluded by mentioning that, after this Yarono Bertalan stirred up the village mob, he and his clan are the ones who escorted her to her trial.

We sat in silence for a moment when I finished my report. Carmilla's index finger circled the rim of her wineglass, and she stared into its rich purple depths, thinking. "Well," she said, "the Bertalan clan has always been loyal to *Dracula*. But why? Why would his agents try to implicate me in such an action? What did they seek to gain?"

"Your sister thinks that this was Dracula's only chance at a legitimate heir," I said. "But then he did what he did. What I do know, 'Milla, is that you were right all along. You did not kill Annalena. And your sister, well, loved you to the point of being willing to die for you." I paused and breathed deeply, exhaling as I said, "As do I."

"Oh?" Carmilla's voice shot two octaves higher as she

216

elongated that simple question. "But I gave my word that if you completed one of your investigations that I would cease to rekindle our romance."

"You did, 'Milla," I said. My heart raced, and my hands trembled. "But there are two issues with that. First, you're not making the attempt. I am. Second, Martin brought it to my attention that I did not follow proper protocol from the beginning. We signed no contract, and I did not receive my advance of half of my fee. So, technically, I helped you pro bono. And, if I'm going to be fully honest with you, as we promised when we swore our oath last night, then I have to admit that I don't know how I will learn to get used to waking up to your cold, lifeless body during the day, but, Countess Carmilla Karnstein, I cannot imagine my life without you in it."

'Milla refilled her glass in silence. She then rose from her chair and started to walk toward the door. My heart stopped, and I held my breath. She walked to the chaise and sat. She sipped her wine, and I exhaled, feeling my heart tremble as it pumped again. She smiled at me and patted the velvet cushion. "Come," she said, "sit beside me."

I quickly topped off my wineglass and sat beside her. I kept my hands in my lap, shifting awkwardly like it was prom night. An inch of electrified space loomed between us. My heart thundered as I looked into her eyes. She reached out and cupped my right cheek with her hand as her lips raised into a smile. I inhaled sharply as we touched. And then she asked, "May I have permission to kiss you?"

"Fucking yes," I said.

We leaned toward each other. I tilted my head upward, parting my lips slightly. As her lips brushed against mine, a loud banging stopped us. We turned to the wall behind us to see Martin hammering a nail into the wall. He hung a sprig of mistletoe from the nail, turned, and said, "Oh, don't mind me, my Countess, Miss Hain. I happened to recall a traditional holiday decoration that you, in your nervous haste, forgot to hang."

* * *

Six days passed since Paul Byron's arrest. He had resisted repeated police attempts at questioning, telling Chief Detective Merkatz nothing beyond what the officer already knew. Given the severity of the charges against him and his choice of targets, the police kept him under guard. Now, as the sun began its descent on Christmas Eve, two officers escorted the handcuffed and smirking Byron to an interrogation room in the Saggen Polizeiinspektion station in Innsbruck where Chief Detective Merkatz planned to conduct another round of questioning.

Merkatz sat at the table in the interrogation room, his blazer draped over the back of his chair. Steam rose from his coffee mug as he scratched the back of his bald head with his ballpoint pen. He sighed as he flipped through the pages of interview transcripts, crime scene photographs, the psychologist's evaluation, and the lab reports on fingerprints and bloodstains. The psychological profile refuted any claim to an insanity defense, as Doctor Katarina Braum believed him to be a disagreeable and belligerent man who wanted her to believe him delusional. However, certain points in previous conversations still concerned Merkatz. The evidence pointed to Paul Byron, and his recent arrest after he attacked both Countess Karnstein and Sam Hain left no doubt in the Chief Detective's mind as to Byron's guilt. Only one mystery remained to be solved, and Merkatz hoped to solve that one this night.

The interrogation room door opened, and Paul Byron entered with a triumphant smirk on his face. The officers removed the handcuffs and stood by the door. Byron spun the chair so that its back stood against the table. He straddled the chair, placed his hands on the top of the chair, and said, "Happy bloody Christmas, Bobby Wanker."

Merkatz narrowed his eyes and said, "I see your manners have remained constant, Mister Byron. May I offer you juice, coffee, perhaps a cocoa? It is Christmas Eve, after all."

"Can't I get champagne to celebrate," Byron asked.

"Celebrate what?" Chief Detective Merkatz took notes in his pocket notebook. "You're scheduled to go to trial on Monday, and you know that we have more than enough evidence to convict you. What are we celebrating?"

Byron snorted while he laughed. He slapped the table with his meaty hand and said, "Oh, you're funny, Bobby Wanker. Oh, sorry, I mean, 'Wanker Bobby.' It's just that you're so bloody funny that you could go on the road and change the world's perception of you stoic bastards. But if you won't give me the bubbly, bring me a cocoa with three little marshmallows."

Merkatz nodded. One of the officers left the room, returning a few minutes later with the requested cocoa. Byron sneered as he sipped his beverage. Merkatz sipped his coffee and then said, "I'm sure you're wondering why I asked to see you again."

Byron slurped his cocoa and smacked his lips. Smiling, he set the cup on the table, leaned forward, and said, "The thought had crossed my mind. I mean, unless you've been lying about this open and shut business. So then, Wanker Bobby, why not enlighten me?"

Chief Detective Merkatz tensed his muscles and relaxed them with a purposeful exhale. "Yes," he said. "We do have enough to convict you and to send you to prison for the remainder of your life. That is not up for discussion. I'm asking you to indulge me with one final loose end, Mister Byron. Why? That is what I want to know. Why did you do this?"

Byron shrugged. His smirk grew wider, and he said, "Would you believe me if I said it was for shits and snickers?"

"Your bruises appear to be healing," Merkatz said flatly as he sipped his coffee.

Chief Detective Merkatz leaned forward, allowing his eyes to search the younger man's physical responses. Byron was larger, younger, and more muscular than Merkatz. His physique suggested some level of military training, but Merkatz found no record of such service. Byron did have a rap sheet that included numerous arrests for fighting, petty theft, and assault from the time he turned sixteen until New Year's Eve of last year. Bruises still darkened his face from Samantha Hain's unorthodox, scrappy fighting style. While most people in his position would remain stone faced, Byron never lost his smirk. His posture remained relaxed as he leaned forward, his arms folded over the back of the chair.

Byron rubbed his stubble-covered cheek, chuckled, and said, "Bitch got lucky. But any fight you can walk away from is a good fight, right? Right?" He looked around the room to see the three officers remaining emotionless and silent. "Bloody wankers," he continued. "No idea how to have a good night."

"According to what you told Doctor Braum during your

meeting," Merkatz said as his index finger glided over the doctor's report, "your actions are for the greater good."

"What of it?" Byron slurped his cocoa. He looked directly into Merkatz's blue eyes, cocked an eyebrow, and said, "Ain't that why you do what you wankers do?"

One of the younger officers by the door clenched his fists. Merkatz sipped his coffee and then rested his chin in the palm of his hand. His eyes remained narrow, but his expression suggested disinterest slouching toward annoyance. "Then enlighten me," he said, "how killing Sofia Pichler promoted the greater good."

Byron shrugged, turning his palms to the ceiling. "I doubt your mind could understand the answer," he said, "so I'll just tell you it was a necessary accident. We good?"

Merkatz recorded the response. He sighed, drumming his fingers on the table as he stared into Paul Byron's mocking eyes. Merkatz nodded. He leaned back in his chair and said, "You told Doctor Braum the same thing. You also mentioned something to her that you did not tell us."

"She asked questions you didn't," Byron said. He turned to the officers by the door, raised his paper cup, and said, "One of you wankers want to become a banger and bring me another cocoa?"

"Only one until you answer some questions seriously," said one of the officers. He was a young man with buzzed black hair and brown eyes.

Chief Detective Merkatz raised his hand and said, "Bring him another. It is Christmas, and we're not monsters, after all." The officer nodded and left. Merkatz continued, "There, now with that attended to, please enlighten me as to who this Order of the Dragon is."

Byron laughed. He shook his head and waved a dismissive hand at Chief Detective Merkatz. He said, "I guess you don't know nothing about your own history, do you, Bobby Wanker?"

Merkatz dropped the pen onto the table, growled, and said, "I know their history from the fifteenth century until the sixteenth. I know of their connection to Vlad Dracula." Merkatz folded his arms across his chest and continued, "And he's been dead for centuries. So, tell me what connection does such an old order of knights have with your murders beyond your pretending to be a vampire?"

Byron laughed again. "I'll tell you this," he sneered as he said, "They're the ones who are going to free me, you, and all the world. When my barrister gets here, I won't see the inside of your courtroom. Your laws are nothing. Now where's my cocoa?"

The two men stared at each other for a few moments. Sitting in silence, they spoke through lip twitches, winks, and finger drumming. After about five minutes, the officer returned. He placed the cocoa on the table and said, "Chief Detective, there's a man here claiming to be Mister Byron's barrister. He demands to speak to his client."

Merkatz nodded and said, "Well, we shall allow him to do so. Perhaps Christmas will be your lucky day, Mister Byron. We shall be outside."

Byron mocked the officers as they exited the room. The door opened, and a man entered. He wore a black suit with red pinstripes. He had slicked black hair and expertly groomed three-day stubble. He had a black leather briefcase with ruby fittings in his left hand. His cologne smelled of sandalwood, sulfur, and wormwood. Byron turned to see him, but the barrister remained just beyond the edge of his vision.

"It bloody took you long enough," Byron said. He searched the room. "Why do you barristers got to be such bloody drama queens. I plan on spending Christmas with my family, so get me out of here."

"Oh, you won't be here much longer," the barrister said, an aristocratic London tinge in his voice. "However, we do have business to attend to first."

Byron tilted his head and cocked his eyebrow. The barrister's voice sounded familiar, but he could not recall its owner. The barrister's briefcase opened with a wailing screech. When he dropped a stack of papers onto the table in front of Byron, the young man saw that his barrister's French cuff shirt had ruby serpent cufflinks. Byron heard the barrister's footsteps move around the table as he picked up the papers and said, "What's all this about? Looks like a contract. I figured the Order would have signed the contract for your services on my behalf."

The barrister remained silent. Byron then looked at the paperwork and read the first few lines. *Paul Byron (hereafter referred to as the "Promisee") and Samael (hereafter referred to as the "Promisor"), under the pseudonym of Nicholas Scratch, have verbally entered into a legally binding Compact (hereafter referred to as "Compact") on this Seventh day of December in the Current Year of that Lord wherein the Promisee agrees to procure the Black Madonna statue from St. Rita of Cascia's Cathedral in Karnsburg, Austria, by the first bell of midnight mass on the Twenty-fourth day of December in the Current Year of that Lord as payment for the Promisor providing Contact Information for one Samantha Blake Hain. The Promisee further promises that should he fail to deliver the promised goods, that his soul is forfeited to the Promisor at the time of the completion of the Compact.*

As Byron's eyes widened in horror, the barrister sat in the chair formerly occupied by Chief Detective Merkatz. Byron trembled as his hazel eyes stared into the gleaming eyes of Nicholas Scratch whose small but elegant horns curled from his forehead As Scratch formed a triangle with his hands, Byron whispered, "I thought you weren't real."

A Cheshire Cat grin spread across Scratch's face as he said, "Well, Mister Byron, you were correct about one thing. You won't see the inside of *that* courtroom. Time's up."

"Now just wait," Paul Byron begged, leaning forward and failing to snatch the compact as Scratch retrieved it, "Can't we work something out? I thought I'd have more time. You asked me to do something impossible. You lied to me!"

Nicholas Scratch laughed. "Oh, that's rich," he purred. "You entered my bar, angry and belligerent, as you attempted to deceive me through a false name and pretense for needing the assistance of one Miss Samantha Blake Hain. I graciously provided you with information you sought for a price. A price you agreed to, I might add, without asking for any further details." He returned the compact to his briefcase, rose to his feet, and added, "Even the court of your god will hold this as fair and binding. So, off we go."

And as Nicholas Scratch reached the door of the interrogation room, a rattle emerged from Paul Byron's throat. The large man fell forward, and as his head slammed into the table, he died.

* * *

I awoke an hour before the sun set on Christmas Day. As my eyes opened to my hearth-warmed, windowless bed chamber,

I smiled into the subtle warmth around me. There she slept, her snores roaring like an ancient dragon. I slid my fingertips over her naked, milky side, and she sighed contentedly, as did I. Christmas Eve was the first night that my beloved Samantha Hain spent the entire day in my bed, and she was still there when I awoke. I know that she worried about the loneliness of waking to my lifeless body, but I hope that we can work out a way for this to continue.

As I brushed the tangles from my ebon hair, memories emerged from the nearly three centuries of my life. Mortals who have learned of my nature always ask about the technological advancements I have seen, the art I have enjoyed, or the horrors I have survived. After the first few inquests, I began to understand their reasons; I have seen things they have only read about in their history books. And yet, most of my early life, I was sheltered in this castle, interacting with peasants and with mortals only when I would sneak out and visit the village at the foot of the mountains. I thought I was sly, but Martin always knew. He always watched out for me.

I remember the day before I turned twenty-five, the day before my turning ceremony, when I grew bored hearing the oral history of my clan recited for what felt like the thousandth time. I excused myself to the privy, and then I exited the castle through my "secret tunnel." I wandered the forest that surrounded our home, picking flowers, dandelions, and mushrooms. It is laughable now how worried I was that I would never again see these flowers or taste these pungent and earthy fungi after I became a vampire.

And then I found a cave in the mountains. Curiosity possessed me, and I entered the cave, shouting that any goblins who lived therein had better not hurt me. There were no goblins, but the bears who lived in that cave returned from gathering fish in the mountain streams. The bears were not happy to see me, and they cornered me against the cavern's wall. I screamed repeatedly, and eventually Martin and several of my father's soldiers rescued me. They only killed one of the bears, and for that, I was also grateful. Father was not pleased with my actions, and my punishment was severe.

"Don't make me eat the pumpkin stem. It's Eastmas or Christer or Santa Bunny Day." I chuckled silently as Sam talked in her sleep. She did not do this frequently, but it was always entertaining and adorable. I applied my makeup, remembering that night we met at The Four Winds. She had just struck her bargain with Nicholas Scratch, an undetermined favor of his choosing in exchange for one hour each year to speak to her deceased mother. The conviction in her words intrigued me, and I approached her. That was seven years ago.

I moved to my wardrobe to dress. As I chose my black pencil dress with a v-shaped panel of lace, I recalled the first night I wore this dress while Samantha and I were first together. Using the magical doors at The Four Winds, I invited Samantha to join me for an evening of Mozart performed by the Vienna Philharmonic at the Salzburg Large Festival Hall. We kissed for the first time that night. I was terrified to fall in love with another mortal woman after Annalena, but I fell. I laughed, remembering how that night brought us many firsts.

I kissed her cheek, and she smiled in her sleep. I descended to the kitchen as Martin directed the thralls to prepare Christmas dinner. As he sampled the pumpkin soup, he spied me from the corner of his eye, turned, and bowed.

"Good evening, my Countess," he said. "I did not expect you to awaken for another hour or so."

"Normally I would not," I replied, "as you well know. However, given what today is, I wanted to oversee the preparations for tonight's meal."

"Well," Martin said, gesturing to the almost mechanized synchronization of the thralls, "the goose is roasting. The seasonal root vegetables will join it in the oven shortly. The desserts and breads are prepared. As is the cheese course. I beg your pardon if this angers you, but I have used two bottles of the 1872 Sanguinovese for the glühwein and I have quite the respectable bourbon to add to the cocoa for your little romp through the forest."

"Are we not having carp tonight," I asked.

Martin sipped the soup again, directing the thrall to add more nutmeg. He winked at me and said, "I assumed you had fish last night."

I narrowed my eyes, pursed my lips, and shot Martin a glare my father would have applauded. He laughed. I turned my nose up and left the kitchen, saying, "I will not dignify that with a response. Bring our meal to the drawing room. We shall dine there."

Sam had awoken and begun applying her makeup for the evening when I returned to my–our–bed chamber. I sauntered behind her and planted a kiss on her neck, allowing my lips to linger for a moment before I pulled away. She turned toward me, smiled, and said, "I saw you in the mirror, you know."

"The mirror is not backed by silver," I said, sitting on the bed. "If it were, I could not see to apply my makeup. The only silver-backed mirror in this chamber is the full-length one by the wardrobe."

She nodded and lined her eyes with thick wings. As she opened her mascara, she said, "So, anything special I should

227

dress for tonight?"

"I thought last night was quite special," I teased.

She turned and narrowed her eyes at me. "It was special," she said, "but in case your memory has deteriorated in your old age, I've never taken part in an Austrian Christmas."

"Samantha Blake Hain," I said in mock annoyance as I sauntered toward her. I cupped her chin in my right hand and whispered into her ear, "In vampire years, I'm almost thirty." I nibbled her earlobe before pulling away to say, "But, in truth, we will dine in the drawing room before taking a walk through the forest outside the castle, and then we will return to exchange gifts."

"That sounds lovely, 'Milla," she said. I loved it when she called me that. I felt like I was a human again, young, and free of most of my responsibilities. "But I know the cold doesn't bother you the way it does me, so I need to dress for that. And I have something special to wear tonight, so would you mind waiting outside?"

I obliged and stepped into the hallway. Samantha emerged twenty minutes later wearing this lovely orange wiggle dress, sheer stockings, and a pair of black t-strap heels. She carried a pair of ankle boots in her left hand and had her blue and gold hounds-tooth trench draped over her left arm. I surveyed her lovely form, but my eyes kept returning to her decolletage accented by a simple, golden pendant hanging between her breasts.

"Eyes up here, 'Milla," she purred, her hand guiding my chin toward her face.

I chuckled and said, "Yes, they are, but your breasts look exquisite tonight."

"That dress is worth every penny," she said with a smile. She grabbed my hand and said, "Come on, I'm hungry."

Martin, as they say, improvised upon my orders in preparing the drawing room for our Christmas meal. He replaced the streetlamps in the winter village atop the mantle with slender taper candles whose soft glow illuminated parts of the scene–the pastry shop, the cherubic-faced choir, and the large Christmas fir under which two women held hands. Sachets of blood orange peels, cardamom, and clove perfumed the air as the blazing orange fires in the hearth warmed them. Our meal, he placed inside a large woven basket set atop a bearskin rug set before the hearth. Sam squeezed my hand, smiled, and led me to take a seat upon the rug.

As we removed our meal from the basket, Martin's voice emerged from the doorway, saying, "I do hope you find the meal to your likings, my Countess, Miss Hain."

"It's lovely, Martin," Samantha said, smiling. "Thank you."

"Yes, Martin," I concurred, "however, we have not had real fur in this castle in forty years, and we have had no bearskin rugs since I returned from Romania. Where did you find this one? It cannot have been an original."

He winked and said, "Oh, I came into a small sum of money this morning from my old gambling habit, so while the two of you slept through the day, I did a small amount of shopping for this evening."

I tilted and scratched my head, replying, "But, Martin, you have not played the dice since I was a fledgling. What are you…"

"You won the fucking pool," Sam interjected, slamming her hands onto the rug.

He smirked and said, "You will find a lighter white Sanguinovese to accompany your meal. I will have cocoa ready

229

to warm you as you leave for your expedition. And there will be glühwein upon your return for the evening's celebration. *Frohe Weihnachten."*

As he walked away, I turned to Sam and asked, "What pool? Do you know what he meant?"

She rolled her brown eyes, chuckled, and said, "Apparently–and I only learned about this right before I left to come here–several individuals have had a betting pool for when we would get back together. I thought it was local to Butcher's Bend, but it seems others were involved as well."

I poured the crisp, white wine into the crystal glasses and handed her one. "Well," I said as I sipped, "I suppose we have been cursed by stubbornness for several years. It must have been frustrating for those who love us."

"I've been trying to work on that since Bannagh," Sam said. She sighed and ran her fingers through her hair as she continued, "You know me, 'Milla. I've always tried to do everything for myself and in my own way. I could've lived in a nicer place, had a newer car, had new equipment for the office if I'd have accepted my dad's help. After what happened on Old Tom's Hill, I'm glad I didn't accept his help, but–who knows?–maybe things would've turned out different if I had."

"I too have had my curse of stubbornness." I poured the roasted pumpkin soup from the insulated container into our bowls and continued, "After returning from Romania, I clung to the strictures and formalities of our society, refusing to deviate from the rules of decorum in all interactions, insisting that all around me do likewise so that I appeared in control and worthy of my title." I sighed, pausing as I prepared my thoughts. Sam leaned forward and clasped my hands in hers. I nodded and said, "The rules protected me, but they isolated me. And then you walked into The Four Winds and brashly entered into a compact with Nicholas Scratch."

Sam chuckled and nodded, sipping her soup. "I still owe him for that," she said, "but I'll be honest, I nearly broke down and accepted your offer to come to Ireland. Not because I felt I needed your help, but because I wanted you there. With me. Now here we are."

"Here we are," I said. We both turned our gazes toward the empty door frame and then toward each other. I heard Sam's heart quicken in her chest as her burgundy cashmere sweater rose and fell. She inched closer to me, and I smelled that sweet but spicy scent of hers, like nutmeg and pear. I licked my lips. Hers parted, and she tilted her head. My stomach tightened as it had not done in centuries.

Our lips melted together as I ran the fingers of my right hand through Sam's thick, chocolate curls. I planted my left hand on the soft rug beside her hips. She purred and wrapped her arms around my neck. Time stopped as her heartbeat and mine synchronized. Heat rose within my body, and I pulled her in, claiming her mouth with a growing hunger for her body. I moaned as I broke from her lips, allowing mine to kiss and nibble a trail along the soft, warm flesh of her neck.

As I licked from her collar to hear earlobe, I whispered, "We have time, but our meal grows cold."

Her chest heaved as she rasped her response of, "Yeah. I think I'm going to need my strength later."

We ate our meal with laughter and flirtatious banter, and although Samantha had yet to drink of my blood, I found that I could taste greater nuances in the food than I could previously. Perhaps this was only temporary, but it was a pleasant surprise as I have missed the tastes of Christmas meals.

The earthiness of the rosemary and thyme on the goose, the subtle creaminess of the Gruyere mornay sauce punctuated by the garlicky pungent nature of black truffle, and the rich chocolate and subtle sweetness of the apricot in the Sacher torte exploded onto my tongue for the first time in almost two centuries.

After our meal, we descended to the kitchen where Martin handed each of us a covered mug of bourbon-spiked cocoa. We walked through the fir and pine forest that surrounded my castle. Sam's cheeks flushed in the frigid night beneath the waning moon. I showed her the infamous bear cave from which, after my rescue, Martin learned of - and helped me better conceal - my secret exit from the castle. She laughed as I shared stories of my human childhood, stories I had not told in centuries. Her trembling body clung to me for warmth, and I held her close. I appreciated this, for I too, for the first time in two centuries, felt winter's bite. I smiled into the darkness.

We returned to the drawing room to find that Martin had placed the presents we were to give each other under the tree. As the hearth fire crackled and dimmed, Sam and I lit the tealight candles and placed them in the glass ornaments on the tree. With the tree lit, a soft warmth filled the room. The citrus and earthy scent of the glühwein in our pewter tankards wafted to our noses. I handed Samantha a long box wrapped in burgundy paper with a golden ribbon. I watched as she tore into the paper and then opened the box, revealing the swept hilt rapier with golden wire threaded through the burgundy leather on both the grip and the scabbard.

Her jaw dropped as she inhaled sharply. Then her eyes narrowed as she read the inscription. She bit her lip as she looked into my eyes and said, "Th-thank you, 'Milla. This is lovely, but it looks old and important. And the inscription... I'm...I'm honored, but I'm..."

"You are my champion," I said as I kissed her cheek. "I know that you lost your rapier during your adventure in Faerie. I commissioned the blacksmiths in Toledo to make you a new one, but recent events have made me realize that a gift worthy of you is the blade of the Champion of House Karnstein."

I beamed as she blushed. Then she cocked her right eyebrow, smirked, and asked, "And how often does the Champion of House Karnstein share the matriarch's bed?"

I sipped my glühwein before shrugging. "It has happened a few times before," I said. And then I added, "but never openly. Therefore, this will be a first for my clan."

Her smile doubled the light in the room. She returned the rapier to its box and set it beside her. She handed me a large box that she wrapped in blue paper and tied with a silver ribbon. She bounced impatiently as I meticulously removed the ribbon. I chuckled at her adorable impatience with my prolonging of the opening process. She squeaked as my hands revealed the mahogany chest onto which someone had burned my clan's crest. I opened the box to see compartments of different sizes. "It's lovely, Sam," I said, "but what..."

"It's for your watercolors, 'Milla," she said. "It's even got wheels and an extendable handle to make transport easier. I thought maybe you'd like to paint different landscapes than those in Austria and Germany, and now you could always come to Butcher's Bend and paint there."

"You really do believe in my art?" I asked, still surprised that someone believed I had enough talent to show to others.

"Why are you so surprised? 'Milla," she said, "I would believe in your art even if you turned me down last night. You're good.

Shit, I almost set you up with a gallery space for an exhibition, but I know you're hesitant to do that. I thought this might be the next best thing. And, well, as your champion, my Countess, I will likely need to accompany you."

Samantha Blake Hain kneeled before me as she spoke. I leaned toward her and lifted her chin with my index finger. As our eyes met, I smirked and said, "I've told you before, unless we are in the bed chamber you do not kneel before me." And then my lips claimed hers again.

Gentle laughter caused us to break the kiss. We turned toward the sound and saw my sister's ghost glide into the drawing room. She sat upon the chaise and smiled at us, saying, "*Frohe Weihnachten*, 'Millie, Samantha."

"Merry Christmas, Elisa," Sam said as I returned my sister's greeting.

"It is bright in here, is it not?" She asked.

"There is some light, yes," I said, confused. "What do you mean?"

She giggled and shook her head. "Oh, 'Millie," she said, "The light is come, and I need my rest."

We then watched as Elisa lay on the chaise, closed her eyes, and disappeared. Sam placed her arm around me and kissed my forehead. I sighed and smiled. And in the calmness of this Christmas night, there was light.